WHAT IF...?

...Germany won the Battle of Britain in 1940, George VI is killed, Queen Elizabeth wounded, Churchill orders an evacuation to Canada ... Young Canadians, Felicity Le Meseurier and John Stafford save Princesses Elizabeth and Margaret from Nazi paratroopers ... Hitler forces Edward VIII and Queen Wallis to be monarchs of fascist New Britain ...Commando units stay behind to form the resistance and Major John Stafford and Captain Felicity Le Meseurier are ordered to free Edward VIII and Queen Wallis from the Tower of London at all costs... !

"Oldham has cleverly tied in a great knowledge of World War II-era history into a very readable, interesting and unforeseen view of how events in the Battle of Britain might very well have gone had certain things gone in favor of the Nazis and against the British.... Touching view of the deposed and disgraced Edward and Wallis Simpson; the German couple loyal to the Fatherland but fearful of life under the National Socialists; the loyal Tower of London employee; the cloak-and-dagger tactics of the British underground; the turn of events in the United States; all make this a very illuminating and thought provoking query into how things might have gone..."

Mark Schmidt, Curator World War II Museum, U.S.A.

"Similar in spirit to Harry Turtledove ... an engaging, and well-crafted story that will entertain sci-fi fans and historians alike. A damn good read!!"
Anthony Heyer, Fantasy/Sci-fi enthusiast

"Robert Oldham's delightfully imaginative World War Two novel will appeal to teenagers and adults. His fictional character, John Stafford from Hamilton, gives a local feel to this exciting rewrite of global history."
Lil Blume, Teacher and Broadcaster

"...well researched work of historical fiction brings to vivid life the characters of Edward and Wallis... A high school history class could have a great deal of fun with this novel in comparing 'what might have been' to how things actually were. This novel is a unique coupling of Oldham's lively imagination sealed with a healthy dose of fact."
Judith Pollard Smith, The Globe & Mail

"Original premise... taut drama-Oldham vividly portrays one of history's 'might have beens'." *John Aimers, Dominion Chairman Monarchist League of Canada*

"A Classic contribution to the ever widening realms of royal fiction and alternative history... a fascinating story of suspense and intrigue in World War II" Arthur *Bousfield and Gary Toffoli, co-authors of Fifty Years a Queen: The Queen Mother and Her Century* *ISBN 0-9690573-3-4*

SAVING THE KING: AN ALTERNATIVE NOVEL OF WORLD WAR TWO

Robert P. Oldham

A Standmar Book

Published by Standmar Publishing
Printed in Canada

Order online at orders@standmar.com
Or visit http: www.standmar.com

Saving the King: An alternative novel of World War II
ISBN 0968938256

10 9 8 7 6 5 4 3 2 1

STANDMAR PUBLISHING

470 Sentinel Road, Suite 1617
North York, Ontario
M3J 1V6

"We must recollect ... what it is we have to contend for. It is for our property, it is for our liberty, it is for our independence, nay, for existence as a nation; it is for our character, it is for our very name as Englishmen, it is for everything dear and valuable to man this side of the grave."

William Pitt, Prime Minister of Great Britain 1806 when Great Britain was threatened by invasion by Napoleon

"Klotze, nicht kleeken" (Hit with the fist, not tickle)

German General Guderian's Panzer Division's unofficial motto

TABLE OF CONTENTS

FORWARD

Thanks are due to my wife Ruth, family and friends for their help and encouragement, particularly Lil Blume, Brenda Brownley (Past Curator Hamilton Military Museum), Mary Ann Chamberlain, Anthony Heyer, Paul Lisson, Dan Malstrom, The Quill Club, Westdale Secondary School History Club, editor Mary Ranni, Francois Roesch and publisher Andy Straisfeld .

This novel is dedicated to the men and women who defended our freedom in World War II and those who continue to do so in our armed forces. It is thanks to them that the following story is a purely speculative account of what might have happened if Great Britain had fallen to the Nazis in 1940.

No disrespect towards any living or deceased member of the royal family is intended, quite the contrary, I hope they have been depicted accurately and with the sensitivity due to an institution which I support and revere.

The author has, to the best of his ability, made up a tale incorporating famous people and fictitious characters in an historic fantasy based upon the accepted historical facts of the period.

Readers are encouraged to find out what really happened by consulting the many fascinating, excellent materials available.

INTRODUCTION

It is only now, 62 years after the momentous events of 1940, when Great Britain came under the Nazi jackboot, that the part played by my father and mother in the story of New Britain's King Edward VIII and Queen Wallis can be told. Due to the Official Secrets Act, some details are still under wraps. I decided to relate this adventure to a friend who agreed to write a fictional account using poetic licence to 'fill in the blanks' and help future generations understand what happened in the days of their ancestors by enjoying an adventure story.

John and Felicity Stafford are now living in retirement on the magical island nation of Newfoundland. They have related to me the facts they deemed suitable. These Canadians made themselves useful when civilization as we know it was in great peril. Their complete recollections are in the archives of the Canadian War Museum, Ottawa and the Imperial War Museum, London to be opened to public scrutiny in 2030.

The handsome, but selfish, eldest son of King George V - David, Prince of Wales, ascended to the throne of the greatest empire the world has ever seen on the death of his father in 1936. He chose the title Edward VIII. However,

Kingship was not a job he enjoyed. When he wished to marry Wallis Simpson, a twice -divorced American woman from Baltimore, Maryland, he was told by the British and Dominion prime ministers to either drop her or give up the throne.

His decision was to abdicate and marry "the woman I love." On 10 December 1937 Edward VIII made his shocking BBC (British Broadcasting Corporation) radio broadcast to the Empire from Windsor Castle in which he renounced the throne and paid homage to his younger brother Albert, Duke of York.

The new king, known as Bertie to his family, emphasized continuity with his much loved and hard -working father by becoming George VI.

David's abdication shocked his mother, the upright Queen Mary, and brought dismay to Bertie who suffered from a stammer and was the shy opposite of the outgoing David. He had only three weeks notice that he would be the sovereign yet, as it turned out, he had the stuff of kings and the support of a wise and loving wife, Elizabeth, daughter of the Earl of Glamis of Scotland.

They were crowned in pomp at Westminster Abbey in 1936, the procession to the ceremony was the first to be televised. It is an irony of history that this unprepared man became an excellent king amidst turbulent times. If he had not been the sovereign, would the Germans have arrived even sooner than they did and would resistance have been as spirited?

George and Elizabeth had two daughters whom they adored. Princess Elizabeth was nine years old when her father became king and she became heiress presumptive. Her younger sister, Princess Margaret, was only seven when her family assumed the role which had been thrust, by fate, upon them.

In December 1936, the disgraced ex-King, now known as the Duke of Windsor, left England, on HMS Brave, for France, where they married. His wife become the Duchess of Windsor but was never accorded royal status as "Her Royal Highness". They visited fascist Italy and Germany in 1937 and were well received. The Duke expressed great concern about avoiding war. He had witnessed the horrors of World War I as a young officer, albeit kept behind the lines against his will, serving on the Western Front. They also expressed some sympathy for social reconstruction in Nazi Germany.

After invading Poland in August 1939, and defeating one European nation after another, the German Third Reich, under the leadership of the dictator chancellor, Adolf Hitler, was master of continental Europe. In June 1940, British troops in France had been pushed to the coast and evacuated by an armada of small and large vessels plying the narrow English Channel. Britain and the Empire were alone in their fight against a monstrous tyranny, which threatened to enslave all non-Germans and replace honesty, honour and freedom with the hateful and empty philosophy of Nazism; as expounded by Adolf Hitler and the Nazi party.

Outnumbered the British may have been, but they had alongside them Commonwealth troops, soldiers, sailors and airmen from the occupied countries of Europe, and volunteer American pilots in the RAF (Royal Air Force). They prepared for the onslaught.

Historians tell us the Luftwaffe, the German air force, succeeded in destroying many Royal Air Force fighter squadrons and the radar stations on the English south coast. Having gained air superiority, Germany was in a position to invade. That, plus good weather and luck resulted in the successful invasion of England on 21 September 1940.

Two radio broadcasts became even more famous than the one in which Edward VIII abdicated. On the day of the invasion, Prime Minister Winston Churchill made a speech on BBC radio, reporting to the nation that the invasion had begun and that King George VI had been killed. Incredulous Britons listened to the German controlled New BBC radio broadcast from the occupied Channel Islands to hear the Duke of Windsor declare that he and his wife were now King Edward VIII and Queen Wallis of a National Socialist New Britain who would appoint a government that would make peace arrangements with Germany once they were established in a liberated London.

Once London was occupied, King Edward VIII and Queen Wallis become 'Quisling' monarchs as New Britain was absorbed into the Greater German Reich. Edward appointed the British Nazi, Lord Eastbourne, as Prime Minister. Every part of the United Kingdom was occupied by the Germans and a reign of terror by the SS and Gestapo began in Scotland, Wales, England and Northern Ireland. The traditional British police forces were replaced by the New British Gendarmerie, armed British blackshirts who supported the new order. Almost immediately, organized resistance cells and Commando units began operating against the Germans and the government of New Britain.

Britain had a staunch friend in the President of the United States, Franklin Delano Roosevelt. Some influential Americans were unsure of direct involvement, so Roosevelt had to help in every way short of declaring war on Nazi Germany. The United States did formally declare war against Germany, when the Republic of Ireland (Eire) was invaded by Hitler and Mussolini in June 1941. The German Fuhrer had lost patience with the country that seemed unwilling to stop the funneling of agents and supplies arriving in Ireland, and sending them across the Irish Sea to help the British resistance.

This then is the background to Saving the King. The story begins in 1938, the last full year of peace before World War II, the child of that earlier, terrible conflict known as The Great War or World War I.

H.G. Stafford
Hamilton, Ontario, Canada
1 October, 2002

CHAPTER ONE THE CANADIAN

The Nazi night parade burned in his memory, as he looked though the window. Singing Fascists held burning torches, the flames demonically lighting up their faces as they goose-stepped through the streets of Munich. Their images overpowered the pleasant scenery of rural France before his eyes. Brownshirts in front of John on a street corner beat the pulp out of a snowy bearded Jewish man who wore the compulsory yellow Star of David armband. John tried to stop them, but policemen had held him back, then laughed as they pulled him into an alley and kicked him unconscious.

Of course he could have made a formal complaint. He was, after all, a Canadian on vacation investigating the possibility of coming back to study. That night, as he put ointment on his aching bruises, he was glad it was time to go and meet his parents in London then take a liner back to Canada so he could start his first year studying History at the University of Toronto in Canada.

John remembered the events of the last year as the cyprus trees flitted by the windows of the train chugging through the sunny fields of southern France, a plume of sooty black smoke curling back from the steam engine as it headed north to Paris. In the dining car, he tucked into a piece of toast liberally dollopped with marmalade, and washed it down with a cup of black coffee. Holding a starched linen napkin in his left hand he dabbed at his upper lip and imagined the short, ginger military moustache he would grow in another year or so.

John Stafford looked like any tall young gentleman of 17 on a continental visit, except more athletic and more ruggedly handsome than average. If someone had sat by him and struck up a conversation, they would have found him charming for his age, and intelligent. His jacket and shirt were tailored. He sported his father's rather battered, dark blue University of Toronto tie. His right arm, in a white plaster cast, was supported by a sling around his neck.

John remembered how his European adventure began in the previous year, 1937, with a visit to Munich, the capital of the German alpine state of Bavaria, where he had stayed with the Schwartzkopfs, the Roman Catholic family who had made him feel welcome during his summer holidays. He had made a big impression upon their son Franz who was two years younger than himself. They were both aware that Adolf Hitler's tyrannical Nazi regime was shrouding Germany in darkness. The memories of his last night of that holiday had curled up and rested in his mind.

Despite that terrible night John had decided to go back the next summer to study German and fencing. Franz had implored him to come back in letters written in broken English, and John wondered whether he could get him out of Germany.

He looked at the issue of the New York Herald Tribune that a traveller had thoughtfully left on his dining car table. Then he self-consciously reached into his jacket pocket for a packet of ten Marcovitch cigarettes he had bought in Malta, an act of rebellion since his father was a notorious anti-smoker.

Holding the cardboard package with the fingers that poked out of the plaster cast on his right arm, he broke the seal, then removed a cigarette out with his left hand and popped it between his lips. He took out a box of matches and struck a wooden Swan Vesta on the smooth sandpaper on the side of the matchbox he held beneath his cast. As he shook out the match, glanced out the window at the passing clouds. He read as he smoked, trying not to choke too much and attract attention
from a French couple chatting at another table.

He coughed. Alarmed by how strong it was, he placed the cigarette carefully in the ashtray on the table, deciding he enjoyed the ritual of striking the match and lighting up more than the actual cigarette.

As the waiter came to refill his cup, he started and his eyebrows came together in amazement. He smiled ironically to himself. On page two a photograph showed tank manoeuvres in Eastern Prussia. An SS officer, binoculars around his neck, was pointing at the horizon. John recognized him as Count Von Darmstadt the Nazi who had engineered the assassination attempt on the Romanian crown prince at the Palatul Victoriei in Bucharest.

His mind was jerked back to June. En route to Germany he had stayed in a comfortable suburban London manor with his father's old friend, Colonel Le Meseurier and his wife and daughter, Felicity. John and Felicity, who was a year his senior, had been childhood friends. The Colonel was a Canadian military attaché to the Canadian High Commission in London. Hearing from John that he planned to study German in Munich for the summer, he invited the young man to visit him at his office in Canada House, the large, elegant grey building in Trafalgar Square that houses the Canadian High Commissioner and various Dominion officials.

"I've got a proposition for you," he said as he motioned for John to take a seat in front of his desk. The Colonel opened a small cardboard box on his desk and removed a fountain pen, a map of Bavaria and some written instructions.

He removed the top from the fountain pen, unscrewed the nib and removed the smallest camera John had ever seen. "This is the latest in miniature cameras, John. I wanted to ask you if you would take some photos of some, uh, secret items the Nazis are working on while you are over there. Lord Beaverbrook, the Canadian publisher of the Daily Express, and Winston Churchill would like photos of some of the new Junkers bombers and Messerschmitt fighters being tested. Our own secret services are reluctant to do much."

John picked up the camera. "Ingenious. The film must be very small."

"Yes, you load and unload the film with tweezers. We can supply you with camera pens and lots of film. The instructions for the camera and how to get to the airfields are written down. Are you interested? You realize that you can say no without any sense of shame? There is some risk. But I would not ask if it were not important. I believe your studying is a very good cover. I know you have no love for the Third Reich."

"You mean we have to do everything we can to stop the Nazis because war is coming?"

The Colonel replied in his French-Canadian accent, "Absolument." John had thought about the old Jewish man who had been beaten, probably killed. He had a score to settle as well. "I'll do it but I wonder if you could speak to Mr. Churchill and Lord Beaverbrook about helping the family I will be boarding with.

Their son, Franz, who is 15, wants to come to England. His parents cannot afford to send him to school here but perhaps they can help."

Colonel Le Meseurier stood up and smiled as he offered his hand to John. "It will be a pleasure to help the young man. Just write his name and address here, we'll do the rest. You can inform the family he should obtain an exit visa and passport and be ready to travel as soon as we have things arranged. A reporter from the Express will be contacting you in Munich, ostensibly to write about your experiences as a student in Germany. Pour it on thick about how wonderful it is. The Nazis love a chance to show off their Reich. He'll bring the film back to us. Good luck, John."

Over the summer on the weekends John would take a bird book, a notebook, the camera pen and binoculars in a rucksack when he bicycled into the country to photograph experimental aircraft at a Luftwaffe airfield near Munich. He had the feeling that his birding trips by bicycle were being watched, so he began exploring different parts of Bavaria, watching birds and making sketches of bridges and railway lines.

September 1938 arrived; Hitler had already gobbled up the Rhineland, then Austria, in an operation of political manipulation and subversion of democracy pithily termed Anschluss. Now it was the turn of the well-defended Sudetanland area of Czechoslovakia. One of Lord Beaverbrook's reporters, who drank copious amounts of scotch whiskey from a silver hip flask during their interview about his studies, was the courier for John's microfilm.

The reporter was also covering British Prime Minister Chamberlain's flying visit from England to Hitler's Alpine retreat at Berchtesgaden. John and the reporter glumly watched the latest newsreel film in a cinema near the huge Munich train station. Chamberlain was shown at Croydon Aerodrome exultantly waving the papers signed by Hitler.

Worthless documents, only as good as the lies Hitler told. France and Britain had shamelessly handed over Czechoslovakia, "a country about which we know nothing" Chamberlain had weakly said, for "peace in our time."

A French train conductor came by John's table. "Ticket please, Monsieur." John was jerked into the present as he reached inside his jacket pocket and pulled out a buff train ticket, one way from Marseilles to Paris.

"How long before Paris?" John asked.

"Two hours, Monsieur."

"Merci," John replied as he leaned and looked out the window at a French village and reflected on his successful summer. He had taken some good photos for Beaverbrook and Churchill, learned a surprising lot of German and travelled around the continent. He was especially pleased that Franz would probably be in England already, attending a boarding school Lord Beaverbrook had recommended.

Colonel Le Meseurier had suggested a trip to Romania at their meeting in London. He had said it would offer an interesting holiday for a student of history and enable John to give Churchill a first hand report of the situation, where the Fascist Iron Guard meant trouble for the Romanian King, Carol II.

Malta was also on Le Meuseurier's list. "You could check on pro-Mussolini fifth column strength on that island. Italian Dictator Benito Mussolini sees the Mediterranean as his own lake and doesn't like anyone else sailing on it."

John hitched up his grey flannel trousers at the knee. He groaned as he looked at their obvious hemlines where his mother had frugally lowered them. He crossed his legs, hoping no one would notice his pant legs, and pulled the right sleeve of his tweed jacket to check his Timex watch. He would be in Paris to catch the boat train by 4 p.m. and in London at 11 the next morning. He took another sip of the delicious Arabian coffee and let his mind drift back a few weeks to his time in Bucharest
the capital city of Romania in eastern Europe.

He had contacted the British Embassy, since there was no Canadian representative. The Ambassador took a liking to the young traveller and invited him to be a guest at a dinner that evening at the Romanian royal palace, the Palatul Victoriei. At the reception John had been introduced to the Romanian Royal Family, minus King Carol II who was in France. He was taken with the direct manner of Crown Prince Michael who, at 17, was the same age as John. Prince Michael was hosting the dinner.

At a distance he had seen the sabre scarred face of the visiting guest of honour, Count Von Darmstadt, who was heading a Nazi mission of friendship to Bucharest. John guessed the dashing count's age as about 26. He was wearing a white tuxedo with a white tie. John was wearing a black tuxedo with a black bow tie borrowed from the generous British Ambassador, Richard Greene.

After being introduced to the Count, the Ambassador warned John, "Now that fellow Von Darmstadt is up to no good. Rumours on the street say that he has come to stir up trouble, perhaps even knock off Crown Prince Michael. King Carol is out of the country drumming up support from France and Britain against the Fascists here. There would be civil war if anything happened to the Crown Prince and that would suit the Nazis."

"The Iron Guard would use the assassination as an excuse for a Fascist coup d'etat, then, bingo, Hitler has another ally," John said.

"You've got it. We should keep our eyes open."

"I've got my revolver with me"

"Good gracious, young man. Do you know how to use that thing?" the ambassador registered his surprise that such a young fellow was packing a weapon.

"It's a Webley and Scott target revolver, very accurate. My father taught me how to use it back in Hamilton. He was a champion pistol shot at Bisley. He gave it to me when I told him I wanted to go back to Germany to study this year. He insisted I take it. I've ... I've never used it in anger. I can hit the bull's eye from 100 hundred yards every time."

During the lavish five-course dinner, John and the Ambassador kept their eyes open for anything unusual. Just before port was poured and cigars lit, John excused himself and climbed up to the upper gallery. He looked down at the head table and the scores of guests seated at long tables on the marble floor. Count Von Darmstadt was talking animatedly to the guests at the table of the German ambassador at the back of the hall.

John took a look around the second floor and noticed a tall man, standing behind a pillar, looking uncomfortable in a tight tuxedo, with a coat draped over his shoulders. The fellow stood behind a pillar. As John watched a palace guard walked over to the man and spoke to him. The guard came up to John and motioned him downstairs saying first in Romanian, then German, that John should be seated for the speeches. John nodded and made off down the gallery and ducked into an unlocked room around the corner, out of sight from the guard. A few minutes later he emerged.

John walked quietly back around the corner and stood behind one of the pillars. The guard was at the top of the stairs, his hands behind his back. The tall man placed his coat on the marble floor and drew out three pieces of a sniper's rifle from an inside pocket. He expertly and quickly fitted the pieces together, adding a black silencer to the muzzle and a small telescope sight above the stock. He quickly balanced the rifle on the balustrade and took aim at Crown Prince Michael.

John's mouth felt dry and his heart thumped. He had only a split second to decide what he should do. It was too far to run and tackle him. He knew what he had to do, stop him, wound him if he could, but stop him. He reached into his tuxedo with his left hand and drew out the pistol from the leather holster hidden under his jacket.

Swiftly he flipped off the safety catch, lifted his arm, levelled the weapon, took aim and breathed out as he squeezed the trigger. The shot echoed around the marble palace walls.

Hit in the hand just as he was about to pull the trigger, the sniper whirled around snarling with rage. His rifle dropped to the floor with a clatter. In a flash, the guard unbuttoned his holster, drew his pistol and ran towards John. He pointed and fired nothing happened - misfire. Several women guests screamed; some men, including the British Ambassador, pushed back their chairs in consternation. The guard confronted John who, with a quick flick of his foot, kicked the pistol out of the man's hand. John punched the treacherous guard with a left hook, causing him to sprawl out upon the floor clutching at his broken nose.

The would-be assassin ran towards another stairway, only to escape right into the arms of the palace guards dashing along the marble hall towards him, led by their captain, resplendent in his formal uniform and high cavalry boots. The fugitive drew a Luger pistol from his pocket and shot at the guards, one dropped to the ground writhing in pain. A volley of gunfire cut down the sniper. Sabre drawn, the Captain of the Guard knelt down by the dying would-be murderer, and cradling his head spoke to him first in Romanian, then in German, "Who sent you?"

The sniper gasped. A bubble of air grew and popped in the corner of his mouth. His eyes looked up in hatred at John who stood in front of him. "Heil Hitler!" he said and his eyes closed in death.

"Monsieur, I believe you have saved the life of our crown prince. If I can ever repay you... my name is Josef Comenici." He gestured with a white leather gauntlet to the guard who sat holding his nose. "And he should have been helping you."

He turned to his guards. "Put this traitor under arrest."

Captain Comenici put his hand out for John to grasp. John shook it. "It was a pleasure, I like your Prince Michael. I wouldn't want any harm to come to him."

The Captain laughed and clapped John fiercely on the back. He issued orders that the Crown Prince be informed of the incident, for extra guards to take position near Michael and for the body of the sniper and his weapon to be taken to the guard room pending investigation by the Romanian Secret Police.

"I will see you to your table my young friend. Come, show me where you are sitting."

John walked down the stairs escorted by the beaming captain while his men grabbed the guard and took away the dead body to the guard room. An aide whispered in Prince Michael's ear. The Prince smiled and stood up as John found his seat. He bowed his head in thanks to John. Count Von Darmstadt, seated at the Prince's left, looked at John with a stare of withering disdain. John ignored him and sat down.

The Crown Prince, surrounded by anxious chattering guests and embarrassed bodyguards, insisted to the Prime Minister that the dinner should continue. The guest of honour, Count Von Darmstadt, was to speak on closer Romanian ties with the Third Reich.

Von Darmstadt did not like having his plans for assassination thwarted, but let the shadow of disappointment flicker only for a split second in his blue eyes. It did not even register on his suntanned brow. Von Darmstadt stood up and smoothly raised his wine glass to the Crown Prince.

His blonde hair was slicked back, shining in the electric lights and candlelight from the table candelabras. He held himself ramrod straight as he proposed a toast in Romanian.

"Please join me in praying that God will keep Prince Michael and all the royal family of Romania safe from

Communist traitors." He raised his glass and the guests stood and raised theirs. Most were impressed with his sentiments and knowledge of their language; and only a few were made cynical by the knowledge of what had really happened. John and Captain Comenici smiled wryly at each other. The British Ambassador crossed his arms and almost imperceptively shook his head.

Prince Michael rose. "I thank our guest from the nation which has, with the exception of the last war, always been our friend." He paused, allowing Romanians to remember how his grandfather had sided with the allies against the Germans and Austrians and brought ruin to Romania. "I also thank publicly those responsible for preventing my assassination and I ask that the evening continue. We look forward to listening to the plans for peace that Count Von Darmstadt says he is bringing to our people."

A servant wearing an eighteenth century wig and a long, blue swallowtail coat placed two large brandy filled balloon glasses in front of John and Richard. John thanked the servant and looked at the ambassador quizzically.

"You don't have to drink it, young man," Richard said.

"Good. I'll just sniff at it. I've seen my father do that. That gun the assassin was using was German and he died mouthing loyalty to his Fuhrer. It's my bet he was acting on the Count's orders"

"I couldn't agree with you more. Let me drive you to your hotel once we leave here. I'll have one of our people stay with you and see you safely to Greece. I don't think you have made a friend of our Count."

The train carrying John to Paris jerked to a stop at a station and his reverie came to a halt. A few new passengers clambered on board and walked through the dining car. His attention was caught by the man in a worn brown leather jacket with a sheepskin collar who had taken a seat at the opposite table. He knew that cheery face. It was large and round, the mouth draped by a large black moustache.

"Josef Comenici! You? Here....?"

The man put a finger to his lips and gripped John's good hand with both his meaty ones. The Romanian leaned forward conspiratorially. "I am on my way to Paris to serve as bodyguard for King Carol. Prince Michael sent me, it's secret, even His

Majesty does not know; he goes to Germany soon and Prince Michael fears for his life there."

John looked concerned. "Don't worry, my best men are at home with orders not to let the Prince out of their sight. Tell me, what have you been doing since you left Romania? Josef caught the attention of a white-jacketed steward and ordered a bottle of red wine, and lunch for them both. John began relating his story.

"The day after the banquet, I took the train to Athens and, after some sightseeing, took a boat to Malta. It was relaxing watching the Maltese ride donkeys up and down the steep hills overlooking Valetta harbour.

"It was there I met a school friend, Robert Petit, a Lieutenant on HMCS Goose. He taught me scuba diving in that lovely topaz water of the Mediterranean. We used state-of - the-art equipment that Robert had picked up in France from an inventor he met. I think his name was ... er ... it'll come, yes, Jacques Cousteau."

"Not Jules Verne, eh?" Josef grunted and poured himself another drink.

"The Captain of the Goose was intrigued with the possibilities of scuba gear. After meeting with the captains of the Royal Navy aircraft carrier Ark Royal and the battleship Repulse, he called my friend into his cabin and told him that an Italian cruiser, the Guiseppe Garibaldi, was anchored at the far end of the harbour for a "friendly visit."

The cruiser was suspected of carrying one of the new two-man underwater chariots. The chariot is basically a propeller driven underwater craft, shaped like a torpedo, straddled and controlled by two men in frogman gear. The Italians think this an ideal craft for spying on the vulnerable hulls of ships and for secretly attaching an explosive device onto the underside of a vessel.

"It was suggested that the two of us in scuba gear take a midnight swim and just happen to patrol around the aircraft carrier and battleship in the harbour and deal with any undesirable visitors."

As John shifted in his dining car seat he felt a twinge in his arm. He adjusted the white sling that supported his broken limb. "That's where I got this, in the fight with two Italians on a motorized torpedo 20 feet below the surface of Malta Harbour."

"We came up behind them. I tore the mask off the rear frogman, oxygen bubbles poured out of his mouthpiece, his mouth opened in shock. When he made for the surface he kicked me with his frantically thrashing legs. His grey flippered feet cracked my arm. The other guy pulled a knife from a sheath strapped to his leg. Robert grabbed his wrists and wrestled
him up to the surface.

The captain of the Goose thanked us when he visited us in the sick bay where the ship's doctor was setting my arm in a cast. The next night Robert helped them winch the Italian chariot aboard. He said the Royal Navy types were impressed. The frogmen maintained they were patrolling around the Garibaldi and got lost. After their interrogation and confiscation of their gear they were sent back to the Italian cruiser. Their captain apologized and weighed anchor. The underwater chariot they called a "pig" is on its way to Portsmouth and the naval intelligence boys will be excited they'll actually be able to test out one of these top secret craft."

"It doesn't sound much like a holiday to me. Ah, we are pulling into Paris soon." They glanced at the growing number of houses, factories and warehouses they were passing. "What plans do you have, John Stafford?"

'I'm on my way to England then back to Canada to join up. I'll be in uniform soon."

"The whole world will be in uniform the way things are going, my friend. Good luck. Perhaps," he said, knocking back the last of the wine in his glass, "we will meet again."

CHAPTER TWO RAVEN

The Yeoman Warder, with his grizzled grey beard and friendly face, was used to lots of visitors, busloads of day-trippers from Birmingham or Americans just off the ocean liner. However, the impending visit to the Tower of London by the German Ambassador to the Court of St. James was not one he relished.

Charlie Gates was the senior Warder that summer of 1937; he held the prestigious position of Raven Master, responsible for the six jet black ravens that strutted about the confines of the Tower green by the Thames.

He lived up to the nickname the warders had been called since the sixteenth century, 'Beefeater'. Charlie loved nothing better than to devour a plate of roast beef, Yorkshire pudding, peas and roasted potatoes smothered in piping hot gravy, then wash it all down with a pint of Burton ale. His rotund stomach stretched his midnight blue tunic which bore the red Tudor rose and the initials of the monarch he served G. R., for George VI, by the grace of God; King of Great Britain, the Dominions and Empire, Emperor of India, Defender of the Faith, ruler of one quarter of the world's population and one fifth of the earth's land mass.

In his gruff, Lancashire accent toned down by years in London, he confided his disgust at the German visit to his favourite raven. "Well, our Croakey, I don't like the idea of Huns coming to poke around the Tower, especially these Nazi types, but I suppose orders is orders. We're not fightin' 'em, for now any road."

The large bird, its whiskers protruding from the root of its ugly beak, looked up, Charlie fancied, in sympathetic disbelief. There had been ravens at the Tower since time immemorial. Croakey himself was old. He was born the year Victoria died, 1901, and had been a fixture ever since. The venerable bird was roosting happily by Traitor's Gate while Charlie was scrambling out of his trench clutching a rifle, tipped with a razor sharp bayonet, on the first day of the terrible Battle of the Somme.

As a warder it was his job to help care for the old Norman fortress, its tremendous collections of swords, muskets, cannons and armour, and protect the crown jewels. The Duke of Wellington, victor over Napoleon in Portugal, Spain, France and finally at Waterloo, had ordered that the ancient office of Beefeater be awarded to deserving gallant and meritorious soldiers of the army.

So Charlie had come to the Tower after soldiering around the world. He was a bachelor, and like his colleagues, had an apartment in the thirteenth century curtain of stone that formed the outer wall of the Tower.

The Raven Master and Croakey watched a knot of VIPs enter the main gate and walk down the path toward them. Charlie noted the tall man with a bowler hat, wing collar and rolled up umbrella - obviously the civil servant from the Foreign Office. He walked alongside a fat man wearing a ridiculously small homburg hat and dark overcoat, a young man in baggy flannel trousers, Norfolk jacket and Oxford tie and an SS officer in black uniform and jackboots, his black cap worn at a raffish
angle. Behind them came Lord Eastbourne.

Charlie remembered seeing newspaper photos of Lord Eastbourne addressing Mosley's Black shirt fascists in Hyde Park. Eastbourne was one of Churchill's enemies. Therefore, Charlie hated him. Churchill had been Charlie's Colonel during the Great War. Many times in the "30s" Charlie had gone to the House of Commons to see Churchill the rotund, balding, pugnacious politician. With his chin thrust forward, his hands on his hips, Winston Churchill growled warnings about a rearming Germany. But Parliament was deaf and the world was asleep.

The officer reminded Charlie of the young Prince of Wales before he became King Edward VIII for just 11 months. He could see more details as they stood in front of him. The uniformed German had a jagged fencing scar on his left cheek. His peaked cap bore silver skull and crossbones.

Just like our Lancers, thought Charlie.

The Raven Master was glad the crown jewels were safely back in the Tower after their use in the state opening of parliament by George VI and Queen Elizabeth in Westminster Abbey. The abdication speech from Edward VIII, George VI's eldest brother, in December 1937, was a severe shock for Charlie and millions around the Empire who had such high hopes for Edward. The day after the radio broadcast, Charlie rose early and counted the ravens twice. He believed the old tale that if the ravens left the Tower, England would fall. William the Conqueror had built this impregnable fortress at London with walls 11 feet thick. It gave Charlie Gates great comfort to see all the ravens accounted for. He walked across the turf of the Tower's green where once heads had rolled, happy to know that England was, for now anyway, secure.

"Fancy chucking the throne to marry that American woman, and a divorced one at that, making his younger brother, the Duke of York, the new King. Well, God bless the new king and his queen!" he had said to his cronies, hoisting a pint of beer in a local pub.

The civil servant smiled at the Yeoman Warder. "Ah, Gates. Good of you to take our German guests on one of your excellent tours. This is the German Ambassador, Herr Steifel." Charlie blinked; it was the only recognition he was going to give him. "SS Captain Count Von Darmstadt and his nephew." The officer clicked his heels in salutation. He was blonde and handsome. Charlie put him at about 26 years of age.

In fluent English the Count spoke, "My nephew has just completed his studies at Oxford. I wanted him to end his time here with a visit to the most interesting place in London."

"And," the civil servant continued, "May I introduce Lord Eastbourne, Chairman of the Friends of Germany Association?"

"Please speak as fast as you like; our English is good," the Captain said, fixing Gates with his blue eyes. "We have a great interest in your Bloody Tower and all the rest. Did you know that the Third Reich has resurrected the axe man as the state executioner, just like in Henry VIII's time?" He spoke with enthusiasm and just a hint of an accent.

Charlie tried not to show disapproval or suspicion. "Right, we'll start with the Bloody Tower, gentlemen."

Croakey hopped over a bronze plaque; his clipped wings prevented his flying. The plaque indicated where Anne Boleyn had knelt to allow her graceful head to be detached with one stroke from the French executioner's sword; King Henry had softened when she pleaded for a sword not an axe. The raven watched the party intently with deep black eyes.

The visitors strolled along Raleigh's walk as Charlie spoke of Sir Walter Raleigh's imprisonment by James I for not finding the fabled city of El Dorado as he had promised. They were enthralled by the story of the murder of the two children of Edward IV and the discovery of their bones just a few years before.

In the Wakefield Tower the Imperial State Crown, the priceless crown of the United Kingdom, encrusted with diamonds, pearls, sapphires, rubies and emeralds, dazzled and stunned the visitors into a gloating silence. In front of the Imperial Crown one of the four "Stars of Africa" shone brilliantly. It had been cut from the Cullinan diamond and presented to Edward VII as a birthday present from the Transvaal in 1905.

Charlie spoke in hushed tones of how the Dutch jeweller commissioned to cut the Cullinan stone spent weeks planning the operation. When it finally split into four precisely as he had hoped, he fell to the ground in a faint. Charlie reverently explained that the spinel stone in the state crown, known as the Black Prince's Ruby, was given by Edward III to his son Edward, the Black Prince, in the 1300s and worn in Henry V's helmet crown at the victory of Agincourt against the French in 1415.

They moved on to St. Edward's Crown. Charlie explained, "It is only used during the coronation, its golden circlet was the saintly King Edward the Confessor's crown. Oliver Cromwell, the republican Lord Protector, had the old crown jewels broken up and sold. The restoration of Charles II in 1666 saw the recovered ruby and new jewels joining the surviving circlet, silver anointing spoon and the eagle-shaped gold ampulla which holds the coronation oil."

Charlie pointed out the royal sceptres, one topped by the dove of mercy and equity and the other adorned with the cross. "The symbol of kingly power and mercy; below the cross," Charlie explained, "is the heart-shaped Star of Africa - the largest" of those four pieces cut from the Cullinen diamond; it weighs four ounces.

"And here is the two-handed, jewelled Sword of State next to the swords," he pointed, "of Justice and Mercy." Charlie
was staggered to see the depth of avarice in the faces of his German guests. Could it mean that one day they intend to take these treasures? he wondered.

At the end of the tour they thanked the warder. Croakey hopped over and stood next to Charlie. The German Ambassador sneered at the bird, "Ha, just a raven. In Germany we have eagles-now they are magnificent birds-more suited to adorn such a wonderful fortress."

There was a flurry of dark feathers, as a darting black beak snapped at a large pink hand protruding from a dark coat. "Gott im Himmel ... he bit me!"

Lord Eastbourne pulled a pristine white handkerchief from his morning coat pocket and wrapped it around Herr Steifel's bleeding hand. Von Darmstadt attempted to kick the bird but Croakey nimbly hopped away.

As they were leaving Charlie had a quiet word with the civil servant. "I know it's not my place, Sir, but I didn't like the way that SS man and his pals looked at the Crown Jewels. It's like he planned to come and get them one day."

"Really, Gates, you'll be telling me next that the Germans are going to invade on the next tide, kill the King and give the crown jewels to the Duke and Duchess of Windsor. Count Von Darmstadt is a big noise in Berlin. I'm sure that he's just very interested in history."

"I don't trust 'em, Sir."

"Same as that bird. What a dreadful incident, the ambassador was not amused. Well, until the next tour Gates. Be sure to keep the ravens away from the visitors from now on."

To the end of his days Charlie told how Croakey winked at him as the bowler-hatted official turned to walk back to his Whitehall office.

CHAPTER THREE LONDON

John was en route to London by rail. When the train pulled in at Waterloo Station he grabbed his brown suitcase from the luggage rack above his head in the second class compartment. He slid open the door to the corridor, then pushed open the coach door and stepped down to the platform. As he walked along it, towards the hissing steam engine at the buffers, the train doors clanged comfortingly as a station guard slammed them shut.

It felt good to be back. He looked past the ticket collector with his head buried in a copy of Picture Post and noticed an attractive, young brunette in a dark green suit with a matching hat bearing a cream-coloured bird's wing and a small, fashionable light green veil.

It can't be?, thought John. The girl raised her arm and held her umbrella aloft. "It is," he muttered, beginning to walk quickly towards her. She returned his smile. "Felicity." He came up to her and shook her free hand. "Scout shake, I'm afraid, it's easier for me; anyway, I'm left handed. I didn't expect you. What a great surprise."

She took his good arm in hers and launched him towards the hubbub of the street. "I thought it would be nice to give you a welcome back. My father is busy at some diplomatic function, so, here I am." She looked at him anxiously. "I heard about your arm, at Malta ... I'll get a taxi. I haven't been so worried about you since you came with us canoeing and fell in that icy water."

"Yes, I remember, I was eleven and I jumped in, you dared me. Your father was mad at you for putting me up to it."

She smiled, "Just testing you - making sure it's the right John Stafford come back to us - good to see you John." She said it with a tenderness that surprised and excited him. He had only ever felt such elation once before, when he had kissed her after a school dance which now seemed a long time ago. But then she had gone away to New York to stay with her mother and John had gone to Europe. They had corresponded occasionally but there was much that had been left unsaid between them.

He looked in her green eyes, put his good hand to her cheek and gently kissed her on the lips. A few people on the platform looked and stared.

"Wow! I didn't expect that," she said groggily. "Careful, too much of this and they'll start to sell tickets! You know how reserved they are here." He kissed her again.

"I forgot myself," John replied, stepping back from her, amused at his unexpected action, "but I'm glad I did."

"Let's go, John," she said returning his smile. Before John could beat her to it, she had stepped out of the station, placed her two baby fingers in her mouth and emitted a piercing whistle. A black, London taxi cab drove up. She opened the umbrella to protect them from the pelting rain and insisted he get in first.

"Don't you let the man do anything for you?" John asked.

"When he doesn't have an arm in a hideous plaster cast I do. But, you could take me out for lunch," she continued, looking demurely at him. "Then there's a great show at the National Gallery I want to see and none of my friends appreciate art like you."

"Where to?" the taxi driver asked through the glass partition. John opened his mouth to say something, but Felicity spoke up quickly, "Canada House, but take us to Piccadilly Circus first, please."

"Right, Miss."

As they drove around the aluminium statue of a cherubic Eros shooting his arrow from a baby bow, Felicity pointed at one of the tall buildings around Piccadilly Circus which were alive with ads and slogans. "WHAT PRICE CHURCHILL?" a huge sign proclaimed. "You see, things have changed in the five months you've been away. Hyde Park was dug up for trenches and air raid shelters last summer. Gas masks have been distributed. Britain is waking up to the danger that waits for us on the continent."

John nodded soberly and then took Felicity's delicate gloved hand in his and smiled at her. "Let's enjoy being together while we can."

"Yes, we shall, John but first you must report to my father." From Colonel Le Meseurier's office in Canada House they could look out upon Trafalgar Square and the huge plinth lifting the statue of Admiral Lord Nelson to the heavens. Four massive bronze lions guarded the base of the statue with its frieze relief of scenes of wooden ships doing battle with the French and Spanish fleets at Trafalgar. Colonel Le Meseurier plucked a cigarette from a round silver cigarette tumbler and lit it with a heavy, round Ronson lighter.

"You've done well. Churchill and Beaverbrook have asked me to thank you for the services you have performed. Due to the nature of the work you've done for us, it all has to be hush-hush."

He looked at his daughter who was pouring tea. "I know, I know, Daddy. I don't know a thing."

"I have a letter from each of them thanking you and, as you see, should you ever be in a position to need help of any kind, they will be willing to do whatever they can." John read the letters carefully and put them in his jacket pocket.

"Thank you, Sir."

"What are your plans now, John?"

"A bit of a holiday here." He saw Felicity's cheeks colour slightly. "Then, a boat to Canada. I'm going to join up in the Canadian army as soon as I'm 18; the big show is coming."

"I'm afraid you're right. Max Beaverbrook has reserved a room at the Savoy for you for a week. It is a small token of gratitude for services rendered. He would like to host a dinner there and perhaps Churchill can come. Now, mes enfants," Colonel Le Meseurier said in his French Canadian accent to Felicity and John, "I have a meeting, and you ... have all London to enjoy."

As Felicity and John walked across Trafalgar Square to the National Gallery, hundreds of pigeons flew up and around Nelson's column. Colonel Henri Le Mesuerier, a close friend of John's father since they had fought together as subalterns at Vimy Ridge in 1917, stepped back from the window where he had watched them cross the square. He poured himself a gin and tonic.

He lifted the glass in a silent toast to the painting of George III on the wall over his bookshelf.
"To King George III who allowed French Canadians their freedom of speech and religion. God bless his descendant George VI and each of us in these uncertain times."

CHAPTER FOUR 3 SEPTEMBER, 1939

The white phone rang and rang, its insistent tones casting circles of sound out of the open French windows into the clear blue Mediterranean sky. The maid picked up the receiver in Antibes on the south coast of France. She ran out to the terrace where the lap of waves onto the shore could be seen and heard. "Monsieur Le Prince de Galles. Telefon. Telefon!"

"Yes, yes. Coming," called a thin, tanned, middle-aged man as he swam to the edge of the sunken pool. Sweeping back his blonde hair, he climbed up the steps, then reached for a bath robe and picked up the elegant white receiver.

"Windsor here."

"Thank God I've got you, your Royal Highness. I've just had word from Whitehall. The Germans have rejected our ultimatum. They have refused to pull their invasion force out of Poland and as of 11 o'clock this morning we are at war with Germany. Prime Minister Chamberlain is addressing the nation as we speak."

The Duke sighed and looked down at his sombre reflection in the surface of the polished table in the hall that reflected his sombre face. He remembered how the mud was stained with scarlet blood, how it grew deeper in colour until it became purple and brown. He gripped the phone tightly. If only Hitler had listened to his pleas for peace. The telegram he had dispatched had not worked, he thought. Perhaps Hitler needed more time. But what was time compared to millions of lives? Another conflict was just too terrible to contemplate."

"Are you still there, your Royal Highness?"

"Yes, I'm here. We want to do something to help, of course. Wallis was just talking of working with the Red Cross; she was being fitted for a uniform. I will get into uniform too of course, perhaps be a liaison officer with the French again."

The ambassador cleared his throat and plunged into difficult waters. "His Majesty is sending an aircraft of the Royal Flight to take you and the Duchess back to England. He's worried about your safety." He tactfully did not add that it was obvious to everyone else that the Duke of Windsor in France was an embarrassment and a danger.

"That seems a bit-far fetched, Muncaster," the Duke said in his high clear voice. He chuckled, his eyes scrunched up, the crow's feet stamped in the corners of his eyes. "No, we can be more useful here. We shall leave for Paris today by car. I shall phone my brother and explain the situation."

"With respect, Sir, the King will be terribly busy. Perhaps you could send a telegram."

Irritated, the Duke thanked the ambassador for phoning. "This line is not good." He raised his voice, 'I shall see you in Paris. Thank you for your call. Goodbye."

"Who was that darling?" a woman's voice with a soft Virginian voice cooed from the French doors. A tall, severe looking woman, with a pink towel wrapped around her head in a turban, stood in the doorway in a loose bathrobe and a purple one-piece swimsuit. She removed her sunglasses and daintily stepped into the room.

"It was the British Ambassador in Paris. The war has begun." The Duke of Windsor spoke in his clipped, tight manner. "I'm afraid in the end it may open the way for communism. It's madness." He stood listlessly looking out the doors to the sea. The Duchess put her hand in his and kissed him on the cheek. He lay his head on her shoulder. "Wallis," he sighed.

She tried to cheer him up, she hated to see him depressed. "We shall make ourselves useful. I don't know how I'll look in uniform but we shall find out," the Duchess of Windsor whispered in his ear.

He brightened up and spoke, "We'll go to Paris. I'll pack as soon as I finish my swim." He kissed her, walked out upon the terrace and dove into the water. She watched his body, distorted by the green water dappled with sunlight, as he swam underwater, over the coloured tiles at the bottom of the pool.

About the same latitude north but an ocean to the west from the Mediterranean, seagulls wheeled over Lake Ontario and James Street in the port of Hamilton, Canada. It was early morning in the industrial hub of Canada.

The ovens of the foundries were belching forth smoke and heat. Shifts of steelworkers tended them around the clock. They were making steel for the factories that would shortly have to switch from assembling trains, cars and refrigerators to producing the multitudes of aircraft, ships and tanks for the conflict that was slowly but surely throttling the world of its last breath of peace.

The orange brick Victorian armoury building on James Street with its green tile roof, stood adjacent to the smoked black limestone blocks of Christ Church Cathedral. The armoury, shared by a Highland infantry regiment, and the Royal Hamilton Rifles, was bustling with activity.

Parliament in Ottawa had not yet declared war, but a statement by Prime Minister MacKenzie King's Liberal government was expected within the week, putting Canada alongside Britain and France. In the meantime, the small armed forces of Canada, shamefully neglected during the '20s and the depression of the early '30s, were preparing for war as best they could. Hundreds of young men were lining up to enlist. Grey-haired veterans of the First War and even a seventy year-old Boer War volunteer had to be turned away.

John Stafford was wearing his new uniform which sported two diamond pips on each shoulder indicating his post subaltern rank, Second Lieutenant. His new, brown leather Sam Brown belt and holster shone as he strode past a line up of civilians waiting to enlist outside the Victorian armoury with its mock castle portcullis.

The soldier on duty brought his Lee-Enfield rifle, from its "slope arms" resting place on his left shoulder, lifted his right boot up and crashed it down as he gripped the rifle with his right hand and moved it into a vertical position in front of the gas mask pack on his chest. John returned the salute, raising his right hand, open palm out, to his peaked brown cap. The private energetically brought his rifle back onto his left shoulder with textbook efficiency. A breathless corporal accosted John in the adjutant's office.

"Have you seen Major Massey, Sir? We need him to interview the volunteers."

"Not yet, I will help once I've assigned men to guard the water plant, electrical works and the train station."

On the other side of the Atlantic, in Berlin, newly promoted SS Major Count Von Darmstadt drove through the strangely placid, crowded streets and through the massive Brandenburg Gate which proclaimed the Second Reich's victories over Austria, Denmark and France in the previous century. He reflected on the might of the Third Reich, which would be able to conquer so much more under the able leadership of the Fuhrer, Adolf Hitler.

Large red Nazi flags, each displaying a black swastika within a white circle, flapped in the light breeze. The Luftwaffe was even now destroying the Polish air force. The Wehrmacht was driving armoured columns into innocent Poland while the Kriegsmarine was shelling forts in the Polish port of Danzig.

There was a sense of shared jubilation in the air among the smart pedestrians: women pushing prams and businessmen climbing onto trams clutching briefcases. A policeman in green military style-uniform and a shako worn over the stubble of his hair grinned at him and halted traffic at the crossroads so that Von Darmstadt did not need to stop his white Alpine BMW convertible.

The policeman recognized the black uniform of a Schutzstaffel officer. The SS Major, sharing the euphoria of the day, returned the grin. It made the scar on his left cheek, running from his ear to below his smoothly shaven chin, a lightning bolt to match the two silver bolts on the uniform's right collar.

He was on the way to army headquarters where, even as Poland was being torn asunder by the Nazis and their Soviet allies, plans were being drawn up for a blitzkrieg through the Low Countries and into France, avoiding the hugely expensive and static defences of the Maginot Line. Von Darmstadt had some ideas about glider landings to neutralize the Belgian forts.

He also had some proposals for a future invasion of Britain, if the British were stubborn and foolish enough to stand up to the might of the Reich, but one step at a time. He turned on the car radio and enjoyed some Strauss waltzes, tapping his tanned hands, in time to the music, on his leather-wrapped steering wheel.

"If this weather continues, not only will we be in Warsaw by the end of two weeks, but it will be ideal for hunting boar on my estate in Saxony. Perhaps Reichsmarschel Goering will wish to join me. Maybe, if I promise him some of the lovely girls on the estate; it does not hurt to court the men at the top."

Over Buckingham Palace the Royal ensign hung, indicating the King was home. Irish Guards in battle dress, their scarlet uniforms had been put away for the duration, kept guard. King

George had exchanged his civilian clothes for the double-breasted navy blue jacket, the uniform of an Admiral of the Fleet. He was having a cup of tea with his wife, Queen Elizabeth, and his daughters.

"My dears," the King looked at Princess Elizabeth, then at the younger Princess Margaret, "Mamma and I would like you both to stay at Windsor Castle; we'll visit you every weekend." Princess Elizabeth frowned, Princess Margaret pouted.

"It will be safer there, but we have to stay here in London," their mother said.

"Can you phone us every day, Papa?" asked Princess Elizabeth. "Can we play with Granny's dollhouse?" Princess Margaret chimed in.

"Yes to both questions," the Queen said laughing, placing her arms around the girls. "We'll come up every week and play with it as well."

"Now you can go for your riding lessons," the King said and smiled as the Princesses kissed him on the cheek.

The Queen poured them both some more tea. She thought how handsome he looked in his naval uniform. She studied the medal ribbons on his chest, remembering how he had fought in the Great War as a midshipman at the naval battle of Jutland. Elizabeth remembered the convalescing officers she had nursed in her Scottish childhood home, Glamis Castle; in the same conflict.

"This will be a long war," the king commented, "we are fighting a terrible enemy but good shall prevail. It must, for our children." He patted his wife's hand.

"Yes," the Queen added, "Canada has all the promise of the new world. The Princesses must only go if Britain succumbs. If there is only bombing they must stay, as we must, to take it with our people. But you and I shall stay no matter what may come."

"Tonight Prime Minister Chamberlain is coming for an audience, I understand one of the many things he wants to talk about is David. He is under the impression the Duke and Duchess of Windsor don't want to come back to England. It might have something to do with more money and recognition of his wife as "Her Royal Highness. It's all very embarrassing."

The Queen placed the silver teapot on the silver tray with a smart clack. "He still doesn't realize he left all that behind when he abdicated and dumped the job in your lap. When will he ever grow up?"

"He should realize that there are many priorities in this war, victory being the major one, not petty aggrandisements to satisfy personal whims. But," he sighed, "he is my," he hesitated but it was only a slight stutter, due to the coaching he had received from an Australian speech therapist, ".... brother, perhaps he can pursue his army career somewhere. He did so well in the Great War. It always irked him that Papa constantly refused him the right to go into action, but he was the Prince of Wales, his life was too precious to waste. I was lucky, I was only the Duke of York then. I saw action."

"By the way," Elizabeth changed the subject, "did I mention our ration books arrive next week? The girls were asking about whether clothes were going to be rationed. They weren't as disappointed as I thought when I said yes. I suppose if we see darning and making do as a challenge that's a good attitude to have."

"We'll all be in rags if the war lasts a long time," the King joked. "I shall ask our gardeners at Sandringham and Balmoral to start growing what vegetables they can in the greenhouses and dig up the flower beds in the spring. We'll have them encourage the fruit trees and strawberries. Now we will be receiving the same rations as everyone else we have to pitch in." He stood up to stretch then bent down and placed his hand lightly on his wife's waist.

"Please excuse me, I have to work on the boxes."

Finding a packet of cigarettes and slipping them into his naval jacket, he walked off to his study to tackle the red leather dispatch boxes of cabinet briefing papers. He was tired after such a sad and momentous day, yet within himself he felt a strong coil of metallic tenacity wound up like a spring. He prayed that that energy would last the duration so he could be the king he knew his peoples deserved.

He sat and pulled the first of the red boxes towards himself and opened it, removing a large sheaf of documents to read and sign.

CHAPTER FIVE   CATCHING A KING

0900 hours. Sunday 10 August 1940, Reich Chancellery, Berlin. General Stoppl, aide to Field Marshal Von Rundstadt, walked towards the ornate desk in the luxurious office used by Adolf Hitler. He clicked his booted heels, gave the Aryan salute and removed his Wehrmacht cap. "Here is the situation report on Operation Sea Lion, Mein Fuhrer."

He placed a yellow folder on the immaculate desktop behind which sat the absolute master of most of Europe. The cover of the folder was plain except for a black eagle clutching a swastika and a red-stamped message: "FOR THE EYES OF THE FUHRER ONLY."

Hitler stood up, reaching only the General's grey-uniformed shoulders. He placed his arms on the desk and pressed his fingers down on the blotting paper. "So ..." He opened the folder with his right forefinger and thumb. As he read he rested a finger on his small moustache. His stomach felt an exuberance bubble up, like the champagne bubbles in the glasses of those who indulged in such pleasures. His hand hovered over his stomach, and rested upon the Fuhrer uniform, a style of double-breasted grey jacket he had sworn to wear until the war was won.

"Our U-boats and surface raiders are strangling the lifeline of freighters carrying oil and material across the Atlantic to Great Britain. Italy will soon join us in the fight against decadence, and the Suez Canal, Malta and Gibraltar will fall into Fascist hands. Our friend, Japan is a constant threat to India, Hong Kong, Malaya and Australia. The U.S.A. has no stomach for a fight. The Soviet Union is our ally-as long as it suits us. England is kaput!" Hitler almost shouted the last sentence.

"Jawohl, Mein Fuhrer. But before she is completely kaput, she can kill a lot of Germans."

Hitler's eyes narrowed as he read. Operation Sea Lion - the invasion of England is being prepared. 800 invasion barges, 200 troop ships, 107 tank-carrying ferryboats and 350,000 experienced men are assembling in French, Belgian and Dutch ports. Britain still has not made up for the massive quantity of supplies and tanks lost in their retreat from France in June.

The Luftwaffe is destroying the Royal Air Force through its sheer might of numbers. The Royal Navy is stretched operating in home waters, the North Atlantic and the Mediterranean, as well as keeping units in the Caribbean, Indian and Pacific oceans to protect their far eastern empire.

However, Admiral Raeder is concerned about the number of Kriegsmarine surface ships available to protect the invasion fleets and changeability of the weather in the English Channel. He is willing to commit 60 U-boats to patrol the edges of the crossing and lay thousands of mines on either side of the invasion fleets. He will provide two battleships, four cruisers and twelve destroyers. The battleship Bismark and pocket battleships will be used to pulverize shore defences and defend the troopships.

Reichsmarschel Goering can provide thirty squadrons of bombers and forty squadrons of fighters, some to be used in a strafing role at the beach heads. The bombers will target military installations at the landing sites. By the 18th of September the destruction of the British Radar Stations and Fighter airdromes in the South and Midlands will be completed. The Luftwaffe will be master of the sky during Operation Sea Lion. The Luftwaffe Paratroop Division is ready to seize the communications centres, selected airfields for Luftwaffe use, railway stations and crossroads.

The General Staff advise launching Sea Lion by 21 September, since after this date the weather and tides will not be favourable. Details and maps are given overleaf.

Hitler stood up, straightening his jacket; he beamed at General Stoppl, who adjusted his monocle. Hitler put his hands behind his back and walked to the window overlooking the Chancellery garden. Some pigeons were playing tag.

He was jubilant, enjoying the tantalizing anticipation of victory made sweeter by the bitterness of the betrayal of 1918. "Now, Herr General, I will make them pay for the disgrace of the Treaty of Versailles. How dare Britain tell Germany that we can be nothing but a second-class nation? Great Britain and Ireland will become vassal states of Gross Deutschland, providing materials and slave labour to the Reich.

The Jew Sigmund Freud will be shot, as will the home grown intellectual scum Earl Russell and that crude clown Charlie Chaplin. The fat imperialist Churchill can rot in the Tower of London. I've forced the French to sign my peace treaty in the same railway carriage as the Imperial German Army was forced to sign their unconditional surrender at Compiegne in 1918. I will place my man upon the throne of that nation of shopkeepers."

Hitler fondled the Iron Cross 1st class on the left side of his uniform jacket. He had won it as a runner in the Kaiser's army on the western front. He remembered how proud he was to have it pinned upon his best uniform, all those years ago.

"Mein Fuhrer?"

"Carry on, General, I have other important business but I will read the rest of this report and meet with the general staff this afternoon at 3 o'clock to personally give my backing."

General Stoppl brightened, clicked his jackbooted heels with panache and bowed. "Heil Hitler!" He saluted and left. Hitler sat at his desk, his folded hands supporting his chin, and proclaimed to himself, "I will be the first conqueror of Britain since William the Conqueror and a millennium before that, Julius Caesar. I will succeed where the Spanish Armada, Napoleon and Wilhelm II failed." He walked over to the eighteenth century globe in its wooden frame. It was newly installed after being confiscated from the Palace at Versailles. He spun it with his hand for several minutes. He returned to his desk and pressed a button.

Heinz Erhardt, a translator in a Wehrmacht grey uniform, opened the tall panelled doors and a secretary in a women's Wehrmacht tunic, blouse, dark tie, wedge cap and skirt, her blonde hair in a bun, came in. "Phone Reichsmarschal Himmler at SS Headquarters, ask him to see me immediately with the Checkmate file, and bring me a glass of water, please."

The attractive secretary put the call through in the anteroom outside Hitler's office at the end of the three block long marble gallery and took a glass of water in to Hitler. Everything in the Reich chancellery was meant to impress and dominate. At each end of the red gallery stood two black-uniformed Lieibstandarte guards holding the muzzles of their Mauser rifles in their white gloves.

In the office he shared with her; the translator poured the secretary a cup of coffee from a thermos. Their office door was open and the guards glanced at each other and smirked. While on duty they enjoyed seeing the shy young man court Ingrid, the secretary. She had long since thwarted any moves of a romantic nature from these men in black. They had given up on her, saving their clumsy advances for easier prey.

"Well, is the old man going to invade England today or make friends with them?" Heinz joked.

She giggled, "Both I think."

He admired her shapely figure and swallowed. He was just about to ask her out for dinner when the doors at the end of the long corridor opened and the guards stamped to attention saluting. A massive door at entrance to the hall opened and the distant clatter of several pairs of jackboots could be heard striding down the gigantic marble hall. Heinz made sure his hair was tidy, straightened his collar and stood to receive the visitors.

Heinz recognized Heinrich Himmler, the sinister head of the Reich's elite special forces, the Schutzstaffel, better known as the SS. Himmler was a short man, with closely shaven hair around his ears and temples. His cruel eyes peered through wire-framed round, spectacles. His immaculate black uniform was trimmed with a white belt, shoulder cord and silver decorations.

Heinz clicked his boots together and threw his arm out in salute.

"Heil Hitler!" he said.

Himmler returned the salute. "You must consider joining the SS. We need intelligent young Aryans. Isn't that right, Major Von Darmstadt?" He swiveled to face the officer with a dueling scar, who wore his black SS cap at a stylish angle.

Ingrid Dietrich looked up at the Major, smiled as he bowed to her and turned to Heinz. The translator was terrified. He knew very well that the death's head badge on their caps was well chosen; it was the mediaeval symbol of mortality.

"It is the best life for a German," Von Darmstadt said.

Heinz decided to emphasize his academic prowess. "I am proud to serve the Fatherland here in the Reich Chancellery. I am pursuing my studies of Goethe and hope one day soon to, er, marry." He found himself looking over Himmler's shoulders into Ingrid's twinkling eyes. He blushed. Heinz managed to stammer, "I'm ... flattered by your words, Reichsmarschal, but I am not a man of action like Count Von Darmstadt who is a hero of the Reich. It is an honour to meet you, Herr Major. This way, please." He opened the doors to Hitler's office and announced them. His hands shook slightly as he poured himself a cup of coffee. Ingrid came over to him with a handful of papers, laid them down on his desk and let her hand rest on his arm. Heinz could not stop his heart from pounding. On top of the papers was a note with the words "I will marry you" written in red ink. "I will marry you." Heinz said to himself. He gulped, and gripped Ingrid's hand.

He wrote below her note in green ink.

Ingrid I love you. I have to talk to you about the future. May I come to your apartment tonight at about 8 for dinner?

She nodded, took the note and put it into her handbag.

"I have brought Count Von Darmstadt with me Mein Fuhrer. He has been invaluable helping me formulate our strategy for Checkmate."

Hitler stood up and shook the Count's hand. "Yes Major. I remember I awarded you the Iron Cross with an oak leaf cluster for leading the Brandenburg Regiment in the paratroop attack on the Eben Emaul Fortress in Belgium. Your band of 78 defeated 1,200 men."

The Count made a curt bow and clicked his heels. "Please sit down," Hitler said as he led them to four soft armchairs, which stood in a semi-circle on the carpeted floor. Himmler opened his black briefcase and took out a file of papers marked 'CHECKMATE-TOP SECRET'." You understand the importance of this plan, Herr Reichsmarschal?"

"Yes, I shall reiterate it for the benefit of the Major. It is absolutely crucial that King George VI and his Queen Elizabeth be killed or captured. Princess Elizabeth, the heir apparent, and her younger sister, Princess Margaret, must also be dealt with. This will happen during the invasion to put the British off balance and give us the initiative. With the present bourgeois royal family out of the way, we can reinstate the true king, Edward VIII, and his American wife, Wallis the Duchess of Windsor, on the throne of a Nazi Britain."

Major Darmstadt spoke with admiration. "I congratulate you, Mein Fuhrer. It is a masterful plan. With an American sharing the British throne it will be that much more difficult for that insipid cripple, Roosevelt, to enter the war against us."

"I am delighted Major that you appreciate the subtlety of the plan." Hitler clapped his hands together and sat down.

"When the Duke and Duchess of Windsor drove from France to Spain and then Portugal our agents were unable to win them over. Unfortunately, one of our men was poisoned by British MI6 agents and the Duke and Duchess were persuaded by Churchill to return to Britain. Now the British have exiled them to the Bahamas where the Duke is Governor, we have devised a plan to make up for those bungled attempts," Himmler said softly, one arm on the back of the chair. "The Major here will take a hand-picked group of SS troops on one of our newest U-boats. It will get to the Bahamas in six days. The Duke of Windsor is lightly guarded. He and his wife will be brought to the submarine pens at Brest, France and then taken to Paris and kept under house arrest, unless, of course they come willingly. If they do that, we will be less obtrusive but nevertheless present."

Hitler picked up the thread. "Events will then be put into place to ensure he does agree to be king. The idea of having Wallis as his queen will appeal to him. His brother and sister-in-law despise her and were aghast that he would give up the throne just to marry the woman he loved. The Duke of Windsor has made no effort to hide the resentment he feels since the British royal family forced them to live in France and refuse to recognize his wife. She is not allowed a royal title. I remember how pleased he was on his visit to the Reich in 1937, when we treated them both as royalty. He is like a child."

Count Von Darmstadt interjected. "Mein Fuhrer, are you counting on the Duke of Windsor agreeing to be king when he finds out that the British people need him, once his brother is dead?"

"Precisely, Herr Major, it is his destiny-he will be our tool-tiresome duties will be done by our advisors-we will make him, and his wife, who hungers for a royal title, happy. When can you leave?"

"Immediately," the Count answered.

Himmler looked at his wristwatch. "I would like the U-boat to leave as soon as possible. You can leave as soon as your handpicked men are ready. I will phone Admiral Raeder immediately to make arrangements for the vessel and crew."

"Tell the Admiral this plan has my blessing. I want to see how quickly his U-boat can get to the Bahamas and return with our royal catch!" Hitler took a drink of water and watched them leave.

That night the German High Command, on orders from the Fuhrer, prepared in earnest for Operation Sea Lion. Count

Von Darmstadt travelled north by train to the naval port of Kiel with his chosen men.

Heinz took a tram car down the Unter der Linden to the middle class section of Berlin. He carried flowers and a bottle of French white wine. It was a beautiful August evening, balmy and serene. He found himself whistling a tune from 'The Magic Flute'.

After a candlelight dinner they talked about their future. "Are we going to win this war; Heinz?" asked Ingrid.

"It doesn't matter whether we win or not, we will have lost our souls on the way. I love you. I want us to have a family; but I have a feeling of impending doom. It is not normal, there is too much...", he waved his hand in the direction of the Reich Chancellery, "too much power here. It is creating a vortex and we will be sucked into it, already it may be impossible to get out without us being shot as traitors".

"But I am not a traitor, Ingrid, I love the fatherland. I just want to be a peaceful German outside of the Reich. My uncle has a business in Sweden, he can get me a job as a salesman, after all, I have been teaching myself Swedish in -a few weeks there and I shall have it."

Ingrid thought for a moment and said, "I will marry you Heinz, even if you are mad. I would go to the ends of the earth to be with you, so Sweden is not so far. I can say that I want to raise sons for the Reich and leave the Chancellery if you wish."

"I will make inquiries about how best to arrange all this without arousing suspicion. One day the Germany will turn on Russia, that will mean the deaths of untold millions. I don't want it to be the end of our future together. Someone somewhere has to keep the truly great traditions of Germany free from terror and the taint of hatred. Say nothing to anyone about the secrets I have told you, Ingrid." He looked at her anxiously.

She placed her long fingers on his over the small table. "Now, my future husband, teach me some Swedish."

Heinz got up and put his arms around Ingrid who turned her face up to him. "First I will kiss you and then I'll tell you how they say that in Swedish." And he kissed her for a long, long time

CHAPTER SIX THE 3RD CANADIAN DIVISION—SUSSEX

The rain lashed down upon the soggy positions on the sea front of Eastbourne, Sussex, on the southeast coast of England. The Royal Hamilton Rifles were part of the 3rd Canadian Division, fresh troops, the front line if there was an invasion. They were under the overall command of one of the few British staff officers capable of defeating the seemingly invincible German troops. His name was to become a household name: General Bernard Law Montgomery.

It was his division of the British Army that had come out of France with the knowledge that they had not only held the line against the German advance but had shattered it whenever they were put to the test

The short, jaunty General Montgomery, or Monty as he was known by admirers and critics alike, trained his army in the South of England to use the few hundred precious Valantine Matilda and light tanks that remained in lightning attacks of his own when and if the invasion occurred.

Rare for a modern man, he put aside time in the day just to think. His desk was clear so everything could be dealt with immediately. He was stubborn, eccentric, a tee totalling egomaniac, as well as a strong anti-smoker after quitting when his wife died. Yet, he was the best hope for Britain in its greatest hour of peril.

John and the rest of the 3rd Division had trained all through June to move whole battalions at night by lorries without lights, to fight at a point of their choosing, to build the best defences possible but man them with an attack mentality that would destroy the enemy at a rate of 10 Germans for every British soldier.

Commandeering double-decker buses to make up for the lorries left in France, Monty had a well trained, but thin, layer of troops along the south east coast from Dover west to Portsmouth where the invasion was expected. It was at the white cliffs of Dover that the Germans would in all likelihood strike. It was the closest link between occupied Europe and Great Britain. Twenty miles separated the armies.

Just months before the impossible had occurred, the German Blitzkrieg had forced France to surrender. Despite Churchill's offer to make all Frenchmen British and indissolvably unite the two countries, it was too late. Prime Minister Renauld capitulated and the Germans marched into Paris and occupied Northern France. In June 1940, 430 thousand British and French troops had been rescued by the Royal Navy from Dunkirk to fight again.

In his radio addresses to the nation, Churchill showed defiance and held out hope. His rallying cry, "we shall never surrender," became a clarion call. John took off his water-beaded helmet, hung it with his dripping plastic gas cape on the back of a wooden folding chair and poured himself a cup of tea in the officer's tent. His twin brother Alan, also a subaltern in the Royal Hamilton Rifles, looked up from the radio set he was tinkering with and grunted. John ran a hand through his thick red hair and rubbed his wet chin. "You've got a dry, easy job there Alan, replacing radio tubes."

The front page of the Daily Mail on the table showed a photo of the Duke and Duchess of Windsor in Nassau of the Bahamas as the Duke took up his official position as Governor. They both looked limp in the hot sun. The Duke was wearing his smart, tropical white dress uniform, white shoes and white hat.

"Remember that night we arrived at Liverpool? Well, this is wetter," John observed.

"Eastbourne is supposed to be the sunniest spot in England."

"Alan, you should know. You played tennis here last summer as a warm up to Wimbledon. The Vickers machine-gun positions are almost afloat, and in a few minutes I make my rounds of the guards down by the pier. Oh well," John said, "at least this is warmer than Norway."

"I still can't figure out how you managed to wangle your way into the British force sent to Narvik to help the poor bloody Norwegians. You must have been the only Canadian there."

"I've told you before Alan," John laughed, "I speak French, I ski and I volunteered, although someone I know owed me a favour and smoothed the way at the War Office. Can't say anything more. It was an interesting time, at least I got to shoot at someone."

"Which is more than we got to do. I couldn't believe it when I saw you gazetted for a Military Medal for storming that Spandeau machine gun nest. Made me sick, I can tell you," Alan joked. "Hello, who's this?"

A BSA motorbike roared up beside their tent and a mud-spattered dispatch rider poked his head through the tent flap, the leather ear flaps of his courier's leather helmet snapped tightly together under his chin.

"Lieutenant Stafford?"

"Yes," the identical twins replied together.

"Crikey," the messenger said, "er, John Stafford?" Alan pointed a screwdriver at John.

Alan thanked the dispatch rider and gave him directions to the mess tent for some refreshment. John slit open the buff envelope, stamped OHMS in red ink, with his penknife and scanned the contents.

"Lt. John Stafford, RHR Canadian Div. is promoted to Captain forthwith and ordered to 1st Independent Company Achnacarry Castle, Fort William, Scotland 1200 hours Sun.1 Sept. 1940"

He beamed at Alan. "I've got my posting for one of those shock troop outfits the Royal Marines are setting up."

"You've done it again, John," Alan said. "I applied but haven't heard a whisper yet."

"I'll see if I can put in a good word for you"

"Yeah, that will be a great help," Alan said sarcastically. "When do you leave sunny Eastbourne?"

"Tomorrow, I'll pop up to London and take the overnight train to Glasgow."

"Oh, good, you can spend the night checking the pill boxes, the mortars and the anti-tank gun positions, and scan the horizon with your binoculars while you stand on the promenade in front of the empty hotels getting soaked."

"By the way I've been promoted to Captain." John ducked as Alan threw his empty tin mug at him.

Rested after two hours sleep following the all-night watch, John shook hands with his brother. He took a two ton lorry drive into Eastbourne to catch his train to the capital. It was a beautiful day, not a cloud in the sky.

He had an hour before the train left. He walked past the empty, boarded up hotels along the street running above the beach of shingle. He looked at the pier, once home to a small fairground, photo machines, ice cream shops and sea anglers with great lug worms on their huge hooks held by thick line. Now it was empty. He saw the gap between the pier and the shore; the connecting girders and floor had been dismantled. It could not serve as a dock by invaders. It was booby-trapped as well, in case the Germans wanted to use it as a beachhead command post.

A Bren gun carrier with two caterpillar tracks roared past the dug up flower-beds that once decorated the centre of the road by the sea front. Now the wet earth concealed anti-tank guns and mortars under camouflage netting. A convoy of lorries drove by on their way east to Brighton, up the chalk hill and along the white cliffs at Beachyhead.

A platoon of Canadian troops marched crisply past. The officer leading them saluted as John walked over to the Grand Hotel. Enjoying the sound of the salt waves slapping on the shore of the nearby beach, he climbed to the top of the roof where five soldiers were on duty with binoculars and a Vickers machine guns in a sandbagged emplacement.

All along the coast a constant watch was being kept. Recce flights were made twice a day over the enemy docks in France. The Royal Navy was intensely patrolling the Channel.

"Come for a look Sir?"

"Yes, one last look. I've been posted elsewhere, just thought I would say goodbye."

"You might miss the party?"

"I think the party will be so big that everyone will be able to come."

John smiled, remembering the picnic in July with his brother and a few Women's Army Corps officers in July on the grass above the cliff. Carefree, they had tossed their empty Bass beer bottles into the sea far below them.

He wished the soldiers in his platoon luck as he walked from the machine gun pill box to the trenches in the park and positions in the buildings along the seafront. Huge rolls of barbed wire ran along the seawall. Every 20 feet a wooden sign proclaimed in red paint: DANGER MINES. Skull and crossbones reinforced the warning.

The windows of the hotels and shops in the town were covered with tape to prevent flying glass if shells or bombs exploded. At the end of the beach, on top of the cliff above the small holiday cottages, was a giant concrete pill-box containing a Royal Artillery howitzer. Its barrel, which pointed out to sea, was draped with camouflage netting.

John looked at his watch and thought of Felicity. He decided to phone her at her father's home from the one hotel still open.

"Is that you, Felicity?"

"Yes, you're lucky you caught me. I'm only in for overnight, I'm taking a break from working at Windsor Castle on the art collection. We're packing it up in crates for the duration."

"Glad to hear it. Look, I'm coming up to London this morning on my way to a new posting. Fancy a bite to eat? You can tell me all about it. A late lunch?"

"The Ritz at two, in the lobby. I'll be in Daddy's office before that. See you, John."

His khaki gas mask bag on his chest and a kit bag over his right shoulder, he walked a quarter-mile inland through the town. The prospect of meeting Felicity made him whistle the whole way. The road signs had all been turned around to give the enemy the wrong directions. His feet led him across a path through a well-kept lawn.

Finches sang as he climbed the front steps into the pointed archway and through an ancient oak door, black with age. He took off his peaked cap and left his kit bag in the narthex. He walked up the flagstone aisle and took a seat. The smells of old stone, wooden pews and the piety of ages filled his nostrils.

He pulled a prayer cushion off the back of the armless wooden chair in front of him and placed it on the cool stone, knelt and looked up at the stained glass, the Norman arches and columns, all leading the eye and thoughts heavenward. He focused on the bronze cross on the altar.

Praying for a few minutes made him feel better, more confident. The bald, middle aged rector, in black cassock and white clerical collar, called out a friendly "good morning," as he approached John.

"Good morning to you. This is a fine church. Look, thank you for having it open. I needed a quiet moment to reflect ."

"That's why we're here. It is a simple church, not Canterbury or Salisbury by any means, but it is still His house in these ungodly times. God-speed." John thanked him again, picked up his cap and kit bag and left to catch the train.

The compartments and corridors were packed like most wartime trains. Soldiers, sailors and airmen were on leave or travelling to new postings. As an officer, John had a first class railway pass, but the coach was jammed with two naval officers finishing leave, a bulky army brigadier and two RAF officers in wearing ornate moustaches brushed up at the ends. Several older businessmen sat by the windows.

John was able to doze and catch up on the sleep he lost the night before. He woke with a start when the naval captains burst out laughing at a joke. The carriage air was oppressively warm and full of tobacco smoke.

He stretched and made his way to the corridor by squeezing past soldiers who were smoking in the corridor. It was a warm day and most of the windows were pulled down. He eased open the button on the right breast pocket of his woollen, olive green, battle dress jacket and pulled out his packet of cigarettes. He lit one and looked out with interest at the rolling countryside and villages that whizzed past.

Many fields had old cars, vans or buses parked in the middle to prevent landings by German troops in gliders.

A group of Land Army girls, working on the farms in place of the men who had volunteered or been called up, were leading some Clydesdale work horses into a barley field. The air was clear. He could make out the lines in their brown corduroy jodhpurs, the fresh complexions of their faces and their cheery smiles. They looked up at the passing train and waved at him. John waved back.

"Got a light, Sir?" John looked round to see a short figure in RAF blue, an observer's single white wing over his left breast pocket.

"Sure." He snapped open the lighter Felicity had bought him in Oxford Street and held its flame under the Player's cigarette the observer held to his mouth with nicotine-stained fingers.

"At Dunkirk were you, Sir?"

"No, I missed that. We were ready to go to France but got orders to stand down. Now we're waiting like everyone else to see if Hitler comes."

"I flew at Dunkirk ... we tried our best to keep the Jerries from shelling our lads on the beaches; we flew 10 missions a day for a week. God, I was tired. But we're ready for 'em now, aren't we, Sir."

"Yes, we're ready. Every week we're stronger, like Churchill says."

"It was a bleeding miracle, Sir. Thanks for the light. You Canadians are pretty decent, even the officers, if you don't mind me saying, Sir,", the fellow said and grinned.

John thanked him and looked out the window in search of more land girls to wave at. His six shot Webley army revolver was secure in its light green holster on his left hip. A cord snaked from the metal ring set in the revolver's wooden butt, up and around his neck and through his jacket epaulets.

John's brown officer's boots shone below green gaiters. His 1937 style uniform was the image of the new soldier. His peaked officer's cap bore the silver badge of the Royal Hamilton Rifles: two muskets crossed over a silver bugle, surrounded by a wreath of maple leaves, with St. Edward's Crown surmounting the circle of the design. On his shoulders he proudly wore the blue flashes with "CANADA" embroidered in red thread.

Hours later the train entered the outskirts of London. The huge art deco Battersea Power Works loomed alongside, its four massive chimneys spewing out smoke as the coal burning station produced electricity for the southern districts of the city. Barrage balloons floated overhead tethered by cables to the power station and other buildings to deter low altitude Luftwaffe attacks.

Sirens wailed as John leaned far out of the window, heard distant explosions and saw the smoke of scores of ack-ack shells exploding in the sky to the east over the Thames. Hundreds of black spots in the eastern sky became larger, he could identify enemy bombers: Heinkel 111s, Junker 88s and Dornier 217s. They dropped what began as minute black eggs which grew as they tumbled down upon the London docks.

The first raid on London, John thought.

RAF fighters tore into the bombers. A Hawker Hurricane roared overhead and shot machine gun bullets into a Dornier which belched smoke and spun, exploding as it hit some buildings on the north side of the Thames. A column of smoke rose from the crash site, joining the rest of the slowly rising smoke from explosions, burning buildings and fuel storage depots at the London docks. The passengers of the train, civilian and in uniform were all squeezed into the corridor watching the aerial battle, cheering on the pilot in his humpbacked machine.

Far above them other RAF Spitfires were dog-fighting with German Messerschmitt 109s. Long white contrails criss-crossed high up in the blue sky. Occasionally a parachute opened and a pilot dangled beneath it. Planes blew up, bombs exploded with distant thumps.

John marvelled at this front row seat for the deadly aerial ballet, but was greatly relieved when he finally got through to Felicity at Canada House on a public phone at Victoria station.

"Why don't we wait until the raid is over? At the all-clear, we can meet at the Ritz. See you then and please take care of yourself John," Felicity cautioned.

"Shouldn't you be in the basement air raid shelter at Canada House?" John said.

"You should be in one too," Felicity countered.

He watched fire engines, with bells ringing, lurch wildly through the streets covered with rubble from bombed buildings. He helped a Civil Defence crew rescue a mother and child trapped under a staircase while their home lay in ruins, shattered plaster, wood and bricks all around them.

"You look a sight," Felicity said to him as he walked into the lobby of the Ritz.

"Yes, a bit of dust ... I tried to clean it off. There was an air raid, you know."

"Yes, I know. Glad you're all right." She pecked him on the cheek.

"Me too. Now how about some lunch, I could eat a horse," John said as he put out his his right arm and Felicity placed her arm on his. "What have you been up to, Felicity?"

"I've been doing a lot of work at Windsor Castle. Canada House got a call wanting to know if I was available to help store the Royal collection of paintings at the Castle for the duration. The curator there taught an art conservation course I took last year."

"You are a woman of many talents," John said. "I've been sloshing around in the rain and getting lost on night exercises since I saw you last."

She saw him off on the overnight express to Scotland and gave him a quick hug and a kiss.

"Wait for me," John had said in her ear as he inhaled her Chanel perfume.

"I'll wait for you. You can write me at Windsor Castle. I'll write to you. Good luck, John."

They waved at each other until the train pulled out of sight from the platform into the blackout darkness and whatever lay lurking in the unknown future. Felicity stood for a minute, her hands stuffed into her coat pockets. Then she briskly made her way to the next train for Windsor, her gas mask box over her shoulder.

CHAPTER SEVEN BAHAMAS

The next day, Sunday September 8th, the dawn broke in the east and the rising sun irradiated the high clouds with pink. The grey Unterseeboot 267, the newest and fastest of the huge Kriegsmarine submarine fleet, sliced through the North Sea after traversing the Kiel Canal. The sleek, steel shark ripped through the waves on the surface. It was equipped with four torpedo tubes, twenty torpedoes and a deck gun. The captain, wearing a black polo-neck sweater, with a black reefer coat over his shoulders and white-topped naval cap, he swept his binoculars across the horizon and the East Frisian Islands coming up on the port bow from his vantage point on the grey conning tower.

He spoke to the SS officer next to him and the two men disappeared down the conning tower ladder. A rating closed the watertight metal door in the conning tower and twisted the round handle hard and tight, then slid down the ladder emerging into the control room.

Count Von Darmstadt who wore his Iron Cross first class at his throat, sneered as he looked around, unimpressed, indeed shocked, by the shoddy appearance of these submariners.

"Now, Captain Herschel, take her to 40 metres and proceed into the North Sea. Steer west north west. I will give our destination to your officers if you would be. He cleared his throat as if being polite was something to work at. Kind enough to gather them in your wardroom."

Captain Herschel seathed inwardly at the arrogance of this trumped-up landlubber, giving orders to him in front of his own crew. Ordering his crew to take the submarine to 50 metres he picked up the microphone to order all officers except , one on watch, to the wardroom.

As soon as the officers crammed into the compartment not much bigger than a wardrobe, the door was shut. Von Darmstadt sat under the framed photo of Hitler and Admiral Doenitz at the launching of the submarine. Captain Herschel spoke, "Men, we have been chosen to carry out a vital, secret mission for the Fatherland. The Major here," he nodded at the brooding SS officer, "has orders direct from the Fuhrer." The

Captain crossed his arms and looked at Von Darmstadt in as detached a manner as he could muster.

"Thank you, Captain. Our destination is the Caribbean, the British Colony of the Bahamas to be precise, the island of New Providence."

A young Lieutenant whispered to the chief engineer, "Treasure hunting!".

Von Darmstadt eyed him icily. "Human treasure, Lieutenant. The ten men of the Brandenberg Regiment on board with me will disembark on rubber rafts just offshore and as near the capital, Nassau, as possible. We shall be, he smiled and continued, escorting the new governor of the Bahamas and his wife back to France on this U-boat."

"And who is this governor, Herr Major?" the Captain asked with an amused expression on his face.

"The Duke of Windsor."

The Captain's jaw dropped.

"Our Secret Service attempts to win him over while he was in Spain and Portugal failed. The Fuhrer believes he can convince him to be of service to his country and to the Reich if he speaks to him face to face."

His composure returning, the Captain asked pointedly, "What good is he? It would be better just to shell Nassau and slip away to sink British freighters."

"It is obvious that naval men don't understand politics. We have the man who was once king of Great Britain, a man whose wife has been slighted by his brother the present king. It is obvious to all but the dullest mind that they would make a friendly king and queen of the vassal state Great Britain will become before Christmas. The Duke and Duchess have been exiled. We shall bring them back to the centre of events."

"It is risky, Herr Major. He may resist," the Captain added.

"It is your job to obey orders. We shall return with them. Tell the crew only that we are sailing to the Caribbean. Now, if you will leave me, I have work to do."

Von Darmstadt opened his attaché case and withdrew some detailed maps of the Bahamas. The Captain rose, lifted his hand in the Aryan salute and left the room followed by his officers, whose eyes shone with excitement at the knowledge of their cloak-and-dagger mission.

The next morning, while they took air into their tanks on the surface in the ocean swell, an RAF Sunderland flying boat lumbered over them and dropped several bombs from the racks on its wings.

The observers on watch in the conning tower had shouted a warning down the voice tube and threw themselves down the hatch as it had approached. The submarine began to fill its ballast tanks and sink. The radio operator of the Sunderland sent off a message to Coastal Command.

Soon the nearest Royal Navy destroyer or frigate would seek U-267. But they would not find it. The submarine had dived deep and set its course west south west for the open Atlantic, heading for the crystal blue water surrounding the Bahamas and a remote sandy beach suitable for a landing party. It took the new class of submarine only seven days to cross the Atlantic. In the early morning of 5th of August the Count and his handpicked troops, diesel fuel smeared across their faces as camouflage, took rubber rafts in silence from the deck of the U-boat and silently paddled into the humid tropical night.

It only took a moment for a German soldier to cut the telephone wire into the Governor's mansion before the guards at the front gate were dealt with by pistols with silencers. The bullets made a gentle phut-phut and the sentries fell. The sounds of the night continued with only a momentary pause of strained silence as the bodies were dragged into the bush. Insects clicked and whirred, the buzz of a cocktail party and clink of glasses continued from the back of the Governor's mansion. The Duke and Duchess were entertaining guests around the floodlit pool. The tiled cipher E R VIII was spotlighted on the wall of the pool.

Four of the raiders followed Major Von Darmstadt through the front door gripping their PK38 machine guns. More raiders slipped into the shadows around the sides of the mansion. Two men put on the uniforms of the dead guards, picked up their rifles, and, to all intents and purposes, looked the same as their victims had moments before.

"Who the hell are you?" growled the Duke's detective in the living room as he reached for the revolver beneath his jacket.

Von Darmstadt shot him and a small red hole appeared between the detective's eyes as he fell backwards onto a sofa.

Wasting no time, Von Darmstadt ran through the French doors leading to the pool. There was panic as the Duke and Duchess and their guests took in the unexpected visitors waving machine guns at them.

The Duke was the first to react and he shouted to his guards for help.

"It is no use, Your Royal Highness. They are no longer here." Von Darmstadt spoke calmly.

The Duke was immaculate in his tuxedo and black bowtie. The smoke curled up from the pipe he had been smoking. Wallis, in a dark blue dress adorned with wearing a diamond-and-emerald peacock brooch, was white with shock.

Her mouth kept opening and closing as if she were some kind of fish. She looked around and saw the stunned expression on the faces of the elite of Nassau who had been invited for cocktails. She moved over to stand by her husband.

Putting his Luger into his holster, Von Darmstadt bowed to the Windsors. "Your Royal Highnesses, I am here to express the Fuhrer's wish that you return to your home in Paris and help him arrange an honourable peace with Great Britain. He knows you share his desire for peace and a new world order where Britain and Germany can stand together against the evil of Communism."

"David ..." Wallis whispered, "I feel faint." He helped her sit down on a wooden lounge chair and stood next to her with his arm placed protectively around her shoulders. She leaned limply against him.

"Our guests," the Duke said, "please release them."

"We have every intention of doing so, but we do have to tie them up. They will be safe, I assure you Sir. My orders are to take you both to Europe. A submarine awaits us. You have three minutes to bring a few precious items ... jewellery, photos, if you wish." Von Darmstadt turned to his men and issued orders in German to tie the guests up and gag them.

"What if we refuse to go?" the Duke asked, with his chin stuck out defiantly. His face had recovered its tan, but his forehead was creased in concern.

"You are coming. We are rescuing you from exile."

The one-time king emperor bit his lip and tried desperately to think of something he could do, anything. A part of him screamed for them to shoot him and get it done with. He looked at Wallis who was dabbing at her eyes with a small hankie. He swallowed. He had made his decision.

"I will come with you, under protest, but only because of my wife." Wallis clutched both his hands.

The Duke took her face in his hands tenderly. "We shall go together. Whatever happens, we will be together I promise." It was a scene, the bound captives told the authorities the next day, out of a romantic novel.

Von Darmstadt led his men and the prisoners to the rendezvous point at 0200 hours. No alarm had been raised. One of his men flashed a Morse code signal from an electric torch. A small flash of light responded off shore. They paddled out to the submarine on the rafts. As they drew nearer, they could see the dark mass of the black U-boat lying low in the water. Naval ratings, in dark overalls instead of their normal white tropical kit, helped them clamber onto the deck and into the hatch.

As U-267 dived and headed northeast for Brest in France, Von Darmstadt allowed himself to breathe easily. The Duke and Duchess had refused any drink or food and retired for bed in the captain's cramped quarters. Tomorrow, Major Von Darmstadt would begin preparing them psychologically for the role Hitler had planned for them. He was looking forward to it. They would be putty in his hands, and he had the hands of a craftsman in the service of the Reich. He fancied himself as Governor of London and he knew just the place from which he could wield the power he looked to using, his headquarters would be the Tower of London. The pitiful man and woman in the captain's bed were destined to be monarchs of New Britain but under his guidance and protection.

All in good time. He poured himself and the Captain another drink of schnapps.

"To victory" he toasted and clinked his shot glass with the captain's.

"Victory."

CHAPTER EIGHT COMMANDO

It was night as the train pulled north over the invisible border and into Scotland. After waiting hours for another train in Edinburgh's railway station John and the other men finally arrived at the tiny Fort William station in the Highlands feeling very stiff and tired.

John breathed the fresh air deep into his lungs and slung his kit bag over his shoulder. "So this Godforsaken wilderness is home for the next eight weeks," a fellow officer in a dark blue naval greatcoat joked. His name was Duncan MacLeod. His brylcreamed black hair was parted in the middle, his furrowed brow and studious glasses gave him a worried, intellectual appearance older than his 20 years warranted.

"Not yet," John said, "I heard we have a lorry ride ahead of us."

They had played numerous games of cribbage on the train from Glasgow to Fort William. An ancient 25 year old Australian lieutenant with a shock of fair hair had mocked them as they played. "Now that's a Pommie game. Let me show you how to play it properly."

In turn, John and Duncan beat him decisively, but made the mistake of agreeing to a few hands of poker. The Australian, it turned out, should have been a Mississippi riverboat gambler. As they played, Duncan told them how he had interrupted his medical studies at Edinburgh University to join up. "I read chemistry and biology, got a first, next stop medical school. One afternoon I was sitting in the university library and I realized everyone else who was fit that I knew was wearing a uniform, so I tried again, in the navy."

He pushed his brown tortoise shell spectacles back up the bridge of his nose. "They took me even with my short sightedness - must have been desperate for officer material the day I went. They didn't know I found out what the optical chart said and memorized it. I went through officer training, hence the lieutenant's ring." He showed the one gold ring around his jacket cuffs. I just don't wear my glasses in front of anyone important. I saw a bit of action on a destroyer. Then I heard about this new outfit for amphibious operations against the Jerries and volunteered."

"Well," Aubrey interjected "I don't have the education you two have had, unless you count the college of hard knocks. I left home at fourteen, too many mouths for my mum and dad to feed. I sheered sheep, lived in the outback with the Aborigines, and then did a bit of cattle work before joining the Royal Australian Artillery right at the bottom of the ladder, as a Gunner in 1937. I decided to succeed - worked my way up by being the best. They made the mistake of granting me a commission when I came out on top of my officer training class."

"What's that object sticking out of your kit bag?" John asked Aubrey.

"Well, since you'll be hearing me play in our off hours, I might as well tell you. It's my didgeridoo," he replied.

"Your didgeree what?" John asked.

"Didgeridoo. It's an Aboriginal instrument." He warmed to his subject as John and Duncan looked at each other in disbelief. "This is just a small one, portable. It's only four feet long. It's a branch from a eucalyptus tree, when it falls down termites eat the wood inside and leave a tough tube. You blow into the tube and it makes great, low rumbling notes."

"Really?" John said sounding skeptical.

"Too right, I ended up the outback when I ran away from home, and got befriended by an Aborigine, George Hudson; he helped me decorate it and taught me how to play it. I can tell you about eating snakes too if you like."

"We'll pass on that right now, Aubrey," John said decisively. Achnarry Castle, the Commando training school, was a draughty ride in a 10 ton lorry from the Span Bridge Railway Station at Fort William. The convoy of lorries lurched their way along the narrow road towards Achnarry and the chilly waters of Loch Lochy, as they sat in the back of the chilly, windblown lorry with only khaki canvas keeping off the evening drizzle, not the wind. The lorries crunched onto the gravel driveway leading to Achnarry Castle and 100 men jumped out with their kit bags and milled about.

They were ushered into the castle hall where folding wooden chairs had been set up in rows. The watchful glassy eyes of ancient stag and bear heads gazed down upon them. The commandant stepped out upon the stage and bellowed at them like a highland beast roaring at unwelcome visitors in his patch.

"Gentlemen, this is an all ranks meeting. I want to welcome you to one hell of a tough course. My name is Colonel Jack Carton. Anyone who is not 'up to snuff' will be returned to their unit, and that unlucky man will have missed his chance to be on the cutting edge of our fight with Jerry."

"We're jamming a four week course into three weeks because Mr. Hitler may want to visit us soon. This outfit was first talked of as a fighting or independent company, even the name Leopards was tossed about. Mr. Churchill chose the name Commandos, no doubt remembering his days in the Boer War when the crack-shot Boer farmers took to their horses with light rations and Mauser rifles to make lightning raids on our positions before we could strike back. They called themselves Kommandos, with a "K". Like them, our job is not to face an army in the field but to take on special missions, hit hard and get out."

There were chuckles from the trainees as they relaxed in the glow of the commandant's enthusiasm and charisma. "That will be the fun part. Here's the bad news, you will be billeted in the town and will miss that delicious British army breakfast you so enjoy. " There was laughter from the lower ranks. "However, you still get up at 0600 hours, and instead of parade there will be a two mile run before breakfast."

The laughter stopped.

"Your classes will be in self-defence and small-arms training including German weapons. You will become expert in mountain climbing and canoeing you will be in very good shape by the time you leave us. Our full-kit marches, rappelling and living off' the land exercises will see to that. We'll be carrying out amphibious landing exercises on the lochs with a ferry boat and some rubber rafts.

"German soldiers are good troops. They have been having it all their own way so far, but they are not unbeatable. Train well, train hard and we can defeat them. Sergeant-Major Lincoln will assign you billets."

The black Sergeant-Major, a rarity in the British army at that time, was as sturdily built and unstoppable as a train engine, stood up gripping a clipboard. "He's not going to be telling us what to do surely?" muttered one of the officers in the row ahead of John. The Commandant's acute hearing picked up the bigoted remark.

"Oh, one more thing. Sergeant-Major Abraham Lincoln is one of the Canadians who have come over to help us. He was heavyweight boxing champion of the British Empire and once bested Primo Carnera in the ring, I trust you will pay him the respect due to your self-defence instructor. He will be looking for volunteers, so don't stand out."

Carton glared at the officer who had muttered out loud; the fellow shifted uneasily, his neck red with embarrassment.

"Officers over there, please. NCOs there and privates over here," Lincoln ordered in what John recognized as a Nova Scotia accent. "He's from the East coast of Canada," John said quietly.

"How can you tell? Sounds American to me," Aubrey replied in thick Aussi twang putting on his Australian bush hat with one side of the rim held up with a brass regimental badge.

"And you sound like nothing from the civilized world," Duncan MacLeod jokingly retorted in his soft, educated Edinburgh burr.

"Just for that you're buying the first shout at the nearest pub, mate!" Aubrey declared.

Duncan leaned against a trestle table with his arms folded. "Brigadier Carton seems a real card."

"He scares the hell out of me; imagine what the Germans will think of him," Aubrey threw in.

"Well you know," John interjected, "he's the one who used a bow and arrows in France against the Jerries on a night raid."

"It wouldn't surprise me, these Commando chaps seem to like the unexpected approach," Duncan replied.

After seeing the men matched with billets, they paraded in the courtyard and John, Aubrey and Duncan marched them into the village. After ensuring all of them found the correct cottages, houses and the one room school where they were to stay, they retired to their billet in the town pub, 'The Highland Cow'. It sported a large painted sign depicting a rust colored, shaggy highland cow with monstrous horns, glowering menacingly through a misty glen.

Despite a lumpy mattress and the air-quaking bass drone of Aubrey's didgeridoo next door, John slept soundly. He dreamt he was swimming up Niagara Falls. Palm trees were growing alongside the chasm where the cool water spewed forth, millions of gallons per hour. The torrent inexplicably flowed into a mountain stream, the palm trees remained, seeming out of place alongside pine trees. Instead of coconuts, the palm trees burst forth with exploding fecundity and sprouted grenades. The Commando recruits stood upon each other's shoulders, picking the deadly fruit and stuffing them into their pockets.

The dawn was foggy and cool. The run led by the Sergeant-Major was at a grueling pace, past herds of nonchalant sheep who hardly looked up at the scores of baggy-blue-shorted soldiers running through blazes of heather and through ice cold burns. For every man who stopped to catch his breath it was 30 push ups.

Aubrey had just enough puff left at the end of the two miles, to wheeze; "that ...," he drew in a quick breath, "Sergeant-Major Lincoln ... he's in good shape." The others were too tired to respond.

After breakfast at the castle, they did calisthenics and lifted logs, tossing them from one team to the other. The first day was exhausting, the second day, torture, as aching muscles screamed silently, but by the end of the first 10 days they were each running 10 miles with energy to spare and lifting logs as if they were branches. They were young, fit and learning to function as a team.

Lincoln, whom John had nicknamed President, had the three friends for self-defence classes in the first week. President Lincoln took great delight in sparring with each of them, showing the fine points of boxing and then demonstrating the throws of judo. After a week under the President's patient instruction, the smallest man in their class, predictably a Welsh miner from the tank corps could throw John, the tallest man, on his back in two seconds.

"Thank God the first thing we were taught was how to fall, Sergeant-Major," John said as he jumped up from the mat where Trooper Owen had triumphantly planted his boot upon John's chest.

"And what do you do to immobilize the enemy, Owen, once he's down?" Lincoln bellowed.

"Kick him in the head, Sergeant-Major."

"Other suggestions?"

"Bayonet him in the chest," a soldier from Newcastle shouted out."

"What did you say?" an anonymous jester called out, ribbing the Geordie for his almost unintelligible accent.

Laughter drowned out the next suggestion, "whack him with your rifle butt."

"Take him prisoner!" Duncan shouted out.

"Very good, Sir, but if that's not possible, kill him and it's one less to worry about later."

After dinner, the trainee officers and enlisted men filled the castle's great hall. A makeshift boxing ring had been set up. President Lincoln wore a tuxedo, borrowed from the laird of the castle's wardrobe, to make him a convincing referee for the boxing tournament.

Five pairs in different weight classes fought it out, and then it was the turn of John and a sergeant with the neck of a bull and a solid punch to match. John, as a southpaw, had the advantage, and since he was a bit lighter, could weave and dodge away from most of the vicious jabs the sergeant threw his way.

In the eighth round John caught one on the chin and was knocked down, but was up again at the referee's count of six. The bell rang indicating the end of the round and John enjoyed the benefit of a sponge of water squeezed over his head by his seconds, Aubrey and Duncan.

"You're tiring him, but don't take any more hits like that or you're a goner," Aubrey said into his left ear.

"Give him some taps, dance around and give him a hard left," Duncan suggested.

"Easier said than done," John muttered as the laird rang a dinner gong to signify the ninth round. John jabbed at his opponent and danced around him. The sergeant tried to connect but it was John who landed a hard hit to his jaw and the Sergeant staggered and fell. Sergeant Major Lincoln counted him down and out, and lifted John's gloved hand in triumph.

Aubrey and Duncan hoisted John on their shoulders, paraded him about the ring and announced to cheers, "Captain Stafford invites everyone to 'The Highland Cow', the drinks are on him."

"Smoke break!" roared the President Lincoln on the obstacle course the next day. The battle-dressed ranks fell out, some standing in knots, others sitting under Scots pine trees. They had just completed making a rope bridge with wooden toggles, over a fast-flowing river in a ravine.

Smoke bombs had been exploded by mortar. Live ammunition mixed with blanks had been fired over their heads and to the sides. Real grenades thrown 100 feet down river had exploded with dramatic effect beside the troops crossing the precarious, hand-made bridge.

John helped a flailing trainee as they clambered across the makeshift rope bridge, one rope to walk on, one on each side to hold onto. His wet boot soles slipped and John fell into the river pulling the soldier with him, they surfaced spluttering.

Aubrey and Duncan laughed as they pulled them up the steep riverbank .

Duncan quipped, "You looked bloody silly falling off that rope bridge."

"I felt very silly. My boot slipped but I learned a good lesson: hang on tight or you're on your arse."

Sergeant-Major Lincoln gathered the Commandos in training, "Right you lot, now we have a special treat-lessons from the man who designed the Commando knife, a clever chap called Captain Sykes. Take a seat on the grass."

"Thank you Sergeant-Major" said an officer standing in front of them as they trainees sat cross-legged on the grass. "I'm Captain Sykes. My friend Captain Fairburn and myself designed this knife especially for you Commandos."

He stepped forward, balancing a dagger in the palm of his open right hand. "This, gentlemen, is one of 500 Wilkinson-Sword carbon knives for use by desperate characters such as yourselves. It is 178 mm long with a brass, gnarled grip and an oval cross guard. He held it up and gripped the handle between his fingers and drew back his arm, then hurled the dagger into a tree 30 feet away."

Lincoln retrieved it as the trainees applauded. It took the rest of the afternoon with the men taking turns as guards and attackers to have them confident that they could silence a sentry forever with the knives.

The next day they used bayonets to find buried land mines. They wriggled over the ground, brown earthworms stabbing into the earth, groping for metal.

As they were scrambling over the ground, Luftwaffe bombers pounded RAF fighter airdromes in the south of Britain, destroying men, machines and aircraft hangars at a tremendous rate.

The raid against London had been a "one-off". A few German bombers, against orders and having lost their targets had dropped their bombs on London by mistake; in retaliation, Bomber Command had bombed Berlin. This infuriated Hitler, who demanded a reprisal attack on London. After all, the Nazi hierarchy had promised not one bomb would drop on Berlin.

Now the Luftwaffe was back to the task, so important if Operation Sea Lion was to succeed, in eliminating the RAF Fighter Command.

The Commandos paddled folding canoes in all kinds of weather, day and night, aching and cursing while on the loch. John did his best to have the boats referred to as kayaks, but was stymied by the commandant who insisted on calling them canoes. The hardest part involved paddling off the west coast of Scotland in the Irish sea at night, then blowing up a dummy German headquarters after "silencing" the guards dressed up in captured Wehrmacht uniforms.

The radio in the officer's mess was playing some light band music as John walked up the massive wooden staircase in the castle a few minutes before 8 o'clock for a few minutes relaxation. As he got himself a cup of tea and sat next to Aubrey and Duncan at a table, conversation ceased as someone turned up the radio to catch the news.

A man's voice speaking in clipped, 'received English' spoke.

Here is the BBC News at 9 p.m. September 14th. The King and Queen spent the afternoon visiting bombed out families in London. Queen Elizabeth told Civil Defence workers; "now we can look the East End in the face," after a bomb landed on Buckingham Palace in the raid yesterday. King George and Queen Elizabeth will continue to stay in London. Their children, the Princesses Elizabeth and Margaret Rose are safe in the country.

The Royal Navy continued its nightly shelling of German invasion barges in European ports last night. The Royal Air Force bombed ports in Belgium and France.

Pilots reported that the French coast was lit up "like a Christmas tree."

News just received - the Duke and Duchess of Windsor have been kidnapped by a German raiding party which landed at the Bahamas by submarine. The Duke of Windsor just began his term as Governor of the Bahamas in July. The Royal Navy is attempting to locate the submarine which is believed to be making for German occupied Europe.

The Nazi Head of Propaganda, Joseph Goebbels, told an American reporter that the Duke and Duchess had asked to be taken back to France in an attempt to negotiate an end to the war. Prime Minister Churchill reported to a hushed House of Commons this evening that this was a lie and that they had been taken at gunpoint. Mr. Churchill stated; "I have the utmost confidence that the man who did such an outstanding job as Prince of Wales for many years and who was our King for a brief time, would not capitulate to any enemy terms and would regard himself as a prisoner of war. His Majesty has expressed great concern about the kidnapping of his brother, and the Duchess of Windsor, and has appealed to Hitler to release them without conditions. His Majesty and the coalition government concur that there will be no bargaining."

The Italian army advancing into Egypt from Libya has met stiff resistance from the Coldstream Guards at Sullum under General Wavell who commands the British, Australian and Indian troops in Egypt. That is the end of the news.

Speculation ran riot, as the officers talked amongst themselves about the latest twist in the war.

"He always seemed a bit undependable. What do you think John?" Duncan asked.

"Well, they did go to visit Hitler and were given a good reception. They got a warm welcome in Venice from Mussolini's lot as well."

Aubrey joined in. "It's hard to believe the Duke of Windsor is for surrender. Perhaps he's hoping that Hitler really is not so bad. Maybe the bloke's unable to believe anyone could be as bad as the press makes him out."

"Well, he is, you know. I've seen what the Reich is really like," John said as he finished his drink.

"I believe you," Aubrey said, "but now the King's brother is in a real pickle and no mistake, and, mates, we will be too if we don't get to bed. I'm bushed and that 20 mile march in full kit tomorrow will be gruelling to say the least."

Instead of the march, however, the next morning the commandant assembled all ranks for a parade. "I've got some important news. General Brooke, the Chief of Staff, has asked that you be passed ahead of time in order for you to take immediate part in the defence of this island. Your class is now A Troop, 8th Commando.

There was a murmur of excitement in the ranks, as they stood at ease, their hands clasped behind their backs. "You will leave as soon as possible. Captain Stafford is given the rank of acting major and will command the troop. Lieutenants MacLeod and Hunter are made acting captains and will each take a platoon. Sergeant-Major Lincoln has asked to go with you and, since we are expecting a replacement physical education instructor with the next detachment of trainees, I agreed.

All of you left in the course were well on your way to passing. Good luck A Troop, 8th Commando. Step forward, Major Stafford."

John marched forward, trying to suppress the mix of excitement, trepidation and surprise, and concentrate on the task at hand. He stood at attention, saluted and shook the Colonel's gloved hand. "They are yours to lead into battle, Major," the Colonel said quietly.

"Thank you, Sir."

"Have the men issued with arms and ammunition by the Quartermaster. Officers to the Adjutant for maps, then my office for a briefing. Transport is already laid on with drivers."

"Sir."

John turned and gave the orders to his men.

President Lincoln marched up and in textbook alacrity and polish stamped to attention his hand quivering in salute.

"Sir!"

His wooden swagger stick, the favourite symbol of privilege for Sergeant Majors in the British and Dominion armies, was tucked rigidly under his left arm. The handle end was adorned with a shiny brass cap.

President Lincoln addressed the 200 men. "Paraaaaade!" he shouted in his foghorn of a voice. Instantly, 200 men stiffened ready for the next order, which they knew would be to stand at attention.

"Shun!" Boots crashed onto the gravel parade ground in front of the castle as the men brought their right feet down to stood stiffly at attention. "Paraaaaaade dis-missed!"

Holding their maps and Tommy guns, John, Duncan and Aubrey stood around the Colonel's desk "Gentlemen, you have an important mission, you have 24 hours to report to Colonel Talbot, commanding the 3rd Battalion Grenadier Guards, at Windsor Castle. Once the invasion flap is over, you are to report to the Commando Depot at the Royal Marines Headquarters Portsmouth.

"In the case of invasion and capitulation Commandos are not, repeat not, to be part of any evacuation from Britain. In this unlikely event, open these sealed orders."He gave a sealed envelope to John.

"If you are about to be captured, or if you are badly wounded, these orders must be passed on to one of your officers , or, if necessary, a non-commissioned officer. If not, destroy these papers."

"The top brass are leaving nothing to chance. I do not know the details but I am told they tell you where you will concentrate if the invasion does succeed, then you will carry on harassing the enemy for as long as it takes. I hope it won't come to that but we are leaving nothing to chance."

The colonel took another deep drag on his cigarette. The young officers looked at him, aware they were on the threshold of a momentous, almost overwhelming moment of history. "If the worst happens and our government is forced into exile, some pro-fascist government will take over and make peace with the Nazis. They will be the enemy as much as the Germans. You Commandos, as well as carefully selected individuals scattered strategically around the British Isles, are to be the nucleus of an underground army, like the Spanish Geurillos who terrorised

Napoleon's armies in the Peninsular Campaign or like the Boers in South Africa. These orders are from the very top. This is top secret. Do you understand? Any questions?"

John and his friends replied, "No Sir,"and glanced at each other grimly.

"I hope to see you when this flap is all over. If we're lucky, Hitler will get cold feet and call off his channel swim."

CHAPTER NINE   PARIS

The triple-engined Lufthansa airliner flew into a bed of soft white clouds as it crossed over Alsace, once more part of the Reich, into the heart of France. Looking out of the window was a face with a flash of black hair over it's forehead. He was looking out, but Adolf Hitler was seeing only the memory of Leni Riefenstahl's film of the great party rally at Nurenberg.

On the silver screen on the innermost white wall of his mind he saw himself swooping out of the clouds, the music of Wagner's "Ride of the Valkyries" swelling up as an offering of the gods to one of their own. Here, on his way to Paris he rode behind a Valkyrie, his arms were clenched around her armoured stomach, of this warrior from Valhalla. He was branded with the symbol of the Neo-Nordic pagan faith, a black swastika on his arm, diving down to his triumphant destiny.

Heinz the translator watched as Dr. Goebbels, the Third Reich's effusive and able Minister of Propaganda, smiled and hastened towards the Fuhrer, who was alighting from the aircraft. Goebbels stopped in front of him and saluted. "Heil Hitler." The Kommandant of Paris shot his arm out in imitation.

"Welcome to Paris Mein Fuhrer," he said, leading Hitler and Goebbels to the two armoured Mercedes Benz cars flanked by a squad of Wehrmacht troopers on motorbikes. "There are umbrellas inside but I think the rain will hold off, Mein Fuhrer," the Kommandant said. "Our royal guests are settling in," the Kommandant replied in answer to Hitler's inquiries. "Count Von Darmstadt is picking up His Royal Highness at this moment. They will be discreetly guarded by Gestapo agents."

Heinz opened the door for Goebbels and then climbed in the back of the car and the military chauffeur drove off following Hitler's Mercedes.

"Nothing must be too much for them," Hitler said.

"Yes, Mein Fuhrer. Her Royal Highness has bought new clothes and they have dined several times at Maxim's. Last night they attended the Paris Opera. They have asked only for their release and a meeting with a neutral diplomat. One of the Portuguese Embassy officials in our pay went to visit them yesterday. He reports that they want to be sent back to Britain."

"Anything else, Kommandant?" Hitler asked.

"Oh yes, they asked for caviar. I obtained some from the Soviet Embassy."

"So, they have a taste for the good life. We can feed them that. You and Count Darmstadt have done well. Do you know what His Royal Highness is thinking?"

"Von Darmstadt believes he thinks he is cleverer than he really is. His wife gives him what confidence he has, but his nervous energy seems incapable of direction. He is angry but uncertain. He is a weakling."

"Like his brother George VI, another weakling. He can hardly speak in front of a crowd. He is nothing without his wife, she is the power behind the throne," Hitler interjected, "I like having malleable leaders to deal with."

"Appearances can be deceiving Mein Fuhrer. Were not Julius Caesar and Napoleon short men, but giants in history?"

Hitler laughed, he was in a jocund mood; "Am I not shorter than most, and greater ... ?"

"Ha, of course, Mein Fuhrer."

At their home on the Bois de Boulogne the Duke and Duchess of Windsor were lounging in the Duke's bedroom after breakfast. The Duke stood in front of an adjustable full-length mirror in the corner of the room, nervously tying a blue tie covered in tiny yellow dots. One of their bulldogs lay with his head on his master's slipper and dozed, slobbering in its sleep.

Wallis sat, her thin legs crossed, on a Louis XIV chair by her husband's bed, reading a May 1939 issue of Country Life. She looked up, sighed and threw it on the bed where it slid onto a white pillow, hiding the needle-worked monogram, HRH.

"Darling, you must stand up to this Hitler." She got up and crossed the room to him, her silk pajamas and dressing gown rustling as she moved. Standing behind him, she placed a hand on each of his white-shirted shoulders and kissed the back of his blonde head. The Duke grunted.

"You invented the Windsor knot, the King's Flight of aircraft for quickly ferrying the monarch around. You are clever enough to do anything you want. You are cleverer than that brother of yours ... If we play our cards right, you will be respected the world over."

"Yes, but which card should I play next? I don't have that many. I was king for 11 months and gave it up, for you. I never wanted to be King-Emperor, you know that. People don't realize what a burden it is, all the duties, those red boxes of dispatches they were always pestering me to open. It was delegations from this group, ambassadors from that country, speeches to give. My God, it was tedious. But, even after I left and we married, set up our home here in exile, cut off from my family and old friends, I still volunteered for service in 1939."

His voice began to rise to a pitch even higher than normal. "You put on a uniform too, didn't you, Wallis, for the Red Cross in Paris? I even went to the Bahamas to be governor, when I really wanted a military post in Wales." He shook his head bitterly. "They wanted me out of the way. And now...?"

"Now you're back, David."

"Back as prisoners, that's what we are. Oh yes, we can walk out of here with our dogs and go shopping, but I can see the Gestapo men following us. We could go dancing all night at all the best clubs, but how can we dance in the middle of a war?"

"No doubt Herr Hitler is going to give me something to think about whence meet at the Eiffel Tower. Are you sure you won't come."

"No, I think I should stay here, I would just be in the way. We don't want the press to drag me into this. This is your day. If I was there it would only go against you. Remember what it was like, how many were against me when I had to leave England in 36. People were throwing things at me, saying horrible things, the Archbishop of Canterbury, your family, the Prime Minister ... you arranged for that destroyer to get me to peace and quiet in France ..." She stopped, upset.

"If we ever get back it won't be like that again, I promise."

"They hated me!" she shouted. "Just because I am an American and had two lousy marriages before I met you." Tears ran down her high cheek bones.

"Because they didn't know you like I know you. Now dry your eyes. Maybe I can get us sent back to Britain. If I could do anything to stop this wretched war. Yes ... that must be it; Hitler wants me to mediate between himself and my old friend Winston. It will be a simple matter of finding what the terms are, then you and I taking a neutral ship from Spain or Sweden back to England.

We shall be received as hero and heroine. We were brought here at gunpoint after all." He looked at her pleadingly. "We didn't ask to be here, did we?"

Wallis dried her eyes and blew her nose. "Now dear, I'll help you finish getting dressed, you don't want to keep the German Fuhrer waiting, even if he is so very common," she sniffed.

"As a matter of fact I do want to keep him waiting, I feel quite stubborn today. It's the least I can do considering several thousand Britons have already died in this beastly war. Why did he have to invade Poland? Mr. Chamberlain clearly warned him to withdraw."

"There." She patted his tie. He admired his wife's handiwork. The tie did look very good. He pecked her on the cheek.

"I'll be all right, Wallis. I'll do the best I can with this Hitler, even put up with his company over a lunch which I couldn't tuppence about."

"Two bits" she laughed.

"Oh yes, you Americans say that don't you?" He laughed too. Wallis checked the shoulders of his natty double-breasted suit for dandruff or stray hairs.

A butler knocked on the door. "Count Von Darmstadt, Your Royal Highnesses."

They both walked into the living room where the Count waited, his SS cap tucked under his arm. He clicked his heel, kissed Wallis's hand and shook hands with the Duke. As they walked through the front door, which the butler had opened, the two German guards stood at attention. Affixed to their Mauser rifles were brilliantly shining bayonets.

On the roof of the house opposite, a flak gun and its gun crew were on duty, watching for any possible RAF raid on the Duke and Duchess of Windsor's house.

Von Darmstadt opened the passenger door of his white BMW sports car for the Duke and then got in the driver's side. Edward looked up at Wallis where she stood gazing through the window in the living room. He gave her a wan smile as she waved goodbye.

As Hitler's motorcade roared under the huge Arc de Triomphe, Napoleon's memorial to his Grand Armee, German soldiers in flared rim helmets and field grey greatcoats snapped to attention. Wehrmacht motorbikes with sidecars armed with heavy MG 34 machine guns, led the Mercedes Benz cars down the Champs-Elysees. A thin line of French fascists along the route gave a ragged cheer of "Vive La France", which rang hollow in the late summer air of defeat. Hitler was in his element. His full-length black leather coat creaked as he leaned forward, and brought his open right hand up in a relaxed Aryan salute.

The Duke of Windsor leaned towards Von Darmstadt on the brown leather seat of the BMW as it purred by the Seine River and over it via the Pont De Bir Hakeim.

"I would like a carnation for my buttonhole," he said to Von Darmstadt.

The Count looked at his Zeiss wristwatch and answered curtly.

"We have a moment only, the Fuhrer detests being kept waiting." He halted the car by a street seller with a stall of flowers. He reached into his black jodhpur pockets and gave the Duke some French coins.

The Duke of Windsor got out and picked out a red carnation from the flower-seller's meagre selection. He proffered the handful of coins and smiled.

"Vive Le Prince De Galles," the vendor whispered. "Merci, Monsieur!" he said loudly.

As he sat in the passenger seat affixing his boutonniere, the Duke spoke to Von Darmstadt. "My father, George V, hated tardiness. He had all the palace clocks set five minutes ahead to encourage punctuality. As soon as I was king, I had every one of those damn clocks in every palace set at the right time." He gave himself a satisfied smile but wondered why his hand shook as he placed it on his knee.

Could it have been the shock the Frenchman would have felt if he had known the Prince of Wales was off to meet the conqueror at the Eiffel Tower? Or, was it the absurd image he saw of his father, the bearded George V, working on his stamp collection in heaven, poking down with his stamp tweezers into the corporeal world, tenderly but firmly lifting him and holding him up to look at his eldest son with wonder, asking the unvoiced question: "What on earth are you doing meeting with that operatic dictator Adolf Hitler in occupied Paris?"

A Citroen saloon car crammed full of trench-coated Gestapo officers was following them. The Duke could see them in the rear view mirror. Irritated he scowled, "Bloody Nazi guard dogs."

The Count looked in his rear-view mirror. "Protection for Your Royal Highness." Von Darmstadt looked narrowly at the Duke.

He continued, "I hope that today's meeting will be a success for world peace. It would be a terrible thing if British raiders were to try and rescue you and something happened to your elegant wife, let alone the chances of a peaceful and just settlement of this unfortunate war." The Duke's face fell.

"Why don't you just shoot me, and let my wife go home to America?"

"That, your Royal Highness, would make a lot of enemies for Germany. We need friends, we value your friendship and leadership."

I bloody well bet, the Duke thought and bit his lip. He sat with his arms folded over his blue pin-striped suit, but he was careful not to crush the red carnation in his left buttonhole.

They crossed the bridge over the Seine and the Count pulled up to the Eiffel Tower where a group of reporters with large cameras and notepads were clustered around Joseph Goebbels. He was waving his arms about in excitement, speaking glibly in German about the importance of this historic meeting of the Fuhrer and the world famous Duke of Windsor, now a guest of the Third Reich in the most beautiful city in the world. Heinz, the translator, stood by a group of American reporters scribbling in their notebooks.

"Look, here comes the Duke of Windsor!" a reporter for the New York Times shouted.

"Die Fuhrer!" cried the Paris correspondent for a daily Berlin newspaper who was looking in the opposite direction. The Americans ran towards the Count's sports car. Flash bulbs created a starry profile in the daylight around Edward's head. The Duke nodded and waved.

"Hey, Duke, where's the Duchess?" the Times reporter yelled out. A German soldier opened the door for the Duke.

"At home," he replied as he stepped out.

He was peppered with questions. "How are they treating you, Sir?"

"When can you get back to the Bahamas?"

"Do you think peace is possible?"

"Have you spoken to your brother the king ... or Mr. Churchill?"

Edward looked around at them and spoke. "I would like nothing better than to serve my country in a military capacity as I did in the Great War. I warned our British generals at the beginning of this conflict about the poorly defended Ardennes region. I was proved correct. I can be of use. Now my wife and I are here ..."

Von Darmstadt had stepped out to him and held up his hand signalling an end to the questions. "A statement will be given to you after the meeting. In the meantime, please take photographs and roll your newsreel cameras."

Just 20 feet away the Japanese, Italian and German reporters clapped as Hitler stepped out of the Mercedes. The Kommandant ushered the Duke, Von Darmstadt, Hitler, Goebbels and Heinz onto the elevator in the south east leg of the tower. An aide unfolded the burnished copper screen of collapsible diamond shapes out and shut. They rose more than 300 feet above Paris.

Heinz had never been outside Germany and was overwhelmed by the architecture of Paris, the splendour of the Seine River with its barges and the delights of Montmartre he could see from the tower. This is incredible, he thought, I only want to be out of this war and here I am right in the middle of it, with Adolf Hitler and the Duke of Windsor. He couldn't wait to tell Ingrid when he got back to Berlin. On the second floor an empty restaurant awaited them.

The Duke's thoughts were more about how he was looking forward to a cigarette as the party followed the maitre d', who wore a large handlebar moustache in the centre of a pale face set on fire by ruddy cheeks. Edward was seated opposite Hitler and in between Heinz and the Count. Edward noticed that Hitler seemed much smaller after removing his coat to sit down next to Josef Goebbels.

"Wasser," Hitler ordered. Everyone else requested a glass of wine, except for Edward.

"Scotch, s'il vous plait." The waiter returned in a flash bearing a tray with the drinks and two bottles of wine. He bowed slightly to the Duke who noted mark of respect by slightly nodding his head. Heinz was relieved to see that the Fuhrer was intent on studying the menu and missed the insult. The French waiter had no intention of paying any respect to the Chancellor of the Third Reich.

"Tell Herr Hitler I would like a cigarette. I know he abhors them so I'll just step out onto the observation deck for a moment," Edward said to Heinz. He duly translated and Hitler watched as Edward went through the door to the platform where Paris lay itself down before him. Edward noticed the rain-coated Gestapo agent outside looking at him.

"It's all right, I'm not going to kill myself," Edward said in the best German he could muster. There was no reaction from the Gestapo officer. Not yet anyway, Edward thought as he turned his back to the wind, cupped his hands and lit his cigarette on the first try.

Edward pondered his position. He knew Hitler was about to offer him and his wife the throne of Great Britain. he could see it coming. He was still angry with his brother for cutting off his money and the royal title for Wallis, and shunting us off to the Bahamas. But still, to betray him ... when all he really wanted was to be left alone with his wife.

Was peace at any price what old Britain needed? If the war was unwinnable what was the point of carrying on? Perhaps they could be victorious, if the Germans didn't invade.

He looked at the Gestapo officer's gloved hand gripping the rail. Was that what being a Nazi King would be like? Always someone watching? What would be the difference to what it was like now, always being pestered, told what to do and when, and how much? He would have to play for time, keep Hitler guessing, perhaps Churchill would send a rescue party...

"Your soup is ready, Your Royal Highness." Count Von Darmstadt had come out to stand by him.

Edward sat down, troubled but wearing a thin smile. His royal training came in handy. Hitler looked intently at him and spoke, letting Heinz translate every sentence, one at a time. "I am eager to end this unnecessary war. In fact, I need an ally against the Soviet Union. My ties with Stalin are only of a temporary nature, it suits both our purposes. But Great Britain is a natural friend, we are Anglo-Saxon nations. Together we could rule the world, each allowing the other our own spheres of interest and let Italy and Japan rule theirs."

He paused to take a sip of water. Edward said nothing. "You are a household name in your country; you could be the intermediary between those who wish to end this war in Britain and myself. I do not wish to invade England, but I will if necessary. It is our destiny to rule Europe but, if Britain allows us ... our successes on the continent, there is no need to fear an invasion."

Edward interrupted, "I can send any message of peace to my brother but he will ignore it. You are treating us well, but we are prisoners are we not? We belong in Britain, not here, Riechkanzellor." Heinz translated. The waiter brought their entrees and they ceased speaking. Once he had gone Hitler spoke again.

"Your Royal Highnesses are under our protection. We believe your own secret service is under orders to kill you both. In the highest circles you are both seen as a liability. It is madness, but, nevertheless, it is true, I assure you."

Edward opened his mouth but said nothing. Hitler continued, "Such a loss of young lives could be prevented. We are both veterans of the Great War. Join us in our bid to make peace."

Edward replied, "I sent you a telegram on September 2nd last year pleading for peace, but still you continued marching into Poland. I will send any peace terms you have via the Swedish ambassador, but in return I ask that we be sent back to British territory."

"You are not safe in their hands."

"We just want to be left in peace, Herr Hitler."

"Peace is a scarce commodity in this violent world and events may thrust you once again onto the centre stage"

Edward hooded his eyes. "How could I be king again, even if I wanted to be, which I do not?"

Hitler leaned confidentially on his elbows across the table, "If your brother is killed accidentally, there will be a great need for an adult monarch, someone with modern ideas, someone the British can trust. You, your Royal Highness, could be king, with your wife Wallis as queen, able to show her gentleness by caring for your people."

Delicately squashing some buttered green peas on the upheld tines of his silver fork with his knife, Edward ate slowly as he tried to think about what Hitler was saying. He could only manage to comment, "These peas are very good."

He cut some lamb, chewed and swallowed. Delicious. What am I thinking? I should be unable to eat. To speak against my brother is treason. I cannot do this. But if the government of Great Britain asked me in an emergency ... who else is there?

Hitler sat back relaxed. "One never knows what the future may bring but one has to be prepared. Lord Eastbourne is ready to take the reins of power as leader of the peace faction. He would make an admirable Prime Minister for you both, ensuring onerous duties were kept for a minimum, allowing you to focus on what really interests you, the living conditions of the working man. Now, let us enjoy this very good lunch and talk about the symphony you are invited to this evening."

As the ramifications of his predicament sank in, Edward felt sick at heart. Count Von Darmstadt drove him back to the Rue de Bologne. He needed to talk to Wallis, he needed her support. He felt trapped, a butterfly pinned to a card printed with his name in English and German.

She listened carefully with a worried concern gripping her thin face. "Oh dear, David. This would put you in a terrible situation. When is your family going to send help, some message of hope? Tell me, if it was truly best for Britain would you do it David?"

He hesitated, momentarily covering his face with his hands as he sat in a chair. "I could get things done: sign a peace treaty, modernize our country, get everyone working, and fight Stalin and the threat of Communism." He brightened at the idea of being useful.

"David, I will be by your side no matter what. The world may call us traitors but we would do it only because someone has to take the responsibility to stop this madness, before we are all destroyed, for peace, for your subjects." He began to weep. "I don't know what to do. Help me."

In a soothing voice Wallis comforted him. "Let us see if Hitler's peace plan is accepted by Mr. Churchill. Then we'll worry about the future. We may find ourselves back in the Bahamas by 1941."

"You're right. If I was back in the Bahamas, at least I could continue my work clearing up the corruption in Nassau and getting the islanders decent wages."

"That's the spirit," She wiped a tear from his cheek with her hankie. "Now let's walk the dogs, I fancy a bit of fresh air, my love."

"Good idea, I'll just phone the Swedish Ambassador and make an appointment with him this afternoon to send the peace offer to Churchill. Hitler gave me the proposal," he patted his suit jacket.

CHAPTER TEN BATTLE OF WINDSOR CASTLE

In the reinforced concrete bunker, forty feet below King Charles Street a brisk walk from the Parliament Buildings by the Thames, a Royal Navy officer walked from his cubicle of an office to the map room where Churchill stood studying the convoy routes across the Atlantic and around the Cape of Good Hope. Commander Nelson Bell coughed discreetly. Churchill looked around, a large Cuban cigar clenched in his mouth, smoke was wreathed around him. A blue-and-white-polka-dotted-bowtie bloomed over his white shirt collar despite the smokescreen.

"Prime Minister, the boffins at Bletchley Park just sent this message on their secure telex machine,"

> *Believe invasion imminent. Enigma codes partially deciphered indicate barges loaded with troops are on their way. Luftwaffe orders indicate bomber squadrons with fighter escorts are gathering over the channel. The Kriegsmarine battle fleet sailed from Kiel yesterday, naval units including U-boats, from European ports are at sea. Indications are for landings in Kent, the Isle of Wight and Sussex with heavy bombing of RAF airdromes in Fighter Command 11 and 10 Groups and coastal defences.*

"Thank you, Commander. Have reconnaissance flights confirmed this?"

"Yes, Prime Minister, some 'Recce' Spitfires just had their photos developed."

He continued reading from the telex message.

> *The invasion force is estimated at 200 thousand men of the German 2nd, 9th and 16th Army Groups, including four Panzer Divisions and 10 mechanized infantry divisions with artillery. Up to four major landings are anticipated: Harwich, Dover, Eastbourne and Portsmouth. Parachute drops are expected on the Isle of Wight and Portsmouth. There are four fleets assembling in the Channel. The one from Cherbourg left first, probable target Hampshire. The*

> *next, from Le Havre, will probably land in Sussex, two fleets of ships from Calais, Brussels and Amsterdam are assembling, targeting Kent and the east coast.*

"When, er, do you think they are coming Commander?" he growled.

The Commander consulted a register of tides. "Uhm, the 'Met' boys are saying light winds tonight with clear skies tomorrow and a calm channel for the next two days. In my opinion, I would think 0530 hours tomorrow morning Sir."

"Well done, Commander. Thank God we are able to crack some of their enigma codes. We have a chance to do them great damage. Get me the First Sea Lord Admiral Pound, General Brooke and Air Marshal Dowding." The Commander picked up different coloured telephones one at a time and announced that the Prime Minister had a priority call. The message to each was the same. Churchill said one brief sentence to each, "Send out codeword 'Cromwell' to home forces and join me here in the cabinet war room as soon as possible." He pressed a button to ring for the secretary on the night shift. When she appeared, note pad at the ready, he asked her to phone the members of the coalition cabinet. "Tell them Churchill says 'Cromwell'. My dear, we are in for a busy time, pray bear with me if I become somewhat irascible."

Churchill paced around the map room. This was the day he feared but he was exhilarated. "The die is cast, Commander. We shall give the enemy everything we have and more, when he comes."

He stubbed out his cigar in the bucket filled with sand and chewed up Cuban cigars and walked down the hall to the operations room. There was a hum of unruffled activity as staff officers made phone calls and messengers walked briskly and quietly past the Royal Marine guards in the passageways of the secret complex below London's streets.

He looked up at the electric clocks set on one wall by the gigantic maps of the world. They showed the time in London, Paris, Berlin, Delhi, Sydney and Washington, D.C. It was 10:33 p.m. Greenwich Mean Time, Thursday September 19th.

Tomorrow would be the most important event in British history since the Spanish Armada was vanquished by storms and

Drake's galleons. Tomorrow, Churchill knew, all hell would be unleashed.

"Get me His Majesty at Buckingham Palace on the telephone."

Some time later the phone rang in Colonel Henry Talbot's bedroom at Windsor Castle. The commander of the Grenadier Guards detachment at Windsor Castle sat up in bed and put the receiver to his ear. "It's 'Cromwell', Sir, we just got word from the War Office" his adjutant reported.

"What time is it Yates?"

"0430 hours, Sir."

"Call out the guard, make sure the anti-aircraft batteries are ready. Let the local Home Guard know in case they haven't heard. I'll be there in two minutes. I'll inform the Princesses immediately."

He dressed quickly, grateful now that they'd had the paratroop alarm installed in the guard room after His Majesty had demonstrated the alarm to the Norwegian king, and no one had responded.

John's convoy of army lorries drove into the town of Windsor at dawn, his driver turned to him. "Sounds like Windsor is welcoming us with bells, Sir." Stafford unwound his window; the bells in every church were pealing.

"That's no welcome. That's the invasion alarm!" John waved his arm through the opened window. "Put your foot down, Corporal, the castle should be just past this corner." He looked back to see the other lorries speed up. They roared through the town past a white-haired officer parading a detachment of Home Guards at a pub.

A milkman galloped his horse and cart towards them, on the right of the road and stopped outside a house. He ran in and in seconds was out again clutching a rifle, ammunition pouches and a helmet. He threw them on his seat and slapped the reins on the back of the horses to the cheers of the Commandos in the lorries.

Stafford looked up in the cloudy sky to the east as the wail of air raid sirens began to mix with the peal of church bells in a strange, repulsive mix of new and old, terror and solace.

Around the corner and up Windsor Hill the magnificence of Windsor Castle filled the landscape and reached up to the heavens. This symbol of British majesty was originally built as a wooden fortress by William the Conqueror. Henry II in the 1100s had begun the imposing stone towers and curtain walls.

By the green bronze statue of Queen Victoria was the Henry VIII Gate. A cluster of helmeted Coldstream Guards in battle dress stood in front of barbed wire as the convoy drove up. A World War I vintage Vickers machine gun was manned in a sandbagged position. One of the guards went inside the guardhouse to get the sergeant to check their papers.

The Sergeant was just handing them back when he glanced up at the sky and his mouth gaped open. "Jerry paratroopers!" he bellowed.

Stafford leaned out of the lorry cab and looked up at the still dim, early morning sky to where the sergeant was pointing. He saw scores of white parachutes dropping grey German soldiers from transport planes flying over the castle. The first German soldier fell like a stone to the ground outside the castle where his partially opened parachute swathed him in folds of white silk.

Overhead, flames poured from an engine of one of the planes as a Hawker Hurricane ferociously tore into it, its bullets eating up the fuselage.

The Junkers tri-motor plane exploded in a ball of blossoming orange, the Hurricane was tossed about by the shock wave as it flew on to another target just as two German Messerschmitt 109s hurtled down from the sun and pursued the Hurricane.

"We're driving in, Sergeant. Clear the way!' The coils of barbed wire were pulled back. The lead lorry screeched into the courtyard and pulled up outside St. George's Chapel some 50 yards into the lower ward. John jumped out of the lorry cab and checked that the safety catch was off his tommy gun. He waved at Aubrey and Duncan.

"Everybody out. Pronto!" Duncan and Aubrey led their men out of the lorries on the double.

"Lieutenant Hunter, take your section to the main gate and help them out. Lieutenant MacLeod, take your men to the battlements up there." Stafford waved his tommy gun to some steps leading to a battlement where Guardsmen were shooting paratroopers as fast as they could squeeze the triggers and pull back the bolts of their Lee-Enfield rifles.

The Czechoslovakian-designed Bren machine guns, manned by the Guards, stuttered into action as the German paratroopers began landing in sections inside and outside the castle walls and returning fire with hastily set up Spandeau heavy machine guns and mortars. Grey-overalled paratroopers with rimless metal helmets stamped with the white Luftwaffe eagle were fighting their way to the southeast of the great Round Tower in the upper ward.

John gave orders to Sergeant Major Lincoln, "Have the lads pick off as many as they can but keep them in defensive position for now, Sergeant Major. I'm going to the Colonel's office over there to get orders."

He ran, crouching, firing his tommy gun at a team of German paratroopers whose sub-machine guns had already slaughtered two young Grenadier Guards at the door. His bullets ripped through their "bone sack" overalls and the paratroopers collapsed to the ground.

The Adjutant poked a steel helmeted head around the corner of the duty office. "You must be Stafford with the Commandos, not a moment too soon."

"Where's the C.O. ?"

"He's gone up to the Lancaster Tower. You can't miss him, he'll be the one waving a swagger stick in one hand and taking potshots at the Jerries with the other."

"What's at Lancaster Tower?"

"Who, you mean? Princesses Elizabeth and Margaret."

Stafford gulped. "Right I'll take my platoon up there."

"Good idea. It's the tower just south east of the large round tower, up the hill turn right." The adjutant said jerking to one side as a row of bullets pocked the open wooden door.

"I've got him," the adjutant pointed his revolver, fired and the enemy paratrooper was dead as he landed.

"Sergeant Major," Stafford called. "We're going up the hill to Lancaster Tower. Get the platoon on the double."

President Lincoln nodded, ceased firing his Bren gun, and shouted at the platoon. "Get a move on!"

The Commandos surged up the hill through a maelstrom of smoke and explosions. Stafford, at the front, thanked God that they were all in such excellent shape. He could make out a portly colonel crouching by the Round Tower puffing on his pipe and taking shots at German troops in the open space between the Round and Lancaster Towers.

"Major Stafford reporting, Sir," he said, throwing himself down as bullets whistled overhead.

"Good man. How many troops do you have?"

"One platoon with me and another helping at the bottom of the hill."

"We have to retake Lancaster Tower. The guards have been overwhelmed."

They looked up to see a cluster of German paratroopers on a third floor parapet by a high Gothic window at the top of the tower. The first invader landed and swiftly unbuckled his harness. Gripping his machine gun he kicked in the window and shattered glass flew all around him.

"Best shots on that man," Major Stafford ordered. But before the rifles could crack, a woman's arm, clad in a white cardigan appeared through the window and a pale, elegant hand could be seen holding a Browning automatic pistol. There was a puff of smoke and the German somersaulted backwards, landing head first on the ground below.

"One less," Lincoln muttered.

"A Platoon, we're going into the tower. Some of the Royal Family need our help. Fix bayonets!" John ordered. With deadly earnest and smooth precision the Commandos pulled their foot-long bayonets from the frogs on their webbing belts and clicked them into position below the muzzles of their Lee-Enfield rifles.

"Charge!" John shouted. The Commandos gave a blood-curdling yell. It was a cold, ferocious anger that swept them over the German machine gun nests and mortar positions outside Lancaster Tower.

The paratroopers were members of the Brandenburg Regiment, veterans of the blitz on Belgium that spring. But this cold steel welcome from the defenders was more than they had ever faced before. A huge German sergeant pulled back his arm to throw a 'potato masher' grenade. Sprinting up from the side a Commando lunged forward with a bayonet and stabbed him in the heart, withdrew and ran on quickly. The grenade fell from his fingers and exploded. Fragments of grey uniform and flesh sprayed out in a red-and-grey shower.

"Up the stairs, Commandos. Grenades!" They cleared the stairs of defenders lobbing back German grenades that bounced down the steps toward them. Several Commandos were killed by German shots as they fought their way up the medieval, winding stone stairway.

Sergeant Major Lincoln clutched his shoulder. A stone fragment, broken off the thick stone wall by the explosions, had sliced into him. He kept going. Filled with the exultation of battle, John's men fought like tigers up to the third floor.

A door was open to a sitting room, domestically surreal amidst the battle, a log fire burned in the fireplace. A loud German voice spoke in good English in clear, commanding tones.

It was a voice John recognized. Startled, he looked towards the figures standing in the room and froze, shocked. Major Von Darmstadt in black SS overalls, had his Luger pistol pointed down at Princess Elizabeth's head. His other arm had the Princess's arm painfully bent behind her back. "Stop! I have the Princess Elizabeth. One move and I'll shall shoot her."

Princess Elizabeth looked older than her fourteen and a half years, her thin face, usually so quick to smile was serious. Her famous curly brown hair was dishevelled. Her blue polka dotted print dress was torn at the waist. Her nine-year-old sister perched on the edge of a sofa, covered by a paratrooper with a shortened Mauser paratroop rifle.

Princess Margaret was pale but maintaining a forced calmness. Time seemed to have come to a standstill.

"Put down your tommy guns and the Princesses will be unharmed."

As John placed his gun on the carpeted floor, the other commandos with him put their rifles down in the hall. He swiftly glanced around the room in search of the woman who had been wearing the white cardigan.

A wood fire was burning in the fireplace to keep out the September chill, but it flickered in vain. Cool air wafted in via the smashed window by the small battlement. An ormolu clock ticked the seconds away on the mantelpiece.

John saw a pair of ladies' shoes protruding from beneath the heavy green curtain drawn across one of the windows.

As he spoke, John tried to calculate how he could grab his commando knife and lunge at Von Darmstadt. "Are you sure you have the real princesses? Surely you must know Churchill has doubles of the Princesses in several locations in this country?"

Von Darmstadt was surprised that the British army officer in front of him would know his name and, taken unawares, took some time to consider Stafford's question. He edged the Princess towards the window. Everyone could see three paratroopers preparing a rope ladder outside leading over the curtain wall to beyond the castle grounds. Von Darmstadt flicked his head.

"See, our ride to our beachhead arrives." They could see a small German monoplane, a Fiesler Storch, fly past the window in British civilian white colours with GB number designation. Stafford saw the figure behind the curtain slowly raise an arm holding a pistol to the side and the other hand reach up to pull back the curtain.

A woman leapt out from behind the curtain and levelled her Browning at Von Darmstadt's chest. The Count's mouth opened, he twisted himself around with Princess Elizabeth.

The mystery woman in white shot Von Darmstadt in his right shoulder causing him to drop his pistol, and give up his hold on Princess Elizabeth. John threw himself at the Count in a rugby tackle. The woman instantly turned to shoot the other paratrooper. Princess Margaret brought her hands to her mouth and recovered herself. She gingerly attempted to pick up the dead paratrooper's Mauser rifle in her small hands.

Princess Elizabeth had fallen and rolled away as the Count lost his grip on her while John caught Von Darmstadt in a wrestling hold. The Count's hand flailed blindly around the floor searching for his Luger. Stafford stabbed Von Darmstadt's hand with his knife, fixing it to the hardwood floor.

Princess Elizabeth reached to grip the Nazi's pistol and stood, a cool, determined light shone in her youthful blue eyes. She held the Luger with two hands and pointed it at Von Darmstadt.

"Tell your men outside to surrender or I will shoot. I am not as good a shot as my bodyguard but I can show you how good I am if I have to."

"Fire, you fools!" Von Darmstadt yelled to the paratroopers outside. They cocked their machine guns and prepared to pepper the room with gunfire just as a British mortar shell exploded on the parapet removing the threat to the future Queen in an instant.

Inside the Princesses' sitting room the blast and noise had knocked everyone down. Von Darmstadt tore the knife from his hand and ran through the still drifting smoke on the parapet. Gritting his teeth from the pain of his hand and shoulder wounds, he painfully made his way down the ladder. As he descended he fumbled for a whistle attached to his overalls and blew it, within seconds German paratroopers began running towards him giving covering fire. John ran to the ladder, calling to his men to follow but was met with a hail of bullets.

A squad of paratroopers made their way with him to a hole in the northeastern curtain wall which had been blasted open by German sappers.

Outside the castle a German field post had been set up with a Nazi flag flying from a radio aerial. A signaller was speaking to the pilot of the first of two small Fieseler Storch aircraft, which were landing on the scenic three-mile avenue lined by trees and known as the Long Walk. With their 240-horse-power-Argus engines still making a high-pitched whine, they turned around on their tall undercarriages.

A thousand feet above, four Messerschmitt 109s circled, ready to escort them south to the German beachhead at Eastbourne. The Storch pilots pushed open their doors and Von Darmstadt was hoisted into the seat beside the pilot. He was holding a heavy bag. Paratroopers pushed several bulky bags into the other plane. From one of the bags protruded the hilt of the large, golden Sword of State. They took off. The machine gunners at the rear of each cockpit waved at their comrades left fighting the defenders of Windsor Castle.

Within 20 minutes hard fighting Grenadier Guards and Commandos surrounded the surviving paratroopers. Colonel Talbot, wearing a bloody bandage around his head and clenching an unlit pipe in his mouth, accepted their surrender.

Stafford cursed himself for letting the SS Major slip out of his grasp but was relieved to see the Princesses were alive and well. He walked back to the Tower to check on his men. After seeing them and ensuring the wounded were taken care of he went to find the identity of the woman who had saved the Princesses.

He felt a clutch at his heart and a look of sheer incredulity flooded his face. "Felic ... Felicity," he stuttered, "it was you. I thought you would be saving the art treasures."

She smiled at him. "I was, until this invasion scare; the Princesses wanted my company. I was here when the paratroopers landed. They killed the bodyguard." She showed John the body in the bedroom. "I had to do something to protect them. John, I'm so glad to see you." She gasped and hugged him.

"She's told us about you, Major Stafford from Canada," Princess Elizabeth said moved by their romance. John blushed silently and Princess Margaret giggled.

"Your Royal Highnesses, may I present Major Stafford?" Felicity asked.

John bowed his head. "Excuse me, Your Royal Highnesses. I have work to do. I'll see you later, Felicity," John said. (rather lamely, he thought later)

He sent a runner to Colonel Talbot to inform him that the Princesses were safe and that his men would stay with them until relieved, then he posted guards around the tower.

Princess Elizabeth and her sister Margaret exchanged their weapons for bandages from a first aid kit and began helping the wounded, starting with a bemused Sergeant Major Lincoln. He kept saying, "Wait 'til I tell the folks back in Halifax, Nova Scotia, that the Princesses looked after me." For once, the tough Commando seemed sentimental.

Through the bedroom window they could see a Spitfire flying at full speed over the castle, firing the eight Browning machine guns, located inside its elliptical wings, at the two white monoplanes, which separated from each other as they were attacked. Incredibly, the first light plane survived the blaze of fire but the second began to emit black smoke, tumbled into a spin and crashed into the ground.

Felicity entered the sitting room where the Sergeant Major was comfortably ensconced on the sofa with one hand balancing a cup of tea and the other resting in a sling. There was a knock on the open door. The Colonel bowed his bandaged head then addressed Princess Elizabeth and her sister. "Your Royal Highnesses, I am afraid we have to evacuate to a safer place. The royal train is on its way to the station now with a Bofors anti-aircraft carriage."

"Thank you, Colonel," Princess Elizabeth said, "Do we have a few minutes?" Princess Elizabeth asked.

"Yes, your Royal Highness."

"Will you be coming? May I thank the guards as I leave? How are the King and Queen?" Princess Elizabeth was full of questions.

"Yes, I will be taking my men with you except for the wounded. The Home Guard are looking after the prisoners and the castle. I will parade the troops for a brief inspection and you can thank them then. I have no news from London except that their Majesties have been informed that you are safe and have approved your being taken to Scotland."

"Thank you, Colonel. While we pack would you help yourself to a cup of tea?"

"Your Royal Highness, I would like nothing better. May I suggest we inspect the Guards in 10 minutes." The Colonel savoured a few mouthfuls and turned to John who had just entered the room.

Colonel Talbot addressed him, "Well Major, I suppose you will be off to Commando headquarters now, you can be useful on the south coast. The Jerries have landed on the Isle of Wight and on the west side of Portsmouth."

John felt a buzz of concern for his brother Alan, as the Colonel continued, "Monty is giving them one hell of a pasting but there are many German divisions with Panzer tanks and their beachheads are growing.

Princesses Margaret and Elizabeth came into the living room wearing their coats and hats, each carried a children's gas mask in a cardboard box attached to a strap over their shoulders.

Princess Elizabeth held out her hand to John, who took it and bowed. "We are in your debt, aren't we Margaret?" She frowned, realising that her sister was finishing a house of sugar cubes on the table for the entertainment of the wounded President Lincoln.

"I'll escort your Royal Highnesses to the lower courtyard where you can inspect the troops," Colonel Talbot said.

Felicity, in her camel hair coat, followed her charges through the door and waited in the hallway. "I'll be right down, Sergeant Major," John said to Lincoln.

"Felicity, I ...," John stammered. He kissed her and held her, it was incredible after all that had happened. Her perfume still smelled as intoxicating, as it had when they had last parted three weeks before. She pulled him closer. "I'm so glad to see you, and your timing couldn't have been better. Thanks. We'll meet again, like the song says," she whispered in his ear.

He found himself saying, "I love you Felicity. Good luck," and they went quickly down the stone stairs which minutes before had been a maelstrom of bullets and exploding grenades.

John could see Aubrey escorting a group of 40 German prisoners with their hands clasped on the top of their heads. "Where are they going Captain?"

"To the dungeon in the Round Tower, Sir." Duncan replied, grinning.

"Good place for 'em. Have you seen Captain MacLeod?"

"He's checking on the wounded. The doctor and nurses from the Windsor Hospital have set up a make-shift ward in St. George's Chapel."

Such were the momentous events of the day that what would have seemed incredible the day before seemed commonplace. The pews in the great chapel of kings and queens, were surrounded by ancient tombs, heraldic devices and mediaeval stained glass. Some of the stained glass portraits had been shattered by bullets. The pews were draped with bandaged soldiers, both British and German. He saw Aubrey conferring with the Coldstream's adjutant.

"Are you all right John?" Duncan asked as he saw John coming.

"Quite fine. And the men? Yourself?"

"Six dead, eight wounded - only two badly. The local hospital staff are doing a great job. First class."

"I think we had better assemble our men, board the trucks and make our way to Royal Marine headquarters in Portsmouth. The Jerries have landed near there."

Duncan whistled. "The balloon *has* gone up."

They paraded the men in a section next to the garrison who were ready to march down the hill to the nearby Windsor Railway station with the Princesses in Colonel Talbot's staff car. Princess Elizabeth, small in stature, looked up at the tall Grenadier Guardsmen and John's Commandos. An even slighter Princess

Margaret followed closely behind her. Princess Elizabeth stopped to say a few words to some of the men.

John conferred with Duncan and Aubrey. "Let's get our men on the road to Portsmouth. They need us there."

"Right. Oh, did you hear, John?" Duncan asked. "That German fellow commanding the paratroopers, Von Darmstadt, he made off with the Crown Jewels."

"The cheeky son of a gun!" John exclaimed.

CHAPTER ELEVEN INVASION

Sensing that his brother Alan was in the thick of the fighting on the south coast, John couldn't help worrying about him, as his own convoy of lorries made the best speed they could on the A3 road through Hampshire to the naval base at Portsmouth on the coast. The road was plugged with tanks and marching men on their way to meet the German 6th Army.

Heading towards them on their right, in the early afternoon of the first day of invasion, was a disciplined stream of refugees walking stoically alongside the green hedgerows. The chestnut tree branches full of yellowing leaves hung lazily over the road, casting shadows on refugees resting by the side of the road. Children were collecting the first chestnut fall of the autumn. With a bit of string threaded and knotted through holes drilled into each chestnut they played conkers, whacking at each other's chestnuts until one cracked. It was an ancient game, the Britons had taught the Romans aeons ago.

Just before dawn, a German invasion fleet, protected by destroyers, the cruiser class warship Hipper, and U-boats, had taken position off the beaches of Eastbourne. Assault troops in small boats powered by outboard engines had landed grey clad sappers and assault infantry. They burst through the smoke screen laid on by smoke shells fired by the Kriegsmarine.

Like clockwork, the first of many waves of Luftwaffe bombers and strafing fighters kept the defending Canadians from concentrating on the task at hand, hurling the enemy back into the sea. The 10,000 ton Admiral Hipper sent salvo after salvo from her four batteries of eight-inch guns into the Eastbourne defences.

Alan Stafford watched in awe with his binoculars as the Dido Class Royal Navy Cruiser, HMS Cleopatra, and two destroyers began shelling German troop barges towed by tugs. The Hipper turned its attention from the defences and set its broadside towards the Cleopatra. The Cleopatra brought her ten 5.2 inch guns to bear on the German ship. Flames belched out of her turrets.

Alan's platoon swept the beach with machine gun fire from their positions overlooking the beach. The six-inch howitzer in its pill box fired its shells into the invasion force every few minutes. It was comforting to the troops defending the beaches to hear it bark at the enemy. Alan drew in his breath as a German Siebel craft, an anti-aircraft platform of pontoons powered by aircraft engines, was hit just below the waterline. "Good shot," he murmured to himself.

An air raid siren wailed and 30 Stuka dive bombers with their ungainly bent wings came into view diving vertically, and dropping bombs and pulling out at the last moment.

"Holy mackerel Sergeant! Look at the Panzer tanks those ferries are unloading down those ramps. Right into the sea!"

"They must be amphibious Sir. What do ya reckon?" his Sergeant asked.

"I am afraid you're right," Alan said. "They'll be on the beach in a few minutes. Prepare the ...," His order was blotted out by a Stuka bomb that slammed into his trench; the Sergeant was nowhere to be seen as Alan tumbled through the air. He could hear nothing. Deaf to the blizzard of shells and bullets on the beaches, he landed on his rump, the air knocked out of his lungs. Gasping, he crawled to the radio man in the next trench.

In shock, he formed the words as best he could as he spoke to the soldier. "Tell the C.O. .... 30 Panzer tanks Mk III's are landing on the beach ... Jerry engineers have cleared a path for them," he drew a breath, "rigged up a ramp over the steps to take them up onto the promenade. Use the French 77 and the 2 pounder anti-tank guns."

The radio man yelled into the mike trying to make himself heard above the noise of battle.

The six-inch gun had ceased firing, the gun crew had run out of ammunition and were firing rifles through the slits at the barges bearing German infantry. A flashing arm of fire from a flamethrower mounted on a barge wrapped around and inside the pill box. Its defenders stopped shooting.

Alan thought of his twin brother at the same time John was worrying about him. Unbeknownst to both, this same type of battle was taking place all along the English coast at Dover to the east, Harwich to the northeast of London and Portsmouth to the west. Paratroopers were being dropped by the thousands behind their defences and seizing railroad stations and airfields for the use of Luftwaffe squadrons who met only token resistance from the few Spitfires and Hurricanes left from weeks of attacks on RAF airfields.

On the beaches, amphibious tanks, crawled on their caterpillar tracks out of the sea. Water streamed off their hulls. Forty foot tall plastic tubes waved fantastically in the air; the tubes had taken exhaust fumes above the waves and pumped air down to the crews sealed into their airtight tanks as they travelled the 80 feet to shore.

Alan's platoon aimed their vintage French 77 field artillery and began to carefully fire their last four shells. They took aim at the first tanks coming towards them. They hit one, breaking its caterpillar tracks, and then were taken out by two Panzer tanks firing as they roared off the ramp from the beach and onto the parade.

Alan felt light headed. Looking down at his foot he realized his left boot was soaked in blood. One of his men tied a tourniquet for him above his ankle and helped him hobble back as the platoon retreated.

Off shore, a British Destroyer torpedoed a ferry boat crammed with German soldiers and it began to list. The same Destroyer received a salvo from the Hipper and began to burn. HMS Cleopatra started to circle, its rudder blown up by a U-boat's torpedo. It brought its guns to bear as best it could and continued to blast the invasion fleet and the Hipper. A second U-boat gave it the coup de grace with a torpedo and the Cleopatra began to sink.

On the A3 road in Hampshire south of London, a boy of eight carrying a tabby cat in a paper bag made his way north. Forlornly he plodded along in rubber Wellington boots which had chafed the back of his knees until they were red. His mother was imploring him to 'get a ruddy move on.'

He looked up at the army lorry and his brown eyes caught John's gaze. John smiled at him and threw him a chocolate bar from his battle dress tunic as they drove by. The boy ran forward, deftly catching the bar in the bag containing the cat. "Thank you Sir"

"Good catch," John called back.

A column of A10 Cruiser tanks were waved along by red-capped military police at the next crossroads. The refugees halted and whooped and hollered, cheering on the tank commanders who wore radio headsets over their black berets. Two slow miles later the Cruiser tanks moved into open fields and headed southeast across country crashing through hedgerows at their top speed of thirty miles an hour. They were going to meet paratroopers who had seized Guildford.

At the next halt in their drive south to Portsmouth, John, Duncan and Aubrey walked over to a Royal Artillery Brigadier whose staff car sat on the side of the road. Its radiator blew out steam as the driver poured in some water from a can. "What's happening, Sir?" John asked after saluting.

"Too bloody much. There is fierce fighting going on in Portsmouth. The Luftwaffe is having a field day bombing the daylights out of our defences. One of my liaison officers with the coastal gun boys tells me that the German battleship, Bismarck, was shelling our batteries at Dover and was attacked by eighteen Fairy Swordfish biplanes, several blew up from the murderous ack ack fire. The others loosed their torpedoes and then two of our battleships had a crack at her. It took five hours of pounding to sink her. That's the only good news I've heard all day. The PM was on the radio earlier. King George is dead and Queen Elizabeth was wounded from a blitz attack on Buck House this morning."

John, Duncan and Aubrey were shocked. Their eyes widened. "No kidding?" Aubrey asked.

"I kid you not. It has been one hell of a day."

As if to reinforce his sentiments, two Messerschmitt 110 fighter-bombers screamed low over the convoy and each began firing the machine guns in their noses at the army vehicles.

Refugees scattered. "Everyone out of the lorries!" John shouted "Take aim ahead of the planes if they come back" The planes doubled back after turning around over the fields. Scores of rifles and Bren guns began to fire, aiming ahead of the attackers. A knot of refugees lying on the ground shook as the bullets from the planes riddled them.

The Brigadier's staff car blew up as an incendiary bullet hit its petrol tank. A Messerschmitt 110 began belching smoke from its starboard engine when it was hit by a lucky shot from the ground. It turned south, losing height, the port engine cut out and it dove into the ground in a graceful arc. There was a crash and smoke curled up from the field. "One for England!" shouted a stout bald man carrying all he had left in the world in a suitcase. The other plane roared overhead unscathed, its rear gunner taking photos to be used by Goebbels the next day on the front pages of German newspapers.

It was one o'clock the next morning when John and his Commando troop finally arrived at the defensive line set up on the cliffs above Havant overlooking Portsmouth. Flames lit up the sky. Italian bombers had been attacking naval diesel fuel depots all day. During the first wave of bombing attacks the Royal Navy fueller ships had filled up under fire and gone to sea to join the fleet.

Thousands of troops from Hampshire and Wiltshire were dug in on the heights. Batteries of 25-pounder howitzers were in place and ready to fire on German held positions in the docks.

John's men were assigned to tents and reported to the temporary headquarters, a red-brick Victorian mansion. Motorcycle dispatch riders roared to and fro bearing messages. Staff cars crunched up onto the gravel driveway, spilling out officers who strode quickly into the building. Inside was a hive of activity. Staff officers with red tabs on the collars of their uniforms moved coloured flags on a map of southern England and gave instructions for orders to be radioed or sent by messenger to units in action and in reserve by the German beach heads.

A sergeant sat at a desk in front of an oak staircase. "Sergeant, I'm Acting Major Stafford of the 8th Commandos, trying to link up with the Royal Marines.

"Right, Sir, I'll have Captain Hawkins see you, Sir. He's with the Royal Marines. Cup of tea Sir?"

John beamed at him. "Good man." The Sergeant brought him a tin mug full of strong, sweet tea.

"Mother's milk, Sir. Captain Hawkins will be right with you."

John was gulping down the scalding tea when Hawkins came to him. "Good morning."

"Good morning, I think. I'm supposed to be reporting to the Royal Marine depot, I'm here with 200 Commandos."

"Jolly good, Sir. The Royal Marines are defending their barracks down there." He gestured toward the sound of distant gunfire. "Jerry paratroopers landed yesterday at Gosport and Portsmouth and since then several divisions have landed at Southsea. There are more reinforcements coming every few hours.

"They have about 200 amphibious Panzer tanks. We were able to blast the first wave with anti-tank weapons but they kept coming. Their paratroopers managed to secure some landing places for them. It was awful down there with squadrons of Stuka bombers diving straight down with those God-awful screamers making that high pitched whine. We prayed for some fighter cover but only got a few Spitfires for about 10 minutes, and then we were alone until my battalion fought its way out.

A squadron of Hampden bombers plastered the Jerries but they had no fighter cover, they were bounced by Messerschmitts. I saw them calmly bombing German troopships in the harbour and then one dropping his bombs on a troop barge was hit. In flames the aircraft picked a German destroyer and dove into her amidships."

Captain Hawkins slumped down in a chair.

"I think you had better grab a few hours sleep. That's an order," he joked.

"Yes, thank you. The Area Commander told me the same thing."

John returned from the Area Commander's office with orders of his own to have his men sleep for seven hours then join a counter attack starting at 6 a.m. After telling Aubrey, Duncan and the President, he lay on the ground in his tent, the orders resounding through his head. "Your Commandos will enter Portsmouth in Bren gun carriers with a squadron of Mark III tanks and relieve the naval forces and Royal Marines holding out in the munitions storage area. A convoy of lorries will follow you in and troops will load them with as much naval ammunition as possible for you to take to Plymouth.

"You will be accompanied by a squadron of Royal Engineers who will set explosives at the docks and in the stores.

"As you evacuate, the whole area will be detonated, your men will escort the Engineers back here. On your left flank you have the Royal Hampshire Regiment freeing the Royal Marines who are trapped in their depot. We'll be giving you artillery cover as you withdraw ... as you withdraw ..." John fell into a black pit of sleep.

At 0500 hours President Lincoln woke up John. "I have the men up, Sir. They're just getting breakfast at the mess tent.

Captain MacLeod told me you wanted them paraded at 0540 ready for action."

"Yes Sergeant-Major, we'll be going down into the docks, to bring out as many naval munitions as we can and then protect the Royal Engineers who are going to demolish the docks and the arsenal. Then we get back in one piece."

"Sounds simple, Sir, where's the challenge?" the Nova Scotian smiled.

John laughed, "Go get some breakfast Sergeant-Major and good luck today."

"Same to you sir. We'll show them what a couple of Canadians can do." John buckled on his web belt with its holster and 38 calibre revolver. He picked up his tommy gun and checked that his pack contained an ample supply of spare round drums of ammunition. After a wash he went to the mess tent where Duncan and Aubrey were ensuring the men got some fried eggs and bacon, fried bread and tomatoes.

"We got you a plate of full English and a cup of tea," Aubrey said.

"Thanks, I could really dig into that." Over breakfast he outlined the details as they consulted maps and synchronised their watches.

The general had promised friendly artillery fire as their force motored south the few miles into downtown Portsmouth and the docks. The comforting crump of artillery shells landing within German-held lines told them the Royal Artillery had the range. The shells whistled over the universal carriers, lorries and leading tanks of the relieving column.

German 88-millimetre guns sent up a steady stream of shells. A Bren gun carrier exploded, its ammunition cracking and whizzing around them. Four British Mark III tanks took on Panzer tanks on the Portsmouth high street. Machine guns rattled and German snipers shot from vantage points in the shops and town hall.

Consulting a map of Portsmouth, John ordered his driver to bear right to the docks where they could hear the sound of Vickers machine guns duelling with the woodpecker sound of heavy German Spandau machine guns.

German infantry were chucking grenades at them, a smoking light British tank blocked the road. When the driver of

John's carrier slumped forward, he was moved to the floor and a field dressing was applied to the wound in his neck. John fired his tommy gun to cover their jumping out and waved his men out of the carriers.

Street corner by street corner the Commandos cleaned out the buildings until they got to the docks. A cheer went up from the light railway yard where naval ratings in their navy blue, bellbottom uniforms and white caps waved their rifles in the air and cheered. A Royal Navy white ensign, rent by bullets and shrapnel, flew from a flagpole on the roof of one of the warehouses.

Smoke from the burning fuel tanks still hung over the harbour like a fog. The sappers roared in with ten lorries full of detonators and wire, to be filled with naval shells for the return trip. John had arrived with his men, now the hard part began.

At this same moment, Winston Churchill spoke by wireless to Great Britain and the world from the underground war room which was connected to the BBC transmitters at Crystal Palace, London.

> *My fellow Britons, it saddens me to tell you that our beloved king, George VI was killed this morning in a bombing raid upon Buckingham Palace. He died in his naval uniform of an Admiral of the Fleet. I had spoken to him an hour before by telephone to inform him of the situation on our coastline where battles are raging against German forces struggling to establish beachheads. His last words to me were: 'We will fight and eventually, with God's help, we shall win.' I say to you, all is not lost, we may have lost a good king, but we are blessed with a brave Queen Elizabeth. Her Majesty is recovering from a wound in a London hospital but will speak to you in a moment to assure you that we shall not give in.*
>
> *Yesterday, German forces began a full-scale invasion of these isles we love. As I speak, tremendous battles are being fought on the south and east coasts. The hearts of free men and women everywhere beat the faster for us as we fight a powerful enemy with every means at our disposal. We are by no means making it easy for the Nazi invader. Our brave army is causing him a great deal of grief. I am assured by our capable General Alan Brooke,*

Chief of the Imperial General Staff, that we still have armoured reserves with which to destroy the foe. Our valiant Royal Air Force is still attacking. Our Royal Navy is sinking many enemy ships and submarines including the mighty German battleship, Bismarck.

All that can be done to expel the invader is being done. Pre-made plans are being put into effect to deal with great crisis. Women and children are being evacuated from the south and east coasts, while able bodied men in these areas are urged to join the Home Guard.

You may ask what you can do? You can behave with courage, be at your post whether you are a fireman, a nurse, an air raid warden, a policeman or doctor. I ask all Britons to fight the enemy. If you see a rifle, pick it up, use it on the Nazis and take one with you. We will fight in the streets and in the hills, and if needs be on and over the oceans, until we have freed our country of the invader. Our sovereign and her loyal ministers will never surrender. So, each to his duty now, let us brace ourselves for the shocks to come, knowing this is the time for great deeds to carry us through the dark days ahead and into the sunlit future days of victory, and freedom that await us and our children. We shall never surrender.

The calm voice of a BBC announcer came on the air. "This is the BBC Home Service. You have been listening to a speech by the Prime Minister, The Right Honourable Winston Churchill. And now Her Majesty Queen Elizabeth, at a hospital somewhere in London." There was the sound of a microphone being moved, then a woman's voice, shaken but clear, spoke.

This is a tragic time for our country, but the late king, my husband would want me to continue at my post as your Queen, and this I swear to do. I shall not leave these islands no matter what the outcome of this Battle for Britain.

The Princesses, Elizabeth and Margaret, who I have just spoken to by telephone are safe and plans to continue their safekeeping are in place. My Prime Minister, Mr. Churchill, has advised me to become Queen

Regent, until Princess Elizabeth is of age to be declared Queen. I have agreed to this. I pray that we shall all stand fast at this time of testing and live to see our endeavours blessed with a free Britain and a peaceful world.

The announcer's voice continued.

"That was Her Majesty Queen Elizabeth speaking from London. This is the BBC Home Service. We will now play a selection of music until the next news broadcast at 10 a.m. We begin with Elgar's 'Pomp and Circumstance'."

In Portsmouth, Royal Navy sailors were firing multi-barrelled Pom pom anti-aircraft guns that had been broken out of packing cases, swiftly assembled and bolted down onto temporary platforms. They were pummelling the German attackers on the ground in the southern docks and any aircraft of the attacking Italian Air Force and Luftwaffe bombers flying overhead.

A harried Petty Officer with a stained and torn, navy blue, double breasted uniform waved John over to the warehouse. "I'm Maxwell, Petty Officer, all the officers have been killed or are with the fleet. I wondered when someone would get through." He thrust a large hand in John's direction, the cuff on his other arm was stained with blood from a wound in his arm. There was no doubting this man was a hero. John took his hand and returned the warm pressure.

John looked at the huge wooden battleship with its three masts and familiar outline in dry dock. "Why, that's the 'Victory,' Nelson's flagship at Trafalgar."

"The Germans don't know it but it contains a squad of volunteers armed with Lewis machine guns. They took a boat out last night and boarded her via the harbour side. From there they can sweep the docks if the Jerries come down that way."

John raised his binoculars and peered through the smoke, waiting for a clear path. They could hear air raid sirens from the northern part of the city. Artillery shells exploded in the German lines and they replied in kind.

"My orders are to have your men load up as much naval ordinance as they can on the lorries we brought. My Commandos will man the barricade. The Royal Engineers are setting up charges to destroy what munitions we can't load in two hours from these warehouses." They watched the sappers' efficiently unrolling wire from hand-held wheels and setting charges. "We have only got two hours, we can't hold them up any longer than that. There will be an attack on the German positions at Southsea in five minutes, to get the Royal Marines out."

The sound of firing came from HMS Victory a quarter of a mile along the docks. John watched through his binoculars as German infantrymen advancing towards the ship fell down or threw themselves down. German tanks charged towards the railway lines by the Victory in dry dock, while supporting grey clad troops took cover. The machine guns on the tanks spat out bullets, splintering the ancient wood of the most famous vessel in naval history. Two more grey tanks appeared around the corner bearing the black cross of the Wehrmacht on their turrets. All four took aim and fired their cannons.

"I think they need a hand, Mr. Maxwell. That train there is not being used to move munitions, we could run it on that rail line alongside the Victory's dry dock."

"Why, yes ..."

"I'm going to use it and bring those sailors back alive."

"Do that and you have my undying gratitude." The non-commissioned naval officer, walked quickly to the small dock train and spoke to the driver.

"Major Stafford wants to take this train and shunt it by the Victory and take off our sailors, I want you to drive it for him?"

The engineers looked at each other and at the bleeding man in charge of the docks. "Aye, aye, Sir," replied the driver.

"Sergeant-Major," John ordered as he strode up to Frances Lincoln, "ask Captain MacLeod and ten men with sticky bombs to join me at that train right away."

While Aubrey set his men defending the barricades, transport corps soldiers loaded the lorries carefully with naval shells and fuses. John spoke to the driver in the small cab of the engine, "Get as much steam up as you can, the track goes behind that warehouse."

Turning to his men Duncan said, "The Jerry tanks will only see us when we're almost there. We'll try the sticky bombs we've been told are so effective. Now, remember your training with the sticky bombs. We're getting covering fire from Major Stafford and Sergeant-Major Lincoln. We'll jump off there," Duncan advised his Commandos as he pointed at an alleyway between two warehouses. "Get as close to throwing distance as you can and let the tanks have it. Remember, when you unseal the sticky bomb, swing it in an arc, don't let the bomb stick on your back you'll blow yourself up!"

John wished them luck.

Frances chuckled, looking forward to action, as he released the safety catch on the Bren gun he always carried. The train shunted out towards the German-held portion of the docks. It slowed as it reached the alleyway. Duncan jumped off with his 10 men. John ordered the train on as they came around the corner of the warehouse into the sights of the German tanks. The sailors on the wooden battleship were firing furiously.

John could have sworn he heard the boom of a muzzle-loaded cannon from the ship. He looked at the tanks and the German infantry who had ceased advancing momentarily, surprised by the appearance of the small, black shunting train.

The cannon shots from the Victory kept the German soldiers ducking. John thought how amazing it was that the cannons from the Napoleonic Wars still worked and how grateful he was at the same time. Frances Lincoln gave a full burst of Bren gun fire from the train, pulled out the empty curved magazine on the top of the .303 Bren and replaced it with a full one. The tanks swivelled their turrets round to fire their cannons at the train. Duncan's men ran up behind the tanks. Clutching the wooden handles of the sticky bombs they threw them onto the sides and turrets of the tanks. In seconds they exploded and the four Mk. III Panzer tanks began to smoke.

As the tank crews scrambled out of the hatches President Lincoln and the sailors on the Victory picked them off. The other Commandos dealt with the German infantry forcing them to withdraw to the safety of a nearby warehouse.

John hailed the sailors on Victory, "Hurry up! Time to leave." Seven sailors ran down the gangplank clutching their weapons and clambered onto the train.

John saw Duncan withdrawing with his men down the alley. "Driver, reverse," John ordered the train driver to slow down to pick up the men just as the Germans unlimbered an 88-mm artillery howitzer, loaded it and fired. John ordered full speed reverse as soon as the Commandos were aboard. The first shell shot over cab of the train by inches.

"Those guys are good," John said. "Too damned good, Sir," agreed Lincoln. A second shell screamed towards them and slammed into the coal tender behind the engine. The train screeched to a halt.

"Jump, run for it!" John shouted, just moments before another 88 mm shell made a direct hit and blew the train to smithereens. Soldiers and sailors rolled away from the blast. John saw Duncan inert upon the ground, he hoisted him over his shoulders in a fireman's lift and moved as quickly as possible towards the British held docks. Lincoln put his arm around a wounded Commando and while supporting him fired his Bren gun at the German infantry advancing towards them.

Ahead of them another 88 mm shell landed, detonated the last lorry full of munitions just as it geared up out of the docks.

"Time to go soon, Captain Hunter," the Petty Officer advised Aubrey commanding the Commandos behind the British barricade at the north end of the docks.

"As soon as Major Stafford's party returns. Here they come now." Aubrey pointed at the Commandos emerging from the smoke of battle surrounding the docks. Aubrey ordered men forward to give covering fire and ran to help John and President Lincoln with the wounded. Once safely behind the barricade the Commandos and sailors squeezed into the Bren Gun carriers and the convoy scraped past the burning vehicle at the gates.

Just outside the gates, the commander of the Sappers squatted and depressed the plunger handle connected by electrical wires to the explosives set to explode in the arsenal. The ground rumbled and shook as the warehouse went up into the sky in a cyclone of destruction. The Royal Engineer ran to the last Bren carrier and jumped in, landing behind John and an unconscious Duncan, as it lurched forward out through the dock gates.

British Mk. 6 light tanks covered their withdrawal by firing into the eastern dockside streets as Panzer tanks began to duel with them. The munitions in the warehouse continued to explode, debris threw itself around blocking any immediate German advance from the docks. John had a feeling of accomplishment knowing they had taken all the ammunition they could and then destroyed the remainder. As they drove to the heights above Portsmouth he checked Duncan to see if he was wounded anywhere. He could find no blood. His friend groaned as he regained consciousness.

"No need to worry, mission accomplished. We'll get a doctor to check you out. Concussion I think," John said.

"What did ... you say?" Duncan murmured and lapsed into unconsciousness. John took off his olive green, wool jacket and tucked it over Duncan. The sun was beginning to come out. John began to compose his report in his head and the letters that he would have to write to the parents of those Commandos that had died that day.

Over the next few days, while Duncan recovered in a field hospital, John and his men learned how the Battle for Britain was proceeding. Oil had been pumped onto the sea and set on fire as the first German troops landed at Dover. Monty had thrown reserves into the Battle of Dover on the afternoon of the first day and threw the invaders who had made it through the wall of fire back into the sea.

The German High Command swiftly realized that the Dover option was useless and ordered reinforcements already at sea from Calais to change to their secondary targets where all was proceeding as planned.

The beachheads at Portsmouth, Eastbourne and Harwich smoothly received extra reinforcements, much to the combined relief of General Rommel of the 6th Army Group at Portsmouth, Guderian at Harwich with the 4th Army and Rundstedt at Eastbourne with the 3rd Army. The weather was clear, the winds low, perfect for barges being towed across the channel.

The amphibious tanks had proven themselves very useful. By the second day the precious few British tanks were outnumbered. The last Spitfire and Hurricane fighters were shot out of the skies by Luftwaffe squadrons utilizing airfields captured by German paratroopers. Apart from losing the Bismarck, the German navy had incredible luck. U-boat captains jubilantly radioed success after success to Admiral Doenitz at Brest, France. Despite losing 19 of their number to the ASDIC-equipped Royal Navy Destroyers and submarine-hunting frigates, which dropped hundreds of depth charges, the U-Boats seemed unstoppable.

General Montgomery commanding British and Canadian forces in the south of England had to decide which beachhead to destroy next. Churchill's intelligence group at Bletchley Park, with its deciphered German codes, informed Churchill that the main thrust for London would be from a combination of Rommel's and Runstedt's armies moving north from the south coast. The feint would be from Harwich which would face any army from the Midlands. Outnumbered, Monty had no choice but to meet the combined 6th and 3rd Army groups and decided upon concentrating his forces at Hayward's Heath, Sussex.

The battle started well on September 27th, when he caught the Germans by surprise in a night counter-attack, reinforced by what troops could be sent by undamaged rail-lines from Wales and northern England. A terrible battle raged. By the afternoon the Germans had lost 26,000 men and a lot of the cocky spirit born of their Blitzkrieg success of the first six days of invasion.

On the second day of the Battle of Hayward's Heath however, disaster struck. Monty's army caravan, his battle headquarters, was strafed by a low- flying Messerschmitt 109 fighter. The General was seriously wounded, with a bullet in his lung, and his second-in-command was killed.

The British General was flown out by a gull-winged Lysander plane, which took off from a nearby field during the battle. One of Monty's colonels took command and was given permission to use mustard gas against the invaders. But the weather was not co-operating, the wind blew from the southeast towards the British lines. By September 30th, day three of the battle, the wind changed and the Royal Artillery fired gas shells into the German positions but extra Panzer divisions and the continued pounding of British troops by Luftwaffe bombers flying from Nazi held airfields, tipped the balance and the British front crumbled. There were just too many fresh enemy troops being poured into the battle.

On October 3rd, the first Nazi troops, led by Von Runstedt, entered London meeting heavy resistance. Rommel's army made a left hook around London, teamed up with Guderian's 4th Army Group and smashed their way to Birmingham, the industrial capital, sweeping all resistance before it.

After the industrialized midlands were taken by mid-October, there was no large armed force in the United Kingdom left to overpower the 600,000 German troops now on British soil. It was only a matter of time before Churchill and the government had to leave the temporary capital in Glasgow, Scotland.

Lord Eastbourne, and the previously imprisoned Lord Mosely, leader of the British Nazi like blackshirts, set up a provisional government in London and made truce arrangements with the German generals. Within hours, Lord Eastbourne agreed to unconditional surrender and declared the state of New Britain, an ally of Nazi Germany. He ordered all Britons under arms to surrender but few did.

John's men were ordered to Bristol with the naval ammunition which he had rescued from Portsmouth, and which was safely taken on board naval vessels. John and his Commandos fought western elements of Rommel's force which struck south west from the Midlands. When word was received that a Fascist Government in London had surrendered, John opened his sealed orders. Following its instructions, he spoke to his acting commander and with his permission withdrew his remaining Commandos and all the ammunition and supplies he could carry on seventeen lorries and five Bren gun carriers. While the regular army followed orders to head for Bristol, Aubrey rounded up a battery of ten 25 pounder howitzers, a large number of shells and artillery lorries, and their crews. John stood on top of a lorry in Taunton and in a rousing speech convinced the Royal Artillery company to go with them to the Welsh mountains in the west of Britain and form a resistance group. He assured them that they would be of more use staying and using their weapons than taking ship to Canada.

By chance, in the chaos of crowded streets that was Bristol that October, John saw his brother Alan. The port city was filled with refugees and exhausted, demoralized soldiers waiting to get on a ship. Constant air raids were met with a defiant barrage of anti-aircraft fire from the defences set up around the port.

"I have orders to go to Wales, Alan. We're carrying on the fight. When you get back to Canada give our parents my love." He hugged his brother.

"Keep out of trouble," Alan told him.

"I have, except for these meetings with annoying Jerries."

"I'm taking my men to Canada, we're supposed to be evacuated on a liner tonight, 'The Empress of Canada.' I should go now to arrange it. Good luck, we'll be back."

"You'd better be Alan! Look for Felicity will you, here's her Montreal address," John printed it out in Alan's pocket notebook, "maybe she got out."

"I'll look for her and look after her, depend on it."

"Thanks Alan. Goodbye," John said with an ache in his throat, wondering if he would ever see his brother or Felicity again.

CHAPTER TWELVE EDWARD VIII AND QUEEN WALLIS

To the pilot of the Lufthansa airliner on day 26 of Operation Sea Lion, everything was wonderful. It was a glorious sunny day, the British army was crushed and Churchill was scuttling off to Canada. The plane was responding well and he had very important passengers.

He had recognized Dr. Goebbels, Minister of Propaganda, wearing a brown, pin-striped, double-breasted suit. The short, black haired Nazi leader was ushering a middle aged couple, a few bodyguards and a young translator onto the plane at Orly Airport in Paris.

He knew that couple from somewhere but couldn't remember where. Their faces were all over the newspapers and in the magazines of 1937, but he had been fighting in the Nazi Condor Legion in Spain for Franco's Fascists and hadn't time for anything except trying to stay alive and down the enemy's Soviet - built planes.

Alongside him flew an escort of Messerschmitt 109s with propellor bosses painted blue. A winged horse decorated the squadron leader's plane. They flew west past the finger of France called Brittany. The island of Jersey grew quickly from a dark smudge into a proper island with a sandy beach. The main town of St. Helier, farms, trees, yachts and trawlers tied up at the dock, houses all became more detailed as the planes side-slipped, descended and landed.

The small airfield on Jersey was the same as it had been during the months of peace before September 1939 except for a piece of cloth snapping in the sea breeze. Instead of the familiar Union Jack, indicating Jersey was part of the United Kingdom, another flag was flying. It was a Nazi flag.

As the Lufthansa liner taxied to the edge of the runway by the concrete observation tower, the Nazi flag was lowered. A metal ladder on wheels was pushed out to the opened door at the back of the plane.

Dr. Goebbels and the bodyguards waited at the bottom of the ladder as the King and Queen of New Britain gingerly poked their heads out from the doorway and descended. At that moment a German military band played 'God Save the King' and an honour guard occupying this part of the British Empire stood at attention.

The red, white and black Nazi flag was lowered on the control tower flagpole. King Edward pursed his lips. Wallis held onto her hat. Another flag was being run up the pole, it was red, white and blue. As it got to the top of the pole the wind blew and unfurled a Union Jack with a black swastika in a white circle staining the centre. "The flag of your kingdom to be New Britain, Your Majesties," Dr. Goebbels said to them as they stood on the cement airfield looking on.

The band began to play 'Deutschland Uber Alles' as Dr. Goebbels ushered them into a waiting car. "We will have refreshment at the hotel in St. Helier, and then to the radio station where you'll shall give your speech this evening. You will be broadcast to your subjects, who should be pleased to know they have a new king. Someone they love."

The Duke swallowed. 'I am King. I am King,' a shrill voice said inside his head. He recognized that voice, he had heard it before in nightmares after his father died. He gulped nervously and tightened his grip on Wallis's hand. Someone had to be King now that his brother was dead. He had died an honourable death. Sadly he wondered about his own fate as they arrived at the hotel.

Press cameras flashed, newsreel cameramen took pictures as they entered the hotel in St. Helier. Dr. Goebbels gave a Nazi salute. David and Wallis looked at him. David, ever so slightly, shook his head. The couple continued to wave their hands as they turned to go.

David leafed through the typed speech an hour before he was scheduled to broadcast from his hotel room. He choked on his coffee and decided not to drink any more. He went over it again:

> *This is your rightful king, Edward VIII speaking to you from the Channel Island of Jersey. My younger brother George VI has tragically died. How many more are to be killed in a senseless war with our sister nation of Germany? Now our nation of Great Britain stands in need of firm leadership. I have been asked by the new government, headed by Lord Eastbourne in London, to*

become Edward VIII once again. I have decided to accept this offer for my people's sake, asking only that my wife be crowned with me as Queen Wallis. I do not wish to burden my niece the Princess Elizabeth, with the terrible cares of kingship in such turbulent times. I also wish to allow my sister-in-law, Queen Elizabeth, to grieve in peace and not have to wrestle with the difficult period of transition which faces a New Britain. Let us build for a future of peace and plenty. New Britain will stand with Germany against the threat of Communism in the east. I have been assured by Herr Hitler that his pact with the Soviet Union is a defensive pact only and that we will enjoy the protection of the Third Reich. So I ask you to pray for our nation that we can reconcile old hates and move on. My wife and I promise to serve you to the best of our ability. God bless you all.

"Is there a problem, Your Majesty?" Dr. Goebbels asked through Heinz as he strode into the room, looking with concern at David's sorrowful expression.

"I'm not so sure I really can say all this with conviction, I mean..."

"I think you will," Dr. Goebbels said in German looking at Wallis as Heinz dutifully translated. "I don't think you wish any stupid Briton to take a shot at you, and your gracious queen, when you arrive on the mainland in a few days."

"You're threatening me!"

"No, Your Majesty, merely informing you of possibilities. Lord Eastbourne is making arrangements now to ensure you are protected as soon as you arrive in London. Now, if you'll excuse me, Sir, I must see that the radio connections are all in order. You are 'on', as they say, in 20 minutes."

The weary new king went and sat next to Wallis and squeezed her hand. "He's got us over a barrel. Fate is against our ever being left in peace," she said.

"Yes," he sighed.

He read the speech into the microphone; it was relayed throughout the United Kingdom as listeners tuned into the Nazi propaganda wireless channel expecting something to laugh at in scorn. He decided that he must be in shock.

He could not even taste his food and everything seemed to be happening in slow motion. He longed for someone to speed the film up, or better yet reverse it backwards, "to when we were married at Cande, and stop it there forever."

Dr. Goebbels sidled up to his table and gripped Edward's arm with two hands. "That was a fine speech, worthy of a king."

"I'm glad you liked it but let's face it you wrote it. However, I'm used to that." He smiled ironically at Dr. Goebbels "I really wasn't at liberty to refuse was I?"

"Champagne!" Goebbels clapped his hands, a waiter brought over four glasses and a green bottle of 1924 Moet in a bucket of ice. Colonel O'Donnell uncorked the bottle with panache and poured some of the frothy liquid into the glasses, then passed them out to the King, Queen and Goebbels.

Holding his glass, up he said, "Here's to the King and Queen of New Britain." Dr. Goebbels drank with relish. King Edward held the glass in his hand, a blank expression on his face as he looked at his queen, who held her hand to her temple.

"A headache, dear? Perhaps a small drink will help. You're under a lot of stress." She reached for her champagne and, as if taking medicine, drank it down. She hoped it would dull the pain.

She offered her glass to their Irish aide-de-camp who dutifully poured her another. "Ahh, I feel better, come along, David, drink up." The new King reluctantly raised his glass and drank.

At Scotland Yard, London the fledgling New British Gendarmerie, a paramilitary police force, acted on lists provided by Gestapo officers, rounding up loyal Britons, intellectuals, Jews, gypsies, the disabled, homosexuals and other 'undesirables'. Reichsmarschal Himmler was personally organizing the transportation of 'Churchill's scum,' either to the Tower of London for questioning, or to the once idyllic Isle of Wight, where British Prisoners of War were being used to build a massive concentration camp.

At the Tower, the new Governor of London, Count Von Darmstadt, was hosting a banquet in honour of Lord Eastbourne's success in gaining power and making peace. The Count was looking forward to visiting the dungeons after dinner. Tonight would be the first time the magnificent, ancient body stretching and breaking instrument known as the rack would be used in over 350 years, an historic moment.

Finally, the interminable speeches and toasts completed, his booted feet clacked down the cold, damp, dungeon stairs to greet the first prisoners.

He felt a surge of satisfaction. Happily, he congratulated himself, I will be the perfect Governor of London. I love history and have great respect for tradition. Those are classic English characteristics.

How odd Lord Eastbourne declined my invitation to see the rack in use. No stomach for the brutal day-to-day necessity of keeping order. I will have to teach him to appreciate realpolitik.

CHAPTER THIRTEEN LAST OF THE YEOMAN WARDERS

Charlie Gates was the last of the Yeoman Warders. He had been thrown on his back by a shell explosion during the last stand made by the Warders as the Wehrmacht rooted out the defenders. The Tower of London was the last part of the city to fall to the invaders. A truce to bury the wounded and a pact to end the shelling of non-military sites was the precursor to the peace overtures put forward by Lord Eastbourne and Lord Moseley. They met with Field Marshal Keitel at Hampton Court.

The next day, October 15th, a peace treaty was drawn up by the provisional fascist government of New Britain. Lord Eastbourne was appointed Prime Minister by King Edward VIII. Eastbourne moved into 10 Downing Street while glaziers were replacing the shattered glass with shiny new panes.

A feeling of gloom had fallen across London. The British army had withdrawn, fighting rear guard actions to the west and north but shattered from the battles in the Home Counties and Midlands which had devoured all its reserves.

The remnants were ordered to the west coast ports of Bristol, Liverpool Belfast and Glasgow where fishing boats, ocean liners, Merchant Marine freighters were waiting to take them on board. The Royal Navy Home Fleet had left its northern anchorage at Scapa Flow in Orkney to escort the convoys.

At St. Bart's Hospital in London on the night of October 15th, Charlie and other patients in the ward, along with nurses and doctors listened to the radio as Churchill spoke from Glasgow. They sat silently, some holding hands, some with tears running down their cheeks. Charlie made careful notes during the speech and was able to produce a very good facsimile of it, which he copied for everyone in the ward the next morning, under the noses of the Gendarmerie constables patrolling through the hospital.

German guards were joking with some local women. One of the New British policemen, wearing a new black uniform, jackboots and a pistol in a shiny black holster on his left hip, stood on duty. Charlie felt sick. He forced himself to walk up to the entrance. Only the thought of seeing his two beloved ravens, Croakey and Jeremiah, gave him the strength to go on. He had found a way to hide them in a secret room with plenty of food and water before the Germans arrived.

He could speak no German, but one of the guards knew enough English to realize that this man was saying he used to work at the Tower. He phoned for an officer to come to the gate. One arrived and invited Charlie with elaborate politeness, for Charlie to come in and have a cup of tea with him. Obviously, Charlie thought, the victors had been told to be nice to the newly vanquished English.

"It won't be poisoned?" Charlie asked.

"No, we have Earl Grey tea or orange pekoe."

"Orange pekoe." The officer gave an order to an orderly and in five minutes a pot of tea and two cups in saucers with biscuits; were brought into the Lieutenant's office. After talking about the weather and seeing that Charlie was uncomfortable having tea with the enemy, the Lieutenant phoned Governor Von Darmstadt's office to inform him that a real Yeoman Warder was sitting with him.

The day before, the Count had complained that without at least one of the original warders the Tower was incomplete. His phone call was immediately returned by Von Darmstadt himself.

"The Governor of London would like to see you."

Charlie protested. The Lieutenant held up his hand. "A friendly talk. He may be offering you your old job back."

"What?" exclaimed Charlie, aghast.

"He has a liking for tradition, especially British ceremonies. You will see."

Unconvinced, Charlie agreed to being escorted to the White Tower which was in the process of being turned into the Nazi nerve centre of London. Workmen were erecting office walls, moving in desks and installing Teletype machines.

They could force me to go I suppose, Charlie thought, besides, this may be a way to look after the ravens. Perhaps if I keep my eyes open I might see something of interest to the resistance.

An inner voice warned him that he was playing with fire and could easily be shot as he slipped up. Nevertheless, he followed the German officer up the spiral stone staircase in the corner to the second floor as best he could, with the aid of his cane.

The Lieutenant took his arm on the last steps as Charlie slowed down and held his back. "We're having a ... what is the word, ah, a lift installed later this week. Then it will be much easier."

"I remember you ...Gates ... 1938." Count Von Darmstadt said after spending a long two long minutes scrutinizing him. "Please sit down."

"Oh yes, it was a tour with Lord Eastbourne. Now it would seem you're in charge."

"How right you are, Mr. Gates."

Charlie held his cane between his legs with his hands clasped over the handle. He reminded himself to act stupid.

"I understand you have been discharged from hospital. We need you back here. You have great knowledge of the Tower and I want you as a tour guide. We are going to have some important people here for the coronation for King Edward and Queen Wallis. The Fuhrer, Il Duce, perhaps even the Emperor of Japan will be here in London. I will invite them here to see the Tower."

Charlie looked pained. "But these are all my enemies."

"Quite right, you should love your country, but this is New Britain. Workers and rulers together fighting communism and social rot, friends of the Third Reich. We all have a duty. You will learn to understand this. Besides, the King and Queen will soon be coming to live here in the Tower, and they need an English friend, someone who can do no harm, like yourself. Their Irish Aide-de-Camp is a martinet and not good company. I want them to settle in first, but I'll let you know when I want you to visit them. Of course you will have light custodial duties, a wage and a place to stay at time when many homes have been wrecked. What do you say?"

"I'll be considered a collaborator."

"A man has to eat and sleep in a dry place. You will be carrying on the traditions of the Tower. What could be more English? You will be the only Englishman here, besides the King. Once the clean-up prisoner of war gangs have left, the workmen inside will all be German. You can have leave to amuse yourself on Saturdays as long as you are back by curfew at 10 p.m. By the way, if you are thinking of any sabotage ... we can easily have you shot or worse. We are using the rack to extract information from terrorists and political prisoners."

Von Darmstadt rubbed his hands together. "An axe man will be arriving from Nurnberg shortly so we can begin using the block once again. Oh yes, the eagles with their handler are on their way from Austria. Your first duty is to ensure that those dead ravens on the lawn are buried; that is a tradition here is it not? You may put wooden crosses on the lawn for them."

Charlie managed to visit the hidden ravens on his first day. The food was used up, the water bowl empty. They had survived by drinking water in a hollow on the stone sill of the small, barred window overlooking the Thames.

"I'll be back soon," he promised, and within twenty minutes he had returned with a bottle of water and a brown bag of seeds pilfered from the gardener's shed.

Croakey and Jeremiah hopped around crazily, happy that someone was finally taking care of them. It's a right mess in here, Charlie thought to himself as he looked at the floor. Trying to figure out how he could bring up some sawdust and a broom, he carefully locked the door and pushed the stone in place so the secret room in the dungeon of the Tower was effectively closed off.

It had been designed for prisoners who could be left there to starve to death. The Yeoman Warders were the only ones who knew of it and he was the last one. Only four inches of sunlight came in through the slit of a window.

Outside, on the green he collected the dead bodies of the four ravens, trying not to breathe in too deeply he buried them and erected small crosses upon which he neatly lettered their names and death dates. He also made two extra crosses for the still-alive Croakey and Jeremiah.

Charlie recollected the words of his doctor at St. Bart's; "If you do get to the Tower and see or hear anything of interest that the Germans are up to, there will be someone at the Old King Lud pub by the Guinness draught bar pump who would like to hear about it. The password is 'Henry VIII,' the reply, 'Six wives.'"

One day, while on his way out of the White Tower, the old warder paused in front of the massive suit of armour worn by Henry VIII that stood in a hallway. He glanced around; there was no one in sight. Swiftly drawing his folded copy of Churchill's speech from his pocket, he opened the visor of the helmet and thrust it inside and heard the comforting sound of it dropping inside the breastplate. He knew his room was being searched, he did not want anything found that could get him into hot water.

He stepped out of the side exit gate into the city. Charlie smiled to himself as he pondered who would find it in the future, if anything happened to him. Would it be a scowling German or British collaborator who would rip up the paper and toss it away, or a free Briton who would wonder about it at some unknown time in the future? he asked himself.

On his first Saturday off he had taken the tube, one of the re-opened underground railway lines that had seen little fighting, to visit a cousin in Hampstead. Charlie kept looking to see if he was being followed but decided he wasn't.

On his second Saturday off, he took a bus to Regent's Park where he fed the ducks. Charlie bought some fish and chips for dinner then took a red double decker bus east to the Old King Lud pub for a few pints, and a possible meeting with the resistance. He shook his head as he looked east and saw the damage done to St. Paul's Cathedral from artillery shells trying to dislodge British snipers.

CHAPTER FOURTEEN RESISTANCE LONDON

Wearing a rumpled, old brown suit, Charlie observed the table by the Guinness draught beer pump at the bar of the Old King Lud Pub. No one came to sit by it. He left at 8:30 so as no to miss the curfew. The following weekend he took a seat by the bar. Two men came, in ordered a half-pint of Guinness each, rolled their own cigarettes and smoked them.

Charlie looked them over. One wore a dark blue London Transport bus conductor's uniform. He vaguely remembered seeing him collecting tickets on a bus he took to the Houses of Parliament in prewar days. The other man was younger and wore a working man's flat cloth cap and a jacket over a pair of blue overalls.

Charlie picked up his glass of Bass beer, sipped some foam and went up to them. "Do you mind if I join you gents? I've a mind to play a game of dominoes." Charlie brought a wooden box of dominoes and placed it on the table by the ashtray. The bus conductor did not look keen but the tradesman nodded in a friendly fashion and motioned to him to sit down. Charlie slid open the wooden lid.

"I believe," Charlie said, breaking the silence at their table, 'this was the favourite game of Henry VIII.'

The bus conductor laughed. "I thought he was too busy with his six wives to play games. My name's Dennis." He thrust out a hand which Charlie warmly shook. "This is Fred."

Fred offered a cold hand and said; "Look, the light's better over there," looking at a table by the wall. It's getting a bit noisy at the bar." They picked up their drinks and the dominoes and moved over. Charlie carefully tipped out the black rectangles with the dots face down on the table, picked out seven dominoes and placed them carefully as horizontal sentries around his beer glass. Fred and Dennis followed suit.

Charlie spoke about himself in a low voice as they played.

"You mean you're the very last Warder at the Tower?"

"That I am."

"You've seen prisoners there?"

"Yes, some slave labour gangs, our lads, prisoners of war. They have just about done the clean-up from the Battle of London, at the Tower anyway. But lorries arrive at night and I've seen intellectual-looking types, men and women, being led into the dungeons in the White Tower. I'm afraid they are using the rack for the first time in centuries." Charlie's fingers were white as he gripped the wooden box.

"My God," Fred said, he gripped Charlie's arm. "It's not your doing, Charlie. Look, we want you to join Resistance London. You just have to come here once a month or so . One or both of us will be here. We will be the only ones you ever meet, it's a cell system. We need to know guard routines, if you see anyone important there. You're a soldier. You know the score."

"Well, did you know that King Edward and Queen Wallis are coming to the Tower?"

Fred and Dennis drew in their breath and picked through their dominoes. They played in silence for several minutes, Charlie placed his last piece in place on the table. "Domino!"Charlie called out victoriously.

"We knew they were in London. They were spotted at Waterloo Station in the middle of the night, but that's all. Even our contacts in the New British Fascist party don't know where they are."

A ripple of subdued laughter drifted over from the bar as someone told a joke. Fred continued, "We believe Von Darmstadt, the Governor of London, will be moving into the Tower from the Savoy Hotel soon."

"Oh yes, on Monday, White Tower, third floor. The second floor seems to be some kind of communications centre, lots of radio equipment. Only German workers and soldiers in there."

"Charlie, you can be a great help to the cause" Dennis said.

Charlie smiled, got up, bought them all another beer from the barmaid and sat down. Fred spoke, "We want you to cooperate with Von Darmstadt. Let him think you are doing all he asks to continue the traditions of the Tower because it is all you have. But be yourself, be crusty, and proud to be British. I think he would respect that."

"He's a strange bloke. He hates some things about us but loves some other things. There is no doubt in my mind that heÕs dangerous. He'll be the death of many Britons. I don't like being near him, he orders the torture and he's even bringing in a German executioner with an axe."

"He's a marked man" Dennis whispered.

Charlie pulled out his waistcoat pocket watch. "I'll just drain this" he said as he reached for his glass, "I must be off."

"Yes, Charlie, we must play dominoes another time," Dennis said. They said goodbye and Charlie walked out into the blackout gloom of occupied London to take the bus to the Tower before 10 p.m. This was when the London transport system stopped running and citizens could be shot on sight by the German army or Gendarmes if caught on the street.

On Monday afternoon, a German corporal knocked on Charlie's apartment door and informed him that the Governor wanted to see him immediately in his office. When Charlie entered, Von Darmstadt was tapping a gold fountain pen upon his blotter.

"Are your legs giving you trouble, Gates?"

"My back."

"How foolish of you Wardens to fight us with pikes and muskets. Foolish but brave."

Charlie did not want to inform him he had knocked off two or three Jerries before he had been thrown up in the air by an artillery shell exploding twenty feet away. "It was a miracle I survived."

"You are like a child if you believe in miracles. But I know one thing we both believe in is this ancient fortress and how important its history is to the whole world. Once the war is over this will be a prominent place for every citizen of the world-wide Reich to visit. I am looking ahead, Gates. The traditions of the Tower must continue no matter who is here. Correct?"

"I couldn't say it any better myself."

"Well, we are bringing in a few improvements: eagles and a handler." Charlie bristled. The Count smiled, "Calm yourself, I will not subject you to helping with their care. This is just a German addition to the traditions ... but I do need your help with the Ceremony of the Keys."

Charlie looked surprised; "The last Ceremony of the Keys was the night before your 2nd Army entered London."

"Yes. We had better start the ceremony once again before too much time elapses. Tell me about it."

Charlie spent half an hour regaling him with the stories of how every evening for hundreds of years a guard of red coated Household Division troops in black bearskin hats had accompanied a warder holding the keys to the Tower. The warder also held a candle lantern and arrived at the White Tower at 10 p.m. The guards to be relieved offered the command "Who goes there?"

When the correct reply, was given, "the King's keys", the warder would be allowed into the Tower with the fresh guards and the door is locked.

"I want you, Gates, to instruct a squad of our men about the procedure. I want the Ceremony of the Keys to begin again and continue daily. I think we can dispense with the red uniforms, we'll have our garrison wearing their best uniforms. But you can be the warder in your best Yeoman's tunic."

"It will be good to see the ceremony continued, Governor."

"Good man. I'll have a squad ready at 9:30 tonight on the green. Bring the lantern and the ceremonial keys."

Charlie wondered, as he carried a bag of seed and a bottle of water under his coat to the ravens, whether his taking part in this charade would be of help to the Resistance at some time in the future. He decided it might be and resolved to take it seriously and do a good job.

Queen Wallis arrived back in the precincts of the Tower, driven by the British Fascist driver who wore the uniform of black jack boots, jodhpurs, a belt with a silver buckle adorned with a lightning flash, black turtleneck and black cap. The chauffeur opened the door of the armoured Rolls Royce for the Queen and Colonel O'Donnell. The Queen exited the car quickly, then ran up the steps of the Bloody Tower and entered the royal apartments. She admired her newly coiffed hair in the mirror as the German maid finished dusting and left.

"David, I've something to show you," she said quietly. He looked up from his father's photo album. She passed him a folded piece of paper torn from a school exercise book. "I fell asleep under the hair dryer, and when I woke up I found this in my hand." The King opened it and looked at the jumble of letters cut from newspaper headlines and pasted down in an uneven message.

Shine a light three times across your window by the Thames at 11:10 p.m. tonight if you are prisoners. Resistance London.

King Edward went to the toilet, tore the note into pieces, and pulling on the Victorian chain handle flushed them into the sewer system.

There was a knock at the door. "Come in," said the King.

"It's just me, Your Majesties" O'Donnell strode in, placed his attache case on the table, unzipped it and removed some papers. He did not notice the Queen's face blanch with shock at his timing.

"Here are the plans for your state opening of Parliament tomorrow. Lord Eastbourne is most anxious for it go smoothly." He jabbed his finger at the route on a map. "Your Majesties will be taken by St. Paul's Cathedral down Fleet Street, the Strand, south alongside Somerset House to the Thames and along the Victoria embankment to the Houses of Parliament in the Rolls Royce with a Gendarme motorcycle escort."

"Good, no carriage," the King interjected. "Old fashioned. I'd like to wear a civilian suit, no uniform."

"Good idea, your majesty. You'll cut a fine figure," O'Donnell said obsequiously, "and one of the best Paris ensembles for the Queen, if I might suggest ..."

"Perhaps the blue outfit with the hat and pearls we brought over David, ... if I must go," Wallis said.

"Of course you must go. You are Queen Wallis, your subjects will want to see you. They will be able to see us, won't they, Colonel?"

"Yes, Sir, there will be schoolchildren lining the route. There will be several BBC television cameras en route and at the ceremony in the House of Lords, as well as several radio announcers. British of course, Edward R. Murrow of the United States, German, Italian, French and Japanese radio announcers. Press journalists will also be there. Look on this as a dress rehearsal for the coronation in the spring of 1941.

Lord Eastbourne will meet you both by the entrance to the House of Lords. There will be a red carpet. He will escort you into the Upper Chamber where the assembled Lords and members of the New British Commons will be ready to give you a warm welcome.

Now I'll leave you to look over the throne speech. The PM thought you would particularly like the legislation planned to aid the unemployed and those Britons without housing, causes close to your heart."

The King nodded. "There are also some routine documents to sign, as per your request only the most essential are being sent to you."

"Quite, ... good, good," the King replied and watched as the Colonel bowed, retreated backwards towards the door and left.

"What do we do about tonight?" the Queen said in low tones to her husband after they heard O'Donnell walk down the hall and away.

"Do? We damn well do everything we can to keep them happy and stay alive!" he hissed.

"Whom do we keep happy?" Wallis asked.

"Why, our captors and Resistance London, of course," the King said in commanding tones.

At 11 o'clock that evening, King Edward put down his pipe, stood up, and brushed down his dressing gown, as he walked to the window holding a lit oil lamp. Queen Wallis opened the curtain and they looked out upon the dark Thames and the huge dim outline of Tower Bridge.

At 11:10 Edward moved the lamp across the window three times. Wallis closed the curtains. Edward read a few more pages of Sir Walter Raleigh's History of the World. The antique, leather-bound volume lay open on his lap as he sat in a stuffed leather chair. "Amazing, he wrote this right here, before he lost his head. I should write a book."

"You will, dear, and you'll keep your head," Wallis purred. "Now, how about a kiss?"

At 11:10 p.m. precisely, when Wallis opened the curtains and Edward moved a lit oil lamp across the window three times. Dennis and Fred were watching from the Tower Bridge control room. They looked at each other then thanked the night shift engineer, who was also part of the resistance movement and made sure their forged work papers were in their pockets. They walked down the stairs carrying bags of tools to bridge level.

"What did I tell you? They're on our side" Dennis said

"Don't believe all you see," Fred countered, "It's possible they told the Governor about this and they've been instructed to play along. Anyway, we'll tell number six. We'll be told be advised what to do next."

They crossed over the bridge to the south bank. All was quiet; only the Thames could be heard gurgling beneath them. The German sentry at the end of the bridge had become used to seeing them every night over the last week

CHAPTER FIFTEEN THE PIPER IN THE BLOODY TOWER

It was December 7th, 1940 the day of the first German Ceremony of the Keys. Charlie was up early, ironing his best uniform and brushing some fallen plaster from his Tudor hat. After that he went for a stroll on the green before cooking up some breakfast. He was allowed generous rations and he was looking forward to fried eggs and bread, tomatoes, sausages and bacon. A real English breakfast. There had been a slight frost and the grass was covered with white rime. It was a bracing morning. Charlie breathed in. If circumstances had been better it would be a bloody perfect morning.

He cocked a hand to his ear. He could have sworn he heard bagpipes. He walked towards the Bloody Tower where the sound seemed to be coming from. He tried to enter that Tower but a guard barred the way and would not let him pass. "Bugger this," he swore to himself.

He entered the adjacent Tower and climbed up to a window which had a good view of the apartments in the Bloody Tower.

Looking out he couldn't believe his eyes. Edward VIII was wearing a kilt and black velvet jacket decorated with silver buttons. He was playing 'Scotland the Brave' as he paced Raleigh's Walk. He's pretty good Charlie thought. He was transfixed as he watched and listened as the King played several laments. He had always loved the pipes. He cleared his throat, emotion had clogged it. Edward was a puppet king, but he was still the old Prince of Wales.

"My God, he's hand in glove with the enemy, the poor sod, doesn't he realize..." The rest of the day Charlie was in a gloomy mood. He consoled himself with feeding the ravens and preparing for the ceremony that evening. He would do a good job. It was what the Resistance had asked of him. Charlie was in his best uniform and hat, clutching the iron ring that held the ancient keys in his right hand. In his left he held a lantern within which a candle glowed. Von Darmstadt, wearing his dress SS uniform, looked on proudly. With him, to Charlie's astonishment, were King Edward and Queen Wallis, wrapped in warm overcoats against the damp air. They smiled at Gates. He had been pointed out to them earlier that day when Charlie had been taking Gross Admiral Raeder and Reichsmarschal Goering on a tour.

The Ceremony of the Keys went well. The squad of German troops had been well drilled. As Charlie walked up to them holding his lantern, a voice shouted in English, with a German accent, 'Who goes there?'

Charlie was tired, and rather light-headed. He felt perversely like giggling. He remembered his friends who had been slaughtered just the month before in the Tower, and the prisoners who had came and never left in one piece. He sobered up and went through the motions.

"The keys, the King's keys."

"You may pass," the German voice replied. The guards turned and stood at attention as Charlie walked past them jangling the large keys on their ring in his hand.

The next day Governor Von Darmstadt thanked him for the ceremony. "We will do it every night. The King and Queen enjoyed the ceremony. They would like to meet you. I give you permission to visit them but remember, Gates, walls have ears. If I hear of any conspiracy to do them harm or some foolish plan to kidnap them, I know where you are and you know what enjoyment my men have with the rack and some of the other instruments in your wonderful mediaeval dungeon."

Gates blinked.

"I have duties to perform as governor, then I will visit the King and Queen. They seem to have only themselves and that Irish Colonel O'Donnell their aide-de-camp, to talk with." Charlie stumped out of the Governor's office with his cane, his left hand holding his back.

On the first visit, Charlie spent time with Edward and Wallis explaining about the previous occupants of the Bloody Tower. Queen Wallis had been particularly interested in hearing about Sir Walter Raleigh who had waited for years at King James' pleasure before his head had been smote off his shoulders on the green. "You see, Mr. Gates, he founded the great colony of

Virginia, which became the state of Maryland, of the southern United States where I was born."

"You've come full circle in a way, Ma'am" Charlie said.

Despite himself he actually liked Queen Wallis. Yes, she was selfish and overbearingly in charge of her husband, but her American candour appealed to Gates. He could not believe she was capable of harming anyone.

The King was pensive and nervous. It was hard for him to sit still. Occasionally the King was driven out for a visit to a Fascist unit, a school or a businessmen's dinner. Once he and his wife both went to the launching of a new battleship which had been almost finished when peace had been arranged.

They had told Gates about the trip by air from Hendon to the Clyde in Scotland and the trip to the shipyard to christen HMS Edward VIII. "We couldn't get the bloody bottle of champagne to break," Edward laughed hysterically. "It kept bouncing off the hull."

"And we would catch it" the Queen told Gates, tears of mirth rolling down her cheeks.

Through his laughter Edward was only able to blurt out fragments. "Then...I...I...gave that bottle on the cord such a shove that it...it...smashed into a...thousand p...p...pieces...there was...even...," he gasped, "a...cheer from the workers."

The atmosphere became supercharged as Queen Wallis stood up and gripped Edward by the lapels of his suit. She pleaded, "David, stop laughing! They were cheering because they were forced to, not because they wanted to."

Edward VIII dabbed at his eyes with a handkerchief and his laughter gradually subsided as he stiffly removed her hands from his suit. "Perhaps, my love, perhaps some of the cheers were just for us."

He looked hurt. Charlie was embarrassed, he bowed and walked silently out of the room, backwards. As he went he could see Queen Wallis comforting the King who sat in a chair with a vacant look on his face staring at the wall. As he went down the steps, Charlie wondered just how his real sovereign, Elizabeth the Queen Regent, was doing.

A few days later Charlie was walking past the choir stall of the Chapel Royal of St. Peter and Vincula on the grounds of the Tower. Charlie was surprised to find King Edward studying an intricately carved wooden cherub by the organ. "That's a Grinling Gibbon's carving that is, Your Majesty," Charlie said quietly.

King Edward started. He had been absorbed in his study. "Oh, Gates. Yes, yes" he piped in his taut voice. "These decorations really are good. You know Gates, you can just call me nothing, Your Majesty, Your Royal Highness-none of it means a thing. For God sake's man, I'm a traitor."

Charlie was silent. He could say nothing of his contact with the resistance, he had not been instructed to tell the King. "You and the Queen are prisoners. It hasn't turned out very well."

Edward chuckled. "Gates, you the last Yeoman Warder, are the only man in the world I can talk to ... can trust. But even you may be a spy for Von Darmstadt, like that loathsome aide-de-camp."

"I am not in the service of the Nazis, Sir. You have my word." The King put his finger to his lips. "Don't say a thing, old man. You never know who is listening." Edward VIII patted the cherub's head that protruded from the wooden wall.

"May I shake your hand, Sir?" Charlie asked.

Charlie left him in the unlit gloom of the chapel. The king knelt at a pew and prayed. That night the King tossed and turned, unable to sleep until dawn. Then he dreamt of a London sky full of helicopters, in Trafalgar Square, large television screens broadcast his face and that of his wife. It was a scene from H.G. Well's Things To Come. The National Gallery was draped in Union Jacks with swastikas and large banners bearing lightning flashes.

He saw himself, old and stooped before his time and Wallis with white hair, waving at a crowd of unhappy, ill-dressed, grey-clad people from the balcony of Buckingham Palace. Letters bearing his likeness on stamps took orders to kill Resistance men and women. Coins stamped with their images were paid out to informers. He screamed, waking himself up, ran to the toilet and vomited.

Wallis soaked a flannel in cold water, squeezed it out and gently placed it on his feverish brow as she helped him to his bed.

"My darling, you are not well."

"No. Things are not well, with me, or you, or our people," he whispered into her ear, fearful of spies. He could hear the clink of breakfast cutlery being set on their table in the dining room by the maid. "If Churchill were to send a rescue party, we should help them shouldn't we?"

"He could have us shot, my love. That is what Colonel O'Donnell said."

"I don't care. Perhaps I should steal a weapon from our captors and..." He could not finish the sentence. "I'll sleep now. Stay with me."

She patted his hand and held it as she sat on the bed. She tried to think of her childhood in Virginia but she kept thinking of walking down the aisle of Westminster Abbey in May 1941, pages holding the long train of a purple gown, her husband King Edward walking next to her, taking their places in the thrones facing the fascist appointed Archbishop of Canterbury stared at by the fascist peers of the realm. She imagined Hitler and Mussolini gazing at her from the front pew, she saw Molotov the Soviet Ambassador sitting next to the Japanese Ambassador. Molotov was whispering loudly to his aide in Russian. She imagined it was about her and was not nice.

Their coronation, wasn't that their destiny? Then David, as Edward VIII, could help his people, as a crowned king he could tell his prime minister what to do. Or could he? Would he? There was no way of leaving the Tower. No one was coming to get them out. They were on their own except for an Irishman who hated them, a power-hungry fanatic of a Nazi Governor and an old man who shuffled around the Tower all day and night remembering the past. With these thoughts wrapping her mind like wet blankets she fell asleep slumped over the husband's sleeping body

CHAPTER SIXTEEN RENEGADE QUEEN

In the Highlands of Scotland on Christmas Eve, the commander of the Black Douglas Commando reported to a dignified lady sitting on the teacher's chair in a small schoolhouse in Tomdoun in Glen Garry.

"We have scouted out the area, Ma'am, and there are no Germans for 30 miles." Lieutenant-Colonel MacCrae said.

"Good. I need to meet some of the Resistance leaders tonight."

"Yes, Ma'am. It is all arranged, a private room at the local pub. It's called the 'Puffin'".

Queen Elizabeth the Regent smiled at him. A pink plastic eye patch covered her blind right eye, caused by a glass fragment from the bomb explosion that killed her husband. She smiled, despite the care and strain the last few months had been on her, that smile could still dazzle. There was a softness about her that concealed a mountain of granite.

"And at the 'Puffin', what a wonderful name, we will be planning our attack on the convoys to the garrisons at Fort Augustus and Stirling Castle on New Year's Day?"

"Yes, Ma'am. But before that there's the Christmas Eve service at the local kirk tonight."

As the Lieutenant-Colonel left to get his briefing notes, the Queen studied the maps of Scotland spread out in front of her. She was the one person who personally knew each of the officers commanding the resistance in Scotland. She was an outlaw. There was a price on her head of £10,000, New British pounds, bearing the heads of her rivals King Edward VIII and Queen Wallis.

Already, songs were being sung of how she quit her palace of Holyroodhouse in Edinburgh vowing never to be taken alive, never to leave Britain, and never stop fighting.

A myth, based largely on fact, was building of how she managed to evade capture, always leaving a stately home or humble farmer's barn just ahead of the arrival of German troops. At Dunfermline in Fife there had been a shoot out and the Commandos had managed to overrun the attackers and make off with their vehicle. Queen Elizabeth had sat in the back of a

German staff car firing her revolver at the enemy as they had driven off. German bullets shot all around them, miraculously missing her and her companions.

To the authorities she was a renegade, a piratical figure with an eye patch. Newspaper cartoons in the state controlled New Times showed her clutching a smoking machine gun standing in a pool of blood, while King Edward VIII offered her an olive branch.

To most Britons she symbolized the resistance that was beginning to hammer large thorns into various parts of the body politic of New Britain.

"I'm quite looking forward to singing carols this evening, Colonel," the Queen Regent said, "what is your favourite?"

"'Hark the Herald Angels Sing", Ma'am"

"Very good choice," she said and turned her face down to study the maps once more with her one good eye.

CHAPTER SEVENTEEN WELSH DRAGON

On a bare wooden stage a desk was draped with a wrinkled Union Jack. A large map of Britain hung on the wall behind the desk. Black dots indicated German garrisons and Fascist British police stations. As John glanced around, he noticed that the walls were rough and there were no windows. A miner would have recognized the seams of a coal mine through the steel pillars and wooden struts that braced the hall. Electric light bulbs in industrial metal cages glowed overhead.

This old mine in Wales was one of a chain of secret headquarters throughout the British Isles used by the British Resistance. Early in 1940 it had been rebuilt and refurbished to serve as a bomb-proof command post in the event the government had to leave London. Now, it was the headquarters for the Red Dragon Commando in Wales.

John had arrived by car with several Commando leaders carrying forged papers indicating they were on a business trip from Liverpool. Resistance men had met them at the rendezvous point in Wales. They had been blindfolded and hidden in the back of a farmer's lorry that drove through the night to the mine headquarters somewhere in the mountains. Later, if John and the others were ever captured they would be unable to reveal its location.

John had left Aubrey, Duncan and their men at the camp in the wilds of Snowdonia. He shifted himself to look around as a buzz of excitement at the back of the group heralded the entrance of a small figure through a doorway. The man who had been fighting a guerilla war against the Italians in Abyssinia, before being ordered back to Britain to organize resistance, entered the hall. He wore a black beard, against British army regulations, and under his arm was tucked a stiff white tropical safari hat. These were his trademarks. It was Brigadier Orde Wingate.

On this day he was wearing British army battle dress, but again, contrary to regulations, his jacket was unbuttoned. He was thin, his face haggard, there were pouches under his eyes but they smouldered in restless energy. He wore a polo- neck sweater under his battle dress tunic. Draped around his neck was a brown scarf with a bullet hole in it, a souvenir from an encounter with the Wehrmacht. Resistance spotters and Commandos were posted for miles on the roads around Mount Drum Dhu and Banc-Y-Celyn leading to the town of Llangynoy by the mine. Wingate looked around the room and into the faces of the thirty men and women whom he had ordered to attend the first national meeting of the Commando leaders.

"First," he cleared his throat, "let me say congratulations to you for the successes in the field since the take-over. I refuse to use the term 'surrender'. Wellington Commando, based in Southern England, already have a reputation for destroying more German convoys than any other. They took out 64 lorries and 30 tanks this winter, as well as capturing some high-ranking German officers who are now interned in Iceland.

In the West country, Drake Commando's specialty is blowing up trains, eight military trains so far. Perhaps there are Lawrence of Arabia types in that outfit." There was laughter from the audience.

"In Lancashire, Red Rose Commando has disrupted steel production by sabotaging factories in Sheffield and Birmingham. In Yorkshire, the White Rose unit has engaged in daring hit and run operations including one on a Luftwaffe aerodrome where a squadron of Messerschmitt 109s were destroyed as well as the pilots in their barracks. They were literally caught napping.

Black Douglas Commando in Scotland has earned the grudging respect of the Germans who now venture out only at night and then only in large numbers.

Across the Irish Sea in Northern Ireland, the Brian Boru Commando has succeeded in destroying the docks at Londonderry in a spectacular raid. They commandeered two freighters which they sank at the mouth of the harbour blocking it for a month. Resistance London is operating mainly with civilian resistance cells and military advisors who are supplying a large organization with weapons, ammunition and training.

We have friends in high places in the New British government and the Gendarmerie. From picking up German military radio signals and cracking their codes, we have a damned good idea what our 'guests' are up to. I can tell you that they are not happy about what we are doing. Our actions are inspiring sabotage and resistance organizations on the continent, which like ours, are being aided by our government-in-exile and unofficially by the United States.

"Monty's hard-won victory at the Battle of Dover, and our defeat at the Battle of Hayward's Heath against the combined German 9th and 6th armies, have taught us the hard lesson of the need for strong air support of our army. Without tactical air power 'on call' to our troops we will never beat the Germans in the field.

"For the future liberation, 150 thousand pilots and air crew are being trained in Canada and thousands of aircraft are being made in the United States and Canada. Aircraft carriers and troop carriers are being constructed as well as long range bombers that can fly from bases in Newfoundland or Iceland to hit military targets here.

"Several armies are being formed in Canada, comprising Britons, Canadians as well as American volunteers. They are being armed with the latest equipment , including thousands of American tanks. Churchill and the general staff in Ottawa, are devising a strategy to liberate these isles and the rest of occupied Europe.

"It will come but it will take years. Japan is already at war with us, and is very close to being at war with the United States. That will slow down the pace of liberation.

"Our job, gentlemen, and ladies," he smiled at the three women seated in the front row," is to hit the enemy and continue hitting him this year, next year, every day he is here. We will make the Nazis, and their Fascist friends who say they govern this land, fear for their lives.

"This has already cost us dearly. We will never forget the massacre at Nottingham, November 11th, when 1,000 men, women and children were locked in the cathedral and machine-gunned, then burned to death after Lady Beltrum stabbed the commander of the Northern German army in bed. She got away and is now fighting with the Red Triangle. The cathedral is a blackened shell. Now for a few photos."

Wingate nodded to an aide and the lights were turned off, a slide projector threw an aerial photograph onto a blank screen. He picked up a pointer and spoke. "These are Concentration camps, Kz1 built on the Isle of Wight off the south coast and Kz2 on the Isle of Man in the Irish Sea. Tens of thousands of suspected resistance fighters and anti-fascist Britons as well as Jews, Jehovah Witnesses, homosexuals, gypsies and disabled are imprisoned there. They are being used as slave labour in underground factories. Some scientists who did not get away in the evacuation are believed to be working there as prisoners. "We think these," he jabbed at the photo with his pointer, "are air vents for underground factories. These are guarded roads leading to the entrances. Also, railway lines now link the camps to the railway system.

These reconnaissance photos from carrier borne Seafires reveal crematoria which are too big to meet just the needs of a hospital. Our intelligence people believe the weak and sick prisoners, no longer able to work, are being gassed or shot and their bodies burnt."

There was a gasp from the audience. "God damn them!" a voice cried out.

"Then the rumours are true," an Ulster voice called out. John felt sorrow and anger rising up to his head, he felt sick.

Wingate put up his hand to quiet the audience. "I am sad to say it is true, we have heard from our colleagues in occupied Poland that it is going on there as well. One thing we shall plan is an attempt to destroy these camps and rescue as many as possible. For that we will need a tremendous amount of coordinated planning and more arms, which are expected via Ireland. Meanwhile, to keep the enemy hopping and flex our muscles, our first nationally concerted operation will be the rescue of the fascist King and Queen from the Tower of London."

There was complete silence as the Resistance leaders leaned forward on their wooden chairs, eager to hear more. "They represent the one link with tradition between Britain and the cruel regime of Lord Eastbourne and the Fascists. If we can get them out of their clutches we will have destroyed the last remnant of so called constitutional legality that the government of New Britain maintains. It will be a great embarrassment for Hitler. He is banking a lot on the propaganda value of having the coronation at Westminster Abbey next May. He will expect us to cause trouble on Coronation Day when London will be well defended. We will attack well before then, in the bad weather that January usually gives us, when they are not expecting us.

Before I finish, I want to bring you up to speed with world events. There is a battle occurring daily in the Atlantic between U-boats and surface ships of the Royal Navy and the Royal Canadian

Navy operating from Halifax, Nova Scotia, Newfoundland and Iceland. The United States has declared a 500-mile safety zone on both coasts and is sinking any U-boats they find inside the limit. The massacre at Nottingham did much to sway public opinion in America to our side.

" In the Far East the Japanese are still on the march after their attacks on Hong Kong and Singapore. Our troops in Hong Kong were evacuated with the help of U.S. ships flying the Red Ensign.

"In the Middle East our troops have succeeded in chasing the Italian army out of Libya. The Germans have landed an Afrika Korps at Tripoli under General Rommel who you may remember fought against Monty at the Battle of Hayward's Heath. Monty will be itching to defeat him after fully recovering from his wound. He arrived in Egypt last week to command the Eighth Army. You will be glad to know he plans to knock the Jerries right out of North Africa."

The audience applauded, several shouted out; "Give it to them Monty!"

"Our resistance groups are being fed information about the enemy from our people in Iceland, who have the most sophisticated radio and code- breaking set up. Agents, weapons, plastic explosives, etc. are being smuggled to us via the Republic of Ireland to obscure parts of our coast. There aren't enough occupation troops to cover every square mile and that is where we have the advantage. It may be only a matter of time before Hitler decides to invade the Republic of Ireland. My sources tell me that, if they do, they will have a fight, only the Irish know how to provide." There were chuckles in the audience. "It could even tip the balance, bringing the U.S. into the war.

"Now, if you would break up into your cell groups, I will turn things over to my second-in-command and staff who will be meeting with you regarding your own parts in the plan. Only a few will know all the plans in case of capture."

Wingate stepped off the stage and came up to John. "Er, Major Stafford, I wonder if you would come with me to my office. There are some representatives from Free London I want you to meet."

John followed Wingate down a dimly lit hallway into the command centre. He could see radio operators monitoring coded signals from overseas and inside Britain, as well as German signals."

"I want you to meet ..."

"Felicity... !" John completed the sentence. His face registered joy and surprise.

The Brigadier asked, "You know each other?"

"Yes, Sir. Before the war in Canada, and during the attack on Windsor Castle."

"Oh yes, Captain Le Meseurier became something of a bodyguard to the Princesses didn't she? She just arrived from espionage training in Canada."

Felicity held out her hand and John gripped it, trying not to grin too much.

"Uhh-hm. Major Stafford. These are the top two men in the Free London group, Mr. Torrey and Mr. White, not their real names."

John reluctantly withdrew his hand from Felicity's and forced himself to pay attention to Torrey and White. He noted with amusement that the two men seemed unlikely agents. Mr. Torrey was thin, he wore a bow tie and a white shirt, with a grey herringbone tweed jacket hanging loosely from his tall wiry frame. Mr. White was large, bursting out of an old suit with a loud tie. His shoes were scuffed and his round wire-framed spectacles, which desperately needed cleaning, seemed too small for his face. Neither one would merit a second glance on the street.

Both men looked at John with intelligent, quick eyes. "MI5 left them in place with a network of agents last October. Now they run hundreds of cells including one that has contact with a Charlie Gates, the last Yeoman Warder at the Tower."

John took a seat next to Felicity as Wingate sat down opposite them and opened his map case. Felicity whispered to John, "Sorry I couldn't contact you, I didn't know how to reach you, this was the only way I could see you. I volunteered as an agent." She smiled mischievously.

"Well, I can't believe it," John muttered under his breath.

Wingate outlined the plan. His black bushy beard wagged as he spoke. "We're calling it Operation Lion Heart. You, Major Stafford, will lead a troop of Commandos into the Tower of London via Traitor's Gate on the Thames. You will do this by impersonating the German navy squad which will be asked to provide the honour guard for the Ceremony of the Keys which occurs at 10 p.m. daily. It will be arranged for a day in January if the Jerries stick to the routine they have started. The Governor of London, Count Von Darmstadt, is big on having different arms of the German and Fascist forces have a go at the ceremony."

John groaned. "An old friend, Major?" Mr. White asked.

"Our paths have crossed."

"We don't want him recognizing Major Stafford," Mr. Torrey put in.

Wingate nodded. "Good point, we'll dye his hair blonde and have him shave off that magnificent ginger moustache." He continued. "Our friend Darmstadt has reinstated the Ceremony of the Keys using honour guards from the German Wehrmacht, Luftwaffe, Kriegsmarine and Gendarmes.

We have a high-speed German E-boat, a motor torpedo boat, that was captured over Christmas at Yarmouth. Your men will assemble in Norfolk and be spread amongst safe houses by the end of next week. We'll provide New British travel passes, money and identity cards here at our forgery factory. Free London will give you the go ahead with two or three days notice. They will get you to the Norfolk coast where you embark. We have experienced sailors, German navy uniforms and weapons. Ten men will be dressed as the Kriegsmarine Honour Guard. I believe you speak German, Major." John nodded.

"We will provide Royal Navy sailors experienced with motor torpedo boats. The real naval honour unit will be dealt with by Resistance fighters in London. The rest of your men will be waiting on board the tied-up boat for the signal to attack. While the Honour Guard tackles the guards you will be quite close to the Bloody Tower here," Wingate placed his finger on the map, "where the so called Edward VIII and Queen Wallis. They'll be warned to be ready. You grab them and high tail it as soon as possible and let the E-boat rip. They are very fast, 33 knots maximum speed. Go east down the Thames at full throttle."

"And we'll be keeping the Jerries busy in the meantime, will we, Sir?" Mr. White asked.

"Absolutely. We want shore batteries along the lower Thames put out of action. Is there anything else you can suggest?"

Mr. Torrey rubbed his hands. "We've had our eyes on some of the arsenals in London; they would make a lot of fireworks. We could warn the civilian population nearby to make themselves scarce."

"Good. It must be after H hour though. 2215 hours would be fine. That would just about when Major Stafford and his charges are heading back to the boats. They will rendezvous with a Catalina Flying Boat which will be landing at the Lower Pool here past all the bridges about two miles down river. It will be a very tricky piece of flying. The only lights they have will be some flares set off by your people along the shores," he looked at Mr. White and Mr. Torrey. "They will indicate their landing path. If for any reason the plane doesn't make it Major, go to the Globe stairs,"he moved his finger to the south bank of the Thames on the map. "Our people will be there as a back-up to hide you in London and get you out one by one. The idea is to get the Duke and Duchess and yourselves on that plane.

Our radio experts will be jamming German signals and pumping out 'black information' to make the Jerries believe that your boat is actually chasing the raiders who have made off with the King and Queen. The Catalina will fly northwest 35 miles to the coast to the River Blackwater by Sales Point and make a rendezvous with a submarine which will take the royal couple to Canada. You, your men and Captain Le Meseurier will take rafts from the Catalina and paddle ashore where the Resistance will take you to safe houses.

Major Stafford and the Commandos will report back to their Snowdonia headquarters, in ones or twos over the period of a week wearing civilian clothes with forged papers." He looked up at Felicity. "You'll take the train back to your London job."

"Any questions?" the Brigadier asked.

"What am I to do during the operation, Sir?"Felicity asked.

"Ah yes, Captain, your job is to help the Duchess of Windsor. We thought it a good idea to have a woman on this operation. We are not sure if Queen Wallis will be keen to come. She may need persuasion. If entreaty does not work you are ordered to bring her under gunpoint. But a woman's touch may be enough.

It is to be hoped that the Duke of Windsor will jump at the chance to leave. We understand he is morose and dispirited. Be prepared to tell him his orders from Churchill are he and his wife to come with you. Arrest him if necessary but bring him back. Is that understood, Major Stafford?"

"Quite, Sir. May I ask about our man in the Tower, Charlie Gates. Do we take him as well?" John asked.

"Yes, he'll have a basket containing the last two ravens at the Tower. We'll warn him what to expect. His life won't be worth a snowball's life in hell once this operation is done, he can't go back. I want you to recommend two officers to go with you."

"I have two in mind, Sir, from our Red Dragon Commando: an Aussie, Captain Aubrey Hunter and a Scot, Captain Duncan MacLeod, they are in my troop. I'd also like to take our Sergeant-Major, a dependable man in action."

"Good. We'll work out any more details after some supper. I'll catch up with you later." The Brigadier-General stood up and made his way back to the meeting room.

"Let's grab a spot of tea," Mr. White suggested to Mr. Torrey who leapt out of the chair with amazing swiftness considering his bulk. "Would you like to join us in the canteen?" Mr. White asked Felicity and John.

"We'll join you in just a moment, thanks, we have to catch up on some news," John said.

John looked at Felicity, whose wavy brown hair was now braided and coiled into a fashionable bun. Her jaunty blue wool beret matched the cardigan she wore over a softly tailored dress. "You look great. Latest style in Canada?"

"Yes, the Ottawa look. I'm a fashion designer here in New Britain, that's my cover. I've been trained in all that espionage stuff at Camp X in Ontario. I was asked if I wanted to come over and be part of the Resistance. Well, is it too late to wish you a Happy New Year?"

"No, it's only the fourth of January. I'm so glad you're here."

She leaned over and kissed him. "I've been wondering if you were all right. I met your brother Alan, I thought it was you at the door at first. He looked me up in Montreal as soon as he could to tell me he saw you in Bristol. Then I pestered my father until he got me into espionage training, anything to get back here."

John's expression was serious as he looked her in the eyes; "I've been hoping you were waiting for me."

"Yes, I have been, but the less said about the ocean voyage to Canada on the battleship the better. I was dreadfully seasick. I'm still a little queasy after crossing the Irish Sea in a fishing smack. At least the submarine trip from Halifax to Ireland wasn't too bad."

"Come and have a cup of tea and a biscuit," John offered as he held out his hand in hand to Felicity, "that will set you right. You know I am now going to worry about you now you are over here in enemy occupied territory but," John smiled, "I know from experience you can take care of yourself." She took his hand and they walked hand in hand in search of the cafeteria.

Hundreds of feet above them a snowstorm swirled. Camouflaged guards in the mountain passes kept watch for German intruders but no one was venturing out on such a dreadful night.

In the Berlin Chancellery, Heinz handed in his letter of resignation to the overseer of the Translator Korps. The overseer read his letter and grunted, "You think you have a future as a businessman in Sweden?"

"Yes, my uncle is established there in the steel export business; he has offered me a job as a translator. I can continue my university studies in Stockholm and get my doctorate. I have all the details worked out with the German literature faculty there. Perhaps I'll obtain a position as a professor there one day."

"The Fuhrer will be disappointed ... but I met a young man last week who is brilliant, he speaks ten languages including Japanese. He's an SS man too, just the right kind of man to replace you." The overseer leaned forward in his chair, "Just between you and me Heinz, that pretty secretary in the Fuhrer's office...?"

"The Fuhrer has given his permission for myself and Ingrid to leave, he encouraged us to have children for the Reich. That pretty secretary is now my wife and I shall have nothing said against her, she is a fine woman."

The overseer shook his head. "I am worried that such a bright young man as yourself is throwing himself away when he could be in my position one day, head of the Reich's translation services at the Chancellery, the centre of the world empire that we are building."

"I am not cut out for a job as grand as yours. I just want to study and teach."

"You are making a mistake ... but I like you, you remind me of myself when I was 23, clever but headstrong. You may use me as a reference in your passport application and in Stockholm if it helps, and if you change your mind about working here at the Chancellery, you have talents we could always use."

"Your kindness is appreciated; I happen to have the form with me." Heinz passed him the paper and the overseer signed it.

"Heil Hitler!"the overseer saluted. Heinz looked at him.

"Heil Hitler. Thank you once again. Auf Weidersehen." Outside, a cold wind bore a few snowflakes. Heinz remembered reading how cold it could get in Russia and shivered.

He had a premonition that if he did not leave Germany he would be freeze to death in some future war with the Soviet Union. He had a feeling that Sweden was pulling him towards its forests and peaceful rivers as if he were an asteroid crazily arcing through space, heading for the cold depth of Pluto but pulled for a few miraculous moments towards a safe, warmer home. He willed that gravitational pull to strengthen and tear himself and his wife away from danger

CHAPTER EIGHTEEN E-BOATS

The Royal National Lifeboat Institute station at Yarmouth, on the windswept flat coast of Norfolk, was a collection of large boat houses alongside each other, whose wooden slipways sloped into the sea for fast launches. Lifeboats manned by local volunteers took to sea whenever a distress signal was received by radio or flare from a vessel in trouble off the east coast of England. The largest and newest boat house still wore fresh paint from the glorious summer of 1939, when it was completed.

A rotund man with only a tuft of hair left around his red ears, waddled in black Wellington boots along the path to the boathouse with three men in tow. It was cold. A brisk January east wind blew over them. John, Aubrey and Duncan had kept their hands in their civvy trouser pockets as they had walked the five minutes from the heart of Yarmouth.

"Here we are, gentlemen, our main boathouse. I must say it's good to get some new crew," the skipper of the station proudly proclaimed as he unlocked the entrance. He tapped his burnt-out stub of a pipe on the cement. A variety of burnt circles indicated previous offerings of tobacco.

"This is the 'Pride of Yarmouth.'" He pointed to a sixty-foot-long-lifeboat. "Now I'll show you our little secret." They walked outside.

"This is our old boat house, we removed the old 'Pride of Yarmouth'. We had one heck of a struggle getting the E-boat in the back of the shed. It's behind all those supplies and tarps. The Jerries call them S-boats. We, for some unknown reason, call them E-boats. Very confusing."

He pointed to the back of the boathouse. John and his comrades moved away some fuel drums and lifted up the tarp, to reveal the sleek grey hull of a German motor boat.

"Beautiful," Duncan said.

"The lads who brought her down from Grimsby last week tell me she can do over 30 knots. She's 93 feet long and weighs about 60 tons. Wouldn't mind one of them myself, whatever you call it," he chuckled.

"Any armament?" Duncan asked .

"She's got one 20 mm anti-aircraft machine gun, and two 19.7 mm cannon," the lifeboat skipper responded.

"And two torpedo tubes?" John asked, peering into the shadows under the tarp.

"Yes, she has torpedoes. The sailors from Grimsby have fired one in practice."

"This E-boat ... wait a minute ... S-boat is bigger than I thought. How did you ever get up the slipway?" Aubrey asked.

The skipper sucked on his pipe. "A lot of ropes and pulleys I can tell 'ee. It took two hours and a lot of sweat in the middle of the night. We'll repaint the names and numbers on the hull to match the upper Thames flotilla to fit into your plans. We don't know what you will be doing and we won't ask. So far the Jerries don't have a clue it's here. Their patrols looking for it have been off the north east coast not down here. The German navy uniforms and weapons that were captured are on board. The four Grimsby sailors who brought them here are ex-MTB, Motor Torpedo Boat crew, they will be here tomorrow to meet you. They'll be going with you on your mission whatever it is."

"Certainly, they know best how to handle it. It's pretty fast, eh?"

"It is, Major, as you shall see when we launch her two nights from now," the affable skipper said, stuffing his pipe full of dark shag tobacco and lighting up a miniature blaze as he stepped out into the dark.

"It just takes twelve minutes to launch the 'Pride of Yarmouth' once the alarm bell is run." He pointed with pride to a gleaming brass bell hanging from an oak transom.

They stepped outside and the captain pretended in a blustery voice that they were to come in for lifeboat training. "So your training begins tomorrow, Saturday, if you would like to be part of our Yarmouth Lifeboat crew. I'll be here at eight in the morning."

Over the next few days, ostensibly training for lifeboat duties, John and his men became very familiar with the E-boat, tried the uniforms on, and went over and over the details of Operation Lion Heart until each participant could recite his or her part and everyone else's down to the last detail.

They launched the 'Pride of Yarmouth' and took lessons from the skipper on handling a boat and navigating the Thames with it's unique currents and tides.

The day of their nocturnal departure, when Felicity arrived by train from London, John met her at the railroad station. "My turn to take your suitcase," he said, kissing her on the cheek and taking her arm.

"Fair enough, just point me in the right direction for my grandparents' home. That's why I'm here. It's what I told my boss at the House of Mayfair."

"House of Mayfair? Felicity, it sounds like Monopoly," he teased as they walked in the direction of the 'safe house.' She was to stay in a bakery.

"I'll have you know our fashions are very chic. Why just the other day Lady Eastbourne was one of the guests at the unveiling of our winter line. Too bad you missed it, but I brought you some photos."

"I can't wait," John groaned.

That evening in the room over the bakery Felicity, John, Aubrey and Duncan went over every detail of the operation using large scale maps of the Thames. Felicity provided a map of the Tower and Traitor's Gate and the latest news from Free London. "The weather will be cold; sleet, moderate winds, no moon tonight for Operation Lion Heart"

"Good," John said, "the E-boat leaves at 1900 hours. We proceed south with full tanks at cruising speed to conserve fuel. We'll easily make the mouth of the Thames by dawn. Then we sail up the Thames to London. The Resistance will ensure that the real naval honour guard doesn't make it from their base at Greenwich. They have been watching the routine. The German navy provides the honour guard for the Keys Ceremony for a week.

"We arrive at Greenwich at 2000 hours and then dock at Traitor's Gate by the Tower at 2130 on the dot. The guards at the Tower will see our tying up as routine. The honour guard of eight, led by an officer, usually have a cigarette break and then form up for the ceremony at 2150. Our man in the Tower is the Warder, Charlie Gates. He'll be shutting off the electricity mains to the lights in the Bloody Tower and Traitor's Gate at 2200, just as the ceremony is underway.

"At precisely the same time there will be some distractions, explosions at the Chatham Wermacht barracks and the arsenal at Woolwich, courtesy of Free London. Felicity and I, with three men, will go into the Bloody Tower and rescue the Duke and Duchess of Windsor.

"Her job is to escort the Duchess, mine to bring the Duke. The rest of the Honour Guard holds Traitor's Gate and the door of the Bloody Tower.

"A squad of Commandos led by Aubrey are to destroy the communications centre on the second floor of the White Tower and to cover our route to the E-boat. Duncan, you'll be left in charge of the boat with the crew.

We get back to the boat with the Duke and Duchess, having destroyed their communications centre, and high tail it back down the Thames to the rendezvous point with the Catalina flying boat in the Lower Pool of the river. The Resistance is setting up a flare path to help him land. The crews have been practising flying in at night, onto a river of the same width in Canada.

"It's flying from Iceland with a stop in a Scottish loch for refuelling then south to pick us up. It takes us north east just off the Isle of Sheppy where a submarine takes the Duke and Duchess to Canada. We paddle to shore to be met by Resistance who take us by fishing boat to Yarmouth and back to our posts. The Catalina flies north to Scotland, refuels and flies from there to Iceland."

"A lot could go wrong," Duncan mused rubbing his chin.

"Wassa matter, mate getting cold feet?" Aubrey joked punching his friend on his arm. Duncan scowled.

"It should be all right," John insisted, "but if the plane misses the rendezvous, we have a back-up plan."

Felicity answered, "the brass have thought of that. We continue in the E-er... S -Boats to a rendezvous site on the north shore at the Limehouse Hole stairs, just a few miles further east from where the seaplane lands. There you'll be smuggled out of London, I'll remain since my cover job is there. Our 'cargo' will be sent to the coast to be picked up by a submarine."

"Good, it's best to be prepared," Aubrey said holding out his tea cup for a refill from John.

John continued, "now, let's go over the crews one more time. I speak German so I'll be the skipper on the bridge in

Kriegsmarine uniform. The pilot at the wheel, our coxswain, is a local sailor who knows the Thames like the back of his hand. Of course, he'll be in a German sailor's uniform. The honour guard, including Felicity, will also be in Kriegsmarine uniform. The rest of the Commandos will be in regular uniforms and out of sight.

"Duncan, you stay on board with the pilot and crew ready to repel boarders. You've got the boat's machine gun in case you need it. Aubrey, I want you to lead the team into the communications room in the White Tower. Sergeant-Major Lincoln will follow behind with two men to pick off any guards who get in the way. I'll be leading the honour guard which will form up at the dock. I march them in for the ceremony. I'll have this ceremonial naval sword." He drew the steel sword from its scabbard. "I hope no one will notice it is Royal Navy issue. I'll put the officer handing over the keys out of action, then you let loose with the machine guns. Our best men, Watson and Crick, will take the door of the Bloody Tower. Felicity and I will bring out the Duke and Duchess."

"It's going to be a wee bit crowded on the boat, John," Duncan commented with a wry grin.

"More crowded than you think," Felicity interjected. "The Yeoman Warder, Charlie Gates, will be coming with a basket containing the last two ravens from the Tower, and some soil and grass from the Tower green."

"We have to take him. His life wouldn't be worth a plugged nickel if he stayed" John added. "And as for the ravens, you know the legend. There have been ravens living there since the days of Charles II, so the ravens take a holiday until we win and get them back to their rightful home."

"Yes," Felicity said. "Another piece of England becomes the Tower for the duration"

"The more the merrier," Duncan joked and they all laughed uproariously, letting the waves of mirth wash away the stress of nerves.

"Now," Felicity proclaimed, "the hairdressing salon is open! One moustache to shave off and one blonde hair dye job." John sighed while Duncan and Aubrey pulled their chairs closer to witness this historic occasion.

"Go away for Goodness sake!" John pleaded.

"No way, mate," Aubrey said.

"He's right. We wouldn't miss this for the world," Duncan joined in as Felicity began trimming John's moustache with a pair of scissors and ginger whiskers flew onto the floor.

CHAPTER NINETEEN   OPERATION LION HEART

The stumpy skipper of the lifeboat station bid them goodbye once the torpedo boat was laboriously launched in the night gloom down the lifeboat slipway. It bobbed up and down in the choppy waters. The skipper rowed out in a small wooden boat to bid them farewell. "Norfolk sailors one day, German sailors the next; funny sort of war, isn't it?"

He waved his hand out to John as he called out, "Good luck." A cold sleet fell from heavy clouds. There were no moon or stars to be seen, it was pitch black.

John, wearing the dark naval uniform of a German Lieutenant, stood at the bridge. The naval pilot at the wheel could see the the glint of excitement in John's eyes from the dim light over the binnacle housing the compass. "Cruising speed ahead," Duncan ordered down the voice tube.

The engineer manning the engine room adjusted the idling diesel motor and they headed south, breaking into the waves of the North Sea. The powerful boat made a v shape with her wake that lifted the lifeboat skipper's rowboat up and down as he rowed back to the lifeboat station.

By dawn they were four miles off shore, heading south, dead on course for a German destroyer moving out into the Channel. John read the name 'Karl Galster' on the two-funnelled warship's hull with his Zeiss binoculars . A signalman on the destroyer expertly flashed a Morse code lamp.

John noted down the message sent one letter at a time; "G.o.o.d. m.o.r.n.i.n.g.S.2.7.w.h.e.r.e. a.r.e. y.o.u.h.e.a.d.e.d.?"

He picked up the Aldis lamp on the bridge and slowly flashed back his reply in German. "G....o....o....d....m....o....r....n....i....n....g....b....i....g....f....i....s....h.... S....2....7.....T....h....a....m....e....s....S....q....u....a....d....r....o....n....r....e....t ....u....r....n....i....n....g....f....r....o....m....t....o....r....p....e....d....o........p....r. ...a....c....t....i....c....e....a....t.... H....u....l....l....r....a....n....g....e."

He jotted down the reply from the destroyer's signalman. "V.e.r.y .g.o.o.d. s.a.r.d.i.n.e. H.a.p.p.y. s.a.i.l.i.n.g."
"H...a...p...p...y...H...u...n...t....i...n...g...H...e...i...l....H...i...t...l...e...r." John flashed.

"I never thought I would say that. I was damned slow as well. Good job we practised Morse code in German last week," he said to Duncan. As they passed the destroyer a few sailors waved. John returned their greeting.

John went below and saw a pale Felicity holding her stomach. "They've gone, if you have to go on deck." She rushed up the ladder in her German naval rating uniform and gagged over the side of the boat.

"I feel terrible," she gasped.

"I'll make her a special cup of tea, Sir," President Lincoln offered. He brewed it up and unscrewed the lid of a hip flask from his pocket. "A little rum will do the trick, Captain Felicity," he said as he passed her the steaming mug. "Just call me sailor," Felicity groaned and sipped at the tea. "Thanks."

John stood on the bridge savouring the stiff salty breeze. The white foam from their way in the channel flew past him whipped up by the wind. This is terrific, he thought, exhilarated by the speed of the E-Boat and the operation about to unfold. Their stern Kriegsmarine pennant, a black cross with a swastika on white, fluttered madly in the wind.

John was enjoying himself and was sorry Felicity wasn't as well. At 0700 hours they were at the mouth of the Thames. John swept the horizon with his binoculars. He noted freighters from France and Germany. A German Arado flying boat passed by overhead but all else was quiet.

It was cold. John was grateful for the heavy black greatcoat. There were some snowflakes in the air. 'New British trade,' he joked with the coxswain at the wheel as they passed a slow-moving tug towing coal barges.

"Got no choice now, do we, Sir?" the sailor replied.

A Commando in German sailor's uniform brought up a cup of coffee, a mug of soup and home-made bread courtesy of the lifeboat skipper's wife. While he wolfed it down the pilot spoke to him. John studied the chart on the bridge as the pilot talked.

"We should go up the Thames at 25 knots per hour keeping to starboard. We'll be at Greenwich at 1900 hours. From there it's about 40 minutes at half speed, less of course at high speed but we'll need to 'pour on the juice' on the return journey to the Catalina."

John went below to check on everyone, squeezing past the sailors and Commandos, asking how everyone was and joking with his men. He made his way into into the crowded wardroom. "Well, how's it going?" he asked.

"Good, Sir, we're rarin' to go,"the Commandos replied. President Lincoln was cleaning his Bren gun, its parts were laid out carefully in front of him. John sat next to Felicity who had been dozing. "'I'm feeling a bit better, I think I'll try some of that soup."

"Good, it will be smoother from now on. We're entering the Thames and will be at Greenwich in ...," he looked at his watch on his left wrist, "Four hours."

He touched her hand. "Got your automatic?" he asked.

"You bet, and this" she patted the German P-38 sub-machine gun on her knee.

"Good luck tonight Felicity, stay close." He stood up. "Good luck everyone. This is an important mission. If Operation Lion Heart succeeds we will really have given Hitler a kick up the rear end he won't forget."

The Commandos roared their approval.

Standing in the shadows of the dungeon of the Bloody Tower Charlie waited for the prearranged time to arrive to pull the handle that would shut off the electricity supplying the lights in the courtyard and the Tower. He glanced at his pocket watch. The hands glowed with phosphorescent paint, the time faintly shone out - only 9:16 p.m. - 2116 hours.

At his feet lay a deep wicker basket containing the two ravens and some hunks of turf from the green. He could hear the birds rustling about as they pecked at the seed he had sprinkled in.

He bent stiffly down and spoke to them, "Won't be long now Croakey and Jeremiah. We'll be off on a bit of an adventure. There might a few bullets whizzing about so keep your heads down." For the tenth time that day he patted the basket and checked that the handles were sturdy. That morning, Charlie had told the King and Queen about the rescue. All day Queen Wallis had been pale and refused to carry out her engagements. The King had thought it wise to keep his. He had visited a Labour Exchange where he had asked about the note he had read in small print on one 'job available ad', for a German tutor in Mayfair: No Jews need apply.

Count Von Darmstadt had assured him it was merely to keep 'rif raf' from the good homes of Britain. With a sinking feeling of depression and doubt, Edward was driven to the Guildhall where he was to have lunch with the newly appointed aldermen of London and give a brief speech.

It was a very brief speech and Von Darmstadt admonished the King for his lack of enthusiasm. To hell with it, Edward thought to himself. I don't need to be told what to do by some trumped up Nazi dictator of London. By God we are going to go tonight and if I die in the attempt then so be it. Then his thoughts turned to Wallis as they drove through the cold drizzle of January and the grey streets of London.

I can't leave her, she must come and I'll get down on my knees to God, to pray for her safety. He was not a man given to excessive concern for religious matters but lately he had found some solace in his predicament by remembering how Christ had been set up, betrayed and sacrificed.

Like a grasshopper, his mind jumped, this time to anger as he considered that he and Wallis had been left all alone cut off from his family. It's about bloody time ordered our rescue, he thought as the armoured Rolls Royce drove into the Tower and the guards locked the gate behind him.

Wallis lay in bed with a perfumed handkerchief on her brow. He sat down next to her. "Charlie Gates says the rescue attempt is tonight at 10 during the Ceremony of the Keys. We can take only ourselves. The electricity will be going out then and that's when the shooting starts. We have to be ready. Can you be brave, my dear?"

"Yes, David, because you will be with me." She put out her hand to touch his.

He gripped it tightly. "That's my Wallis," he said gently. "You didn't have your heart set on wearing a crown, did you?" She said nothing but gripped his hand. He sat there until she fell asleep. Then he got up, smoked cigarettes one after the other and drank whisky, wondering what the night would bring.

After an hour he came to another decision. We'll take the bloody Crown Jewels with us. Von Darmstadt's got the crowns and sceptres in the White Tower. I'll get O'Donnell to have them brought over right away - tell him we felt like practising wearing them. He felt a bit unsteady. Too much whiskey old man, he told himself.

He left their apartment to look for Colonel O'Donnell. Twenty minutes later two soldiers arrived with a grey canvas bag containing the crowns and the sceptres. They bowed and left the bag. Edward eagerly unzipped the bag and stared at the dazzling objects within.

The pilot steered the boat at 20 knots on the north side of the Thames, past the dockyards which were still being repaired from the artillery and bomb blasts during the Battle of London and past the Freighters from Europe which were docked there. A Fascist Gendarme police boat with machine guns mounted on the cabin roof sped by them on patrol. Her crew waved at the S-boat passing them in the night. To them everything was as normal.

At the Thames S-Boat squadron station at Greenwich, Lieutenant Blucher, commanding the honour guard, was cursing the rating who brought him the news that the fuel tanks had been sabotaged.

"How did resistance fighters get close enough to put sugar in our tanks? God damn it, we'll have to phone the Tower and tell them we'll be late."

He phoned and got through to someone he believed was the duty officer at the Tower of London. He was actually an intelligence officer at the Free London phone exchange below the Underground tunnels, who had tapped into the massive telephone system that crisscrossed the occupied capital.

The operator, in impeccable German, urged Blucher not to worry and come again the next night. "The SS troops here miss doing it. Fix your tanks, I'll smooth any ruffled feathers the governor might have, his guard will do it, he'll make sure of that. See you tomorrow night."

The commander snapped at his men to flush out the tanks and refuel and in a foul mood went to the officers' mess for a drink of schnapps to recover his equilibrium.

At the Tower the SS guards and Governor Darmstadt were getting ready to receive the naval honour guard. As S-27 came up to Tower Bridge, John spoke into the voice tube in German, "Slow speed." A sailor went down below to tell the Engineer to slow down in English. Quietly, Duncan ordered the coxswain at the wheel to "bring her in alongside the quay there by

Traitor's Gate," as he gestured towards the dock by the Tower on their starboard side.

In the cramped engine room the engineer slowed the engines, then brought them to a stop in response to another order which would let them glide smoothly up to the quay which the Germans had built by Traitor's Gate just for German naval participation in the ceremony.

A Commando in German sailor's uniform tied up the boat. John led his honour guard ashore and ordered them to muster on the quay. He chatted to the German guard on duty, who paused to talk for a minute then continued his rounds pacing the dock.

John noted the floodlights on the wall of the Bloody Tower illuminating the quay and knew if something happened to Charlie Gates, Duncan would shoot them out in a hurricane of bullets.

John checked his watch, five more minutes. John saw one of his commandos climb up the dock as planned at the far end in the shadows clenching a Commando knife in his teeth. He crept up behind the guard, overpowered him and silently dragged his lifeless body into the shadows. In a moment, he had strapped on the German 'coal scuttle' helmet and put on the Wehrmacht tunic. He continued the pacing, the Mauser rifle resting on its strap over his left shoulder.

Von Darmstadt looked every inch the Nazi Governor of New London. The silver lightning flashes on his lapels shone fiercely on his dress black uniform under the glare of the floodlights he had erected around the Bloody Tower. His ceremonial dagger hung from his belt, the swastika design in the handle reflecting the light. He stood proudly alongside his SS guard.

John's throat tightened and his heart pounded. He unsheathed his sword, holding it up in front of him. He imagined himself on parade, but in the German Navy. John led his honour guard in a goose step into the courtyard from Traitor's Gate. They marched over the grass to just outside the White Tower where Von Darmstadt had the Crown Jewels on display for special guests.

This is it, John thought as he ordered 'Halt' in German.

"Who goes there?" John called out in English with a German accent, carrying on the tradition of centuries.

"The keys, the King's keys,"the German officer replied in English as Charlie Gates had painstakingly instructed him. Von Darmstadt stepped forward to inspect the guard. He spoke to John in German.

"You are new, Lieutenant?"

"Yes, sir. It is an honour to be part of this ceremony. I have just been posted to London from the Reich. Lieutenant Blucher trained me and allowed me to come in his stead."

"Good, good. This will be a most interesting posting for you," Von Darmstadt said. However, a hunch made him question who this naval officer was. His accent was Bavarian, unusual to have a naval officer from that landlocked State but not impossible." He stood before John and looked him up and down closely.

The Governor was sure he had seen him before. John and his squad remained at attention. The seconds ticked away. John felt perspiration trickle from his armpits, dripping onto his shirt underneath his tunic. Von Darmstadt walked around them and stopped again in front of John, scrutinizing his blonde hair and eyebrows, his clean shaven face, his blue eyes.

He turned away clenching his gloved hands, feeling a familiar twinge of pain in his hand from the wound at Windsor Castle. Now he remembered the Canadian officer who had attacked him there. The Count pulled out his dagger and then jumped back as he thrust his face into John's. He pressed the SS dagger point against John's stomach and hissed,

"I never forget a face. You are the Canadian meddler who spoiled my plans in Bucharest and at Windsor Castle."

John stamped on the Count's foot with an almighty crunch. He stepped back and gripping the Count's wrist which held the dagger, he slashed at him with his sword in his left hand. Von Darmstadt let out a gasp of pain and grabbed John's sword with a gloved hand, pushing with all his strength so that John was forced down to the ground. A dark stain spread across the palm of the glove as the sword cut through the white leather. Just then the Commandos began firing their machine guns into the surprised SS formation.

At that moment, seeing his watch's second hand come to two minutes after 10, Charlie Gates pulled the handle on the electric mains plunging the courtyard into darkness.

In the dark , Von Darmstadt pulled his Luger pistol from its holster and aimed at John's head. John was ready for him. He gripped the Count's right arm and thrust his sword upwards into the Count's stomach with all his might. The skewered Governor of New London, impaled upon the Wilkinson sword, flopped dead onto the ground. His limp black body joined the SS guards who had fallen under a hail of their own P-38 machine gun bullets in a common pool of blood.

"Come on!" John shouted, waving his reddened sword with a tremendous slice in the air. There were shouts and shots from German guards running out of the White Tower. Two Commandos dressed as German sailors ran to the entrance of the Bloody Tower and mowed down the guards who ran out.

Commandos chucked in grenades then waded through the smoke made by the explosions. Felicity and John followed. "Stay here," John ordered the Commandos. "We'll be back with the goods in three minutes." The commandos, Watson and Crick took up defensive positions at the door.

From the White Tower came the sounds of more explosions as the three remaining commandos from the honour guard fought their way into the communications centre, machine gunned the men on duty and set the dynamite charges with which to blow up the radio transmitters.

In Raleigh's apartment in the Bloody Tower Colonel O'Donnell had drawn his revolver at the first sound of firing and looked suspiciously at the King and Queen.

"What is going on, Colonel?" Edward asked as the colonel drew the iron bolt on the inside of the door to lock them in.

"You mean you don't know?" asked the Colonel. "It is obviously a rescue attempt."

"Well if it is, I want it to succeed, you traitor" the King snarled and grabbed the Irish colonel's arm which held his Luger. The pistol went off and the bullet slammed into the wall and ricocheted over their heads. Edward forced the pistol from the aide-de-camp's hand, but O'Donnell, a sturdier and younger man, grabbed the King by the throat and wrestled him to the outer door leading to Raleigh's Walk.

"I shall kill you and we can blame it on your rescuers, Your Majesty," O'Donnell said, becoming breathless as they struggled. "The door, Wallis, the door," Edward squeaked. She ran to the door, drew open the bolt and John burst into the apartment. Felicity followed him and placed herself between the fight and Wallis. John ran up to the pair wrestling outside on the parapet. He placed his arms around the Colonel's back and broke his hold on the King. Gripping O'Donnell by his jacket, he lifted him up and, with an almighty heave, threw him over the edge.

The Colonel screamed sharply before he struck the ground by Traitor's Gate and lay still.

The King, verging on hysteria as he straightened his jacket said, "Good. I never liked him. Have you come to rescue us?"

"Yes, Your Royal Highness," John replied.

"I'm back to being the Duke of Windsor again, am I?"

"Yes, Sir. I think it's better than being a pawn in Hitler's game."

"I really don't know. I don't care any more ... the only thing, person, I care about is my wife. Where is she?"

A huge explosion in the east end made a dull roar.

"That's the arsenal at Woolwich going up, Sir. That will keep them busy, but we have to leave."

"I've got her," Felicity said. She was putting a coat over Wallis's slender shoulders as she came out of the bedroom.

"We have to go dearest," the Duke said, "we have to escape."

Wallis burst into tears, speaking as she sobbed, "We'll be shot, we're traitors. David, what about your being King and me being Queen?"

"It's a farce. I see now that Lord Eastbourne is not interested in my advice. God knows what he and his people have been doing in my name ... our names. I feel like the scales have dropped from my eyes."

"We have to go. We've got a boat." John pointed at the door with his sword.

"Come, Wallis. I've got the Crown Jewels in this bag, Major."

"You have the Crown Jewels?" John asked incredulous.

"I do, both crowns and the sceptres. The rest was blown up during the attack on Windsor Castle."

"Well done, Sir,"John said as he sheathed his sword.

"Here ... Your Royal Highness," Felicity said gently, putting her left arm around Wallis to support her. Then, holding her Browning .45 automatic pistol in her other hand, she propelled Wallis down the stairs.

Just outside the doorway were the Commandos in German naval uniforms firing their sub-machine guns at the enemy. "We'll run for it - cover us then come yourselves!" John shouted over the gunfire, gripping the bag with one hand and clutching the Duke's arm with the other.

A shot from a German guard caught a Commando who groaned and fell to the ground. Several other Commandos kept on firing while another hoisted the wounded man over his shoulder and took him to the boat.

A hail of fire flew around the royal couple. A bullet ricocheted off the stone wall of the Tower and hit Wallis. The Duke stooped in shock as a dark stain grew over his wife's chest.

"Wallis, this is my fault. You should never have married me."

"But ... I love you, "she whispered in his ear as he knelt.

The Duke watched as John nimbly picked her up in both arms. Grinding his teeth in anger the Duke pried a rifle from the hands of a dead German soldier. He took aim at the garrison firing at them from the White Tower. He had not used a rifle since hunting tigers in India but squeezed off his shots as if he had been doing it all his life. Felicity fired her automatic pistol at an advancing German soldier and dropped him.

Sergeant-Major Lincoln came running from Traitor's Gate with his Bren gun firing into the German attackers. Another Commando threw smoke grenades into the courtyard and covered the rescue party who carried the wounded duchess onto the boat .

Edward was still firing the Mauser rifle, shooting, ejecting the cartridge, reloading from the black leather ammunition pouch on the dead German's belt and firing. A rictus of rage transformed his usually placid, thin face. John pulled Edward's arm and pushed him onto the boat.

"I'll take this rifle with me, Major," he declared. Aubrey and two Commandos continued giving covering fire as John and the Duke ran up the gangplank.

Duncan was on the deck, he had ordered the boat's engines readied and ensured a Commando manned the 20 mm machine gun. It fired into the smoky black void of Traitor's Gate over the heads of the last Commandos as they clattered aboard.

John shoved the bag containing the Crown Jewels into a sailor's hands, "Take this down below, guard it with your life." He lowered Wallis's unconscious body down the hatch into the arms of President Lincoln's who lay her on a bunk.

The Tower's garrison rushed through Traitor's Gate desperately attempting to stop the rescuers. They were too late, Duncan ordered, "Cast off—engine room full speed ahead - Coxswain turn her around, get us in mid-river past Tower Bridge." Aubrey pulled up the gangplank and sailors cast off the moorings as the boat's propellor blades began to bite hard into the water. S-27 moved away from the quay and roared in a tight turn to port turning back down the river. As bullets from the garrison shot into it the boat began to plane as it gained speed under the magnificent Neo-Gothic Tower Bridge.

They were away but not out of danger. Sentries on Tower Bridge unslung their rifles from their shoulders, ran over to the eastern side of the bridge and fired at the torpedo boat whose nose was just racing out from beneath it.

One soldier slumped over the bridge, knocked unconscious from a bullet hitting his helmet. He would wake up with a vicious headache. The other fell into the Thames, dead before he splashed into the cold, murky water swirling around the huge stone pier.

On the stern of the deck Duncan slapped Aubrey on the back as they sped down the Thames, "I didn't know Aussies could shoot."

A distant blast followed by a loud chain of explosions could be heard above the sound of the boat speeding down the river.

"That's Free London blowing up the shore artillery battery at Greenwich," John said to the Kriegsmarine-uniformed Commandos clustered around him.

"Well done, everybody."He dug out a packet of German cigarettes from his overcoat pocket and passed them around. "As promised. Now get down below. We are a ship in the German navy for a few minutes yet. As far as the enemy knows we're on the look out for whoever blew up the arsenal and the battery. Let's hope the Catalina makes it to the pick-up point on time. Aubrey, ask the torpedo experts to be at action stations, we may need them."

CHAPTER TWENTY 'THE NAVY'S HERE!'

HMS Stingray, one of the Sea Lion class of Royal Navy submarines manned by a crew of 40, was on station at periscope depth waiting for the flying boat to deliver its passengers after the rescue. It's 800 ton bulk hovered in the water, fifteen feet below the surface off the coast of Kent, close by the isolated Isle of Sheppy, where the River Medway meets the Thames.

Captain Hardington collapsed the cross-hatched metal hand arms to the periscope, through which he had been looking with hunched shoulders, and let the smooth hydraulics lower the periscope down.

He stood straight and addressed his lieutenant. "No enemy ships. If all is well the E-Boat is on its way to rendezvous with the Catalina. It should pick be picking them up and landing here in approximately one hour. We'll take her up to the surface in 45 minutes. Keep scanning at periscope depth every 10 minutes and let me know of anything. Carry on, number one, I'm getting a cup of tea. "

Meanwhile, at Greenwich, jumpy German troops were shooting off flares over the Thames, looking for those responsible for the attacks on the shore battery howitzers and the arsenals that were in flames.

Below deck, as S-27 sped towards the rendezvous point, past the bend that threatens to pinch the Thames' flow in hundreds of years time, Felicity tended the Duchess. It was obvious she had lost a lot of blood. The wound, a bullet in her chest, was mortal. Wallis was barely conscious and breathing in shallow gasps.

A Commando hung up a blanket privacy while Felicity examined the wound and bandaged it up. The Duke sat next to his wife holding her hand, silent. Felicity sat beneath the first aid box she had replaced on the cabin wall. They could feel the vibration of the engines. The box shook as the hull of the boat shivered.

Felicity broke the silence. "We rendezvous with a seaplane in about 15 minutes. It will fly us out to the coast where a submarine will take you both to Canada."

The Duke nodded. "Thank you, but I fear I will be the only one going to Canada." He closed his eyes and put his head down, still holding onto his wife's fragile hand.

On the bridge, John and Duncan peered with binoculars into the night being lit up by flares. Commandos and sailors in German navy uniform were also scanning the river and shore from the stern, sides and bow. They were looking for the bow wave of an approaching S boat, the flash of artillery from the shore or the tracer bullets of a night fighter.

The black Catalina flying boat had been stripped down and equipped with extra fuel tanks. It had taken off from the aerodrome near Reykjavik, the night before Operation Lion Heart, flying without lights. Once within range of the chain of new Luftwaffe radar stations at Orkney and northern Scotland, it had dropped to sea level, skimming over the waves.

A navigational error meant the craft had to retrace it path. With its fuel tanks dry as bones the pilot had to glide onto Loch Maree to have the plane refuelled as planned by Commandos who had two petrol lorry bowsers covered with camouflage netting. The next day the crew rested until the early northern darkness set in and then resumed their flight to London, flying low and avoiding built up areas. The flames east of London at the arsenal at Woolwich and the light from the explosions at the Greenwich battery made it easy to find the Thames.

As nervous searchlights swept across the sky, miraculously not catching them, the pilot and co-pilot headed for the flares on either side of the Thames indicating the Lower Pool.

At the German Naval base at Greenwich, Lieutenant Blucher was relieved to hear from his Petty Officer that the tanks had been cleaned out and refilled. "About time. The phone has been ringing off the hook. Resistance fighters are on the Thames. Come on!" He ran from the base office, slipped and recovered himself on the wet wooden dock, cursing the time wasted. He ran over the gangway onto his motor torpedo boat, a sister ship to John's S-27.

"Start the engines! Action stations. We're after Resistance fighters who just blew up some shore guns and the Woolwich arsenal down river." There were shouts as the crew rushed to get aboard and cast off into the river.

"Take her up river. S-32 and 34 are patrolling the river east at Tilbury," he said to the rating at the wheel. He turned to his Petty Officer. "Sweep the river with the searchlight for suspicious vessels. Post men aft and forward to keep watch."

To the west and upriver, John was relieved as they throttled up past towards the rendezvous. They had seen only Gendarme patrol boats whose crews had no clue S-27 was in the hands of the enemy. So far his radio operator, tuned into the Kriegsmarine band, had heard nothing to indicate the liberation of King Edward and Queen Wallis had been reported. He had heard only messages from two S boats operating near Woolwich had nothing to report. As they entered the Lower Pool he ordered the craft to slow down. He checked his watch, it was 15 minutes to rendezvous.

A stabbing white light carved out the bridge amidst the dark shadows. John put his hand up to cover his eyes and at the same time yelled, "Hard to port! We've got company." Their motor torpedo boat veered to the left but the searchlight stubbornly stayed with them.

"My God, it's one of our S-boats!" Lieutenant Blucher exclaimed as he read the registration number "S-27" with his binoculars. "How can that be possible? Of course, the Resistance captured one of our boats on the North Sea in December. They repainted the registration number to match one of our squadron. Fire the machine gun and get the gun crew working."

"Herr Leutnant?"

"Fool! It's the enemy."

Dutifully, the petty officer gave the order, "Give them a burst across their bow. Gun crew fire at will." The machine gun went into action and bullets flailed John's boat until it finally jerked away, when thanks to the coxswain's violent evasive action by wrenching on the ship's steering wheel. A shot from their cannon splashed harmlessly where they once had been.

Duncan fired the machine gun at Blucher's boat, his bullets were short at first, then a few ripped into the enemy craft. The German machine gunner's body jerked and slumped forward as enemy bullets riddled his body.

"We'll launch two torpedoes at them. Ready torpedoes," John shouted, "I'll fire a flare. Coxswain, point her straight at the enemy. Ready?"

"Aye, aye, Sir."

John raised the flare pistol and a small green ball of fire shot lazily into the night sky flew over the German boat in an arc and burst into a bright green shower of light.

"Fire both!"

The port torpedo shot out into the dark, fell into the river with a splash and was closely followed by the second.

The searchlight of Blucher's S boat stabbed into the darkness until one of Aubrey's bullets shattered it. "Fire torpedoes" Lieutenant Blucher yelled.

As the flare fell and fizzled out into the murky water of the Thames S-27's torpedo homed onto its target, the Nazi torpedo boat.

On Blucher's boat the bridge look-out shouted, "Evasive action -torpedo - starboard bow!"

"Hard to port!" Blucher ordered his Coxswain. His S boat heeled over sharply. The first torpedo missed, the German crew cheered as it bubbled uselessly past them.

"Circle back!" Blucher shouted. Too late. At that moment the German motor torpedo boat exploded in a fury of molten metal and fuel. S-27's other torpedo had hit home straight into Blucher's fully loaded diesel tanks.

"We got him, Sir. Now they know 'the Navy's Here!'" John's coxswain yelled in exultatation as the enemy torpedo shot past them missing them by two feet.

"Now that was close. Good work, everyone. Keep our course for the Lower Pool, I'm just going below for a moment," he said to the coxswain.

Then John noticed Duncan's crumpled body on the fore deck. There were tears in John's eyes as quickly climbed down the metal ladder onto the deck. He took off his naval greatcoat, rolled it up and placed it under the unconscious Duncan's head.

"Is he ... ?"John asked Aubrey who had been applying a tourniquet to Duncan's thigh to staunch the bleeding.

"He's alive," Aubrey said, feeling the pulse in Duncan's wrist. "He must have caught a Jerry bullet. Stay with him I'll get some bandages from below."

Aubrey returned with a medical kit and began applying a bandage to his wound.

John put a hand on Aubrey's shoulder.

"I want to check on the Duchess, I'll be back on the bridge directly." Below deck he found Felicity comforting the Duke of Windsor.

She stood up and came to John. "The Duchess is dead," she told him. "Is everyone all right up top?"

"Duncan is in a bad way . A bullet wound in the leg."

Felicity looked up slowly and sadly. "I'm sorry John."

"Aubrey's looking after him but I don't think we should move him until we get to the flying boat."

He glanced at the drawn-looking Duke of Windsor. Felicity spoke quietly to John. "Wallis's death was no one's fault. We still have the Duke. We have to get him out of this alive to make her death meaningful." He put his left hand on one of her's and squeezed it, and went back up to the bridge.

The pilot spoke as John stepped up the ladder and onto the bridge. "There, Sir!" he pointed, "there's the flare path." A quarter mile ahead for 200 yards on both sides of the Thames were white flares.

"She's landing," John said. A dark shape flew over them and touched down 400 yards east of them. He could barely make the plane out as she taxied on the Thames, except for the movement of the water and the path she had cut through it.

"Our ride home is here. Let her rip," he ordered down to the engine room. The Coxswain expertly brought them closer to the plane that floated on the Thames.

"Slow ahead," John ordered as they got within 50 yards of the plane. The boat gently bumped into the great black hull of the large American flying boat. A door opened on the side of the Catalina and the RAF crew helped the Duke, Wallis's body and Felicity on board. The Commandos gently lifted Duncan on board and climbed on board with their weapons.

Only John and the MTB sailors were left. "Open the sea cocks. Scuttle her," John ordered the crew. "Now let's go." As the S-27 began to settle into the Thames the sailors left and climbed aboard the plane. John was the last to jump aboard the flying boat. The pilot opened the throttles and the two engines roared into full life. The great blackbird of a plane skimmed over the water and took off. They flew east over the Thames for several minutes, the crew and the Commandos watching the flames licking the sky red around Woolwich.

That will keep them busy, thought John, as he breathed a thank you to the eccentric but effective team of Mr. Torey and Mr. White. Then they headed north- east into the night. The pilot hedge-hopped as much as the large craft would allow, to avoid being caught on German radar. If caught they would be chased by Junker 88 night fighters sent up to find and destroy them.

John checked on his men, the Duke and Felicity. Duncan was conscious and in pain was lying under a blanket at the rear of the plane. A doctor who had flown from Iceland on the Catalina in case the Duke and Duchess needed medical care, examined him, gave him a shot of morphine. "He'll need to have the bullets removed as soon as you land on shore in Kent and a blood transfusion too. It will be touch and go. Can you get him to a hospital when we land at the coast?"

"Yes, we're being met by the Resistance. They are prepared to take any wounded to a doctor standing by near the coast. They have an operating room, I am told, with everything that might be needed." The doctor listened to Duncan's chest with his stethoscope and drew a blanket up to his chin. "He'll sleep now." President Lincoln and Aubrey, sat exhausted on aluminium seats along the side of the fuselage. At the front of the plane Wallis's body lay under a blanket below the feet of the weeping Duke. Felicity was holding his hand. John, feeling drained, had no words for them. Instead, he went up to the cockpit. "Thanks for the lift, fellas."

"No problem. Hold on," the pilot warned him. John's stomach lurched as they picked up 200 feet and then dropped like a stone.

"Bit of a church steeple back there. Thought you might fancy some steeple- chasing," the co-pilot said.

"Terrific fun, glad you saw that church," John said trying to quell the uneasy feeling in his stomach.

As he walked back the navigator looked up from his maps and passed John a huge thermos. "It's whisky and tea." The navigator bent down and picked up a large plastic bag of sandwiches, offering them to John. "I brought these from Iceland, thought your troops might be hungry."

"Thanks a lot. We could do with this. I'll pass them around."

*

HMS Stingray's periscope swivelled above the waves and withdrew back down into the water. "All clear, Number One. Take her up," the captain said to his Lieutenant. The submarine blew some ballast while sailors trimmed the stabilizers and the craft rose to the surface.

On the conning tower in the dark grey twilight of the early morning, Captain Hardington scoured the western horizon over the coast of Kent with his binoculars. His ears cocked, straining to hear the flying boat. "Good, I hear them. Signalman - two flashes 30 seconds apart for five minutes." The Able Seaman began flashing with an Aldis Lamp from the conning tower.

The Captain gave another order. "Number One, get the men ready on deck to take on the Duke and Duchess. I want them on board in double-quick time. Then we're out of here. The Jerry fleet will be nosing around the coast with all the commotion going on in London."

"Aye,aye, Sir."

On the Catalina the navigator spoke to the pilot using the radio in his oxygen mask. "We are just coming up to the coast now. You should see the submarine soon." The pilot of the Catalina replied. "Got it, I'm heading for the flashing light." The Catalina descended to sea level and with engines throttled down and with it's wing flaps up, landed in the waves. It puttered its way towards Stingray homing in on the flashing light.

The plane's engines idled as the fuselage door opened and the crew pushed out a life raft and inflated it. "I'll say goodbye Your Royal Highness," John said to Edward. "I only wish..."

The Duke nodded. "Thank you for helping me come to my senses. What happened to my wife was not your fault but mine. I will pass on the Crown Jewels to the authorities, Major Stafford." He smiled sadly at Felicity. "Thank you, my dear."

The Duke of Windsor was helped into the raft and the body of the Duchess was gently passed down to the commandos ready to paddle to the plane. John thrust the canvas bag containing the Crown Jewels into Aubrey's hands as he knelt in the raft next to the Duke and the body of the Duchess. "Pass this on to one of the crew," John instructed him. "Tell them the contents are very valuable and guard them as if they were the crown jewels."

Two more life rafts were pushed out of the Catalina and inflated. John and Aubrey supervised the loading of the inflatable rafts with Commandos and sailors. The wounded Duncan, wrapped in blankets, his pale face showing in the dark, was laid in the first raft containing John and Felicity. Aubrey commanded the second, full of sailors and President Lincoln with the Commandos. The three rafts floated over the waves as the men paddled the 200 yards to shore to be greeted by the Resistance.

The Duke followed in shock as his wife's body was carried down the ladder leading from the deck hatch of the submarine to the captain's cabin. He watched as it was carefully placed on the captain's bunk. The canvas bag with its precious contents was locked in the captain's cabin and Edward was ushered to the control room to meet the captain.

Stingray took on seawater as ballast and headed out to sea. Topside, the Catalina flying boat revved up its engines and took off showing no lights, heading north to Scotland for more fuel.

"Welcome aboard, Sir," Captain Hardington said, saluting, as Edward entered the submarine's bridge and stood by the periscope.

"To Canada, I presume, Captain er...?" the Duke of Windsor offered his hand to the captain.

"Hardington, your Royal Highness. My orders, Sir, are to take you to Canada. Allow me to express my condolences on the death of the Duchess.

"Indeed it was, Captain but, if you'll excuse me I want to sit with my ... with my wife,"he replied.

"I quite understand, Sir."

"Thank you, Captain. I brought an important bag with me."

"What's in it, Sir?"

"What's left of the Crown Jewels."

Captain Hardington's thick, black, bushy eyebrows shot up. "We weren't told about that, Sir, but I suppose anything can happen in a war."

Edward sighed "How right you are, Captain. How right you are."

CHAPTER TWENTY ONE   AT BATTLE

John stood with Felicity on the grounds of Battle Abbey in Sussex, looking down at King Harold's grave. A small palm tree grew alongside the ancient stone commemorating where the last Anglo-Saxon king had been buried after being, as legend had it, struck in the eye by a Norman arrow during the Battle of Hastings. A swallow swooped over them clutching a twig in its beak to make a nest .

"Life continues even under the jackboot of the Fascists," John said. "Beauty still exists," Felicity said as she stooped down and picked some purple pansies.

"Yes, the flowers and birds are untouched but we are perverted by the occupation."

"That's why we're fighting for freedom, John," as she said this, Felicity placed a handful of purple pansies on King Harold's grave.

He held her hand and they strolled past bunches of brilliant yellow daffodils towards the site of the Battle of Hastings several hundreds yards away. They meandered through a copse of oak trees following a footpath leading to Senlac Hill. A group of four German soldiers on leave, walked past them heading back to the abbey and the town of Battle. One, a corporal, thought of asking Felicity and John for their papers, but shrugged. He surmised they were probably a young couple on their honeymoon.

John and Felicity had not slowed their pace. They had excellent forged documents, and one genuine document, a marriage certificate obtained yesterday from the local Fascist Marriage Registrar. Although the certificate lied in detail, giving John's occupation as a history teacher at a private school in Wales , they really had been married at a small church in Battle the day before.

So the corporal was correct, they were newlyweds. But he did not know that they were wanted by the authorities for crimes against New Britain as part of the Resistance movement. They walked slowly up the path enjoying the fresh, young spring air. Bluebells grew in vivid blue clumps in the wild green grass.

"So this is where it all happened all those, well, almost 900 years ago, when Duke William the Bastard of Normandy took England from his cousin King Harold?"

"Yes," John replied. "See those cows grazing quietly down there in the shafts of sunlight slicing past that cloud?" He pointed down the hill and she nodded leaning on his shoulder. "That's where the Norman cavalry attacked Harold's men on this hill. They kept attacking, but to no avail, until William ordered the archers to fire volleys of arrows in the air to break the Saxons. That worked, one of the arrows mortally wounded Harold. Once he was down, the House Carls, his bodyguard, fought on halfheartedly but were over-run by Norman cavalry wearing helmets and chain mail. My father brought me here as a boy. I wanted to bring you."

They rested against a wooden stile in the wooden fence enclosing a field. Suddenly they were aware of the sounds of horses' hoofs pounding the earth, the jingle of harnesses, the sounds of men shouting and iron swords smashing against shields.

"I don't see any horses, Do you?" Felicity asked. John stood up on the stile and surveyed the rolling green and brown fields below them.

"No, isn't that strange." He climbed down and stood next to Felicity who was leaning against the fence and listening carefully. The noises were very distinct, but subtle, like small waves on the shingle at the beach, lapping, advancing and being sucked back, advancing, retreating.

They scarcely breathed. Gradually the clamour faded and they could only hear the sound of distant sheep bleating and cuckoos calling. The gentle sounds of spring 1941.

Felicity put her hand to her mouth, surprised at the power of the vision that had been given them.

"Are you all right?" John asked.

"Yes, perfectly, it's just that ... that was a spiritual experience, John, and we both heard it." They did not speak for several minutes." I told you about the Spiritualist Church I belong to didn't I?"

"Oh, yes, the Sir Arthur Conan Doyle medium stuff or the Madame Blavatsky Theosophy line?"

She smiled. "You know perfectly well. It's the kind of spiritualism Conan Doyle was interested in, the afterlife, spiritual healing. My grandfather set up the first Spiritualist church in Montreal in 1912."

"My grandfather was involved in helping set up the World Council of Churches about the same time," John said.

"Don't you believe that, 'there is more to heaven to earth than we have ever dreamed of?"

"Yes, especially now, after what we heard, and especially now I've got you."

She looked at her Welsh gold wedding ring with its slightly ruddy warm tinge on her left hand. "Yes, I'm glad we both heard it. One day we'll bring our children here, when the war is over."

"Yes," John said with his arm around her shoulder. "When we've won.Until then we've got each other."

They walked alongside the field and then back to the town for a cup of tea and a few days of blissful peace before melting back into the deadly shadows of the resistance.

Across the North Sea at the ferry terminal at Malmo, Sweden, Heinz was overjoyed to see Ingrid waving at him. She was one of a knot of passengers waiting for the gangway to be lowered on the ferry boat from Copenhagen. There were still holes in the bridge where British gunfire had raked her when it let off amphibious Panzer tanks at Harwich the previous September. Ingrid carried two suitcases and wore a brown coat in the windy cold air.

Heinz ran forward and picked her up and whirled her around in joy, forcing her to drop her suitcases. "Heinz, you are mad," she laughed.

"No, it is not I that is mad, but them." He looked south back over the Baltic.

He was unusually serious. "They will not be satisfied until they rule the world and destroy millions in the process; they have plans to destroy the Slavs and the mentally ill, the Jews, Gypsies, homosexuals, Catholics and the intelligentsia. Tell no one of this , but I have had access to many secret papers. We will not talk of this any more. Now, Sweden is our home." He brightened up. He took the suitcases and loaded them into the back of the car. "Our new house is just a few hours away."

When she saw the wooden house Heinz had bought, had been carried over the threshold by her young husband and laughed at the colourful parrot preening itself in a huge cage in the sunlit kitchen, she knew she would be happy to stay the rest of her life in Sweden .

They burnt the suitcases in the garden that night to the annoyance of their neighbours. "It's all right. We are not burning books, just our suitcases. We are so happy to be here, we will never leave," Heinz shouted out in perfect Swedish.

CHAPTER TWENTY TWO ROADBLOCK

The early morning call of the roosters on Gaitskill's farm near Goathland, Yorkshire in northeastern England woke Charlie Gates. He swung his legs over the edge of the bed and shook his head. As he did every morning, he reached for his wooden cane. He squinted at the calendar pinned on the door. Today was June 1, 1941. His eyes moved over to the framed print of Holman Hunt's 'The Light of the World' above the brass bedstead. He stood up and wrapped a woollen dressing gown over his red-and-white striped pyjamas.

Slipping into his shoes, he made his way to the outhouse. After a brisk wash in cold water he padded to the kitchen where his farmer hosts were sitting down to a hearty breakfast of eggs and back bacon. "You sit yerself down Charlie. Those birds can wait a few minutes," said Mrs. Gaitskill as she set another plate on the wooden kitchen table. A white-and-black cat rubbed itself against Charlie's leg. Jack Gaitskill, the owner of the farm, stood up and went to the window to ensure no nosy Fascist gendarme was bicycling up the road. He turned the radio on, switching the dial to catch the Free Britain station beamed from 'somewhere in the British Isles.'

Like millions around the United Kingdom they did not know that the Iron Duke Resistance group, operating in the south of England, was broadcasting from the Forest of Bere in Hampshire. They knew enough, however, to admire the courage of those who broadcast the truth under the noses of the occupying forces.

> *'Here is the Free Britain news broadcast from somewhere in the British Isles. German forces have invaded the Republic of Ireland in an attempt to stop the smuggling of arms and agents into British territory. Only last week Nazi Prime Minister Lord Eastbourne promised the puppet Parliament in Westminster that Germany had no intention of invading Eire and were negotiating a way to stop 'international piracy' with the Irish Premier. The*

United States has broken diplomatic ties with Germany and has warned Hitler that this could mean war.

The Minister of Propaganda, Josef Goebbels, in Berlin has stated that the United States should not involve itself in European affairs. Josef Stalin, the Soviet leader, has expressed surprise at Hitler's invasion and has ordered the Soviet Forces at full alert.

Prime Minister Churchill, at a Commonwealth leaders meeting in Australia, has urged President Roosevelt to declare war on a deceitful and power hungry Third Reich before the United States is next. The United States Congress and Senate are in an emergency joint session today. This is Radio Free Britain."

Jack Gaitskill put down his mug of tea, turned the tuning knob of his wireless radio as if he had been listening to the propaganda of the New Home Service and shut it off. "Well, isn't that a turn up for the books?"

Charlie shook his head in agreement. "If the Americans enter it, we've a chance to win this war. Maybe the Russians might come in with us."

Jack Gaitskill laughed as he put on his work coat and opened the front door to deal with milking the cows. "The Russians are rubbing their hands at all the capitalists killing each other, you mark my words. Any road, I've not been one to support the Irish; too many of our lads were killed in the Easter Rising in 1916 and the Civil War in the twenties. But they're good fighters. A lot of 'em were in the trenches with you and me, Charlie. I reckon now they just might be on our side. "Tis a good thing that. I'm off, love," he called to his wife.

Charlie dressed and shaved. Looking in the mirror he shook his head. He still missed the white beard he had worn as a Warder. He had also lost 50 pounds, which he didn't miss, so that he no longer resembled his photo on the wanted posters or the description sent to every Gestapo, Gendarme and German Army station. His counterfeit papers said he was Charles Gaitskill, brother to Jack Gaitskill. Even the local church register had been carefully faked to indicate his christening and birth and which had been clandestinely inserted into the archives at Somerset House, London.

Now that Charlie Gates no longer existed officially, he was finding that living once again in the north was bringing out the childhood accent that had been softened by decades of living in London.

He went out to an old pig barn with a courtyard surrounded by a low stone wall. There were no pigs. He opened the gate.

"Croakey, lad, where are you?" At his voice the raven hopped out of the barn and onto the wall. Behind him flapped the other raven, Jeremiah, that Charlie had brought in a wicker basket in the escape from the Tower. Inside the basket had been some earth and grass from the Tower. He had placed the earth and the grass in the courtyard and tended it.

The spring sun and rain had been kind to it and now the Tower grass was spreading. He had been told by the resistance man who had dropped him off at the farm that the Gaitskill farm had been decreed a precinct of the Tower of London by the Queen Regent, and that he was still the Yeoman Keeper of the Ravens and should protect them with his life.

"There's no way those Nazis can have the satisfaction of saying their eagles have kicked our ravens out of the Tower. They can say what they like but we know better, don't we, lads? This is a bit of the Tower right here!" They cawed back at him as he tossed out some handfuls of seed and filled their tin bowl with cold water from the river that flowed through the moors and past the farm.

He gently but firmly picked up each bird in turn and clipped its wings. "Good! You won't be able to fly away. Shouldn't be long now and you shall have some company. We should have six ravens to be proper, not just two. Now for some work on the tractor."

In Llanfaeog, Anglesey on the north Welsh coast, a transit point for arms from Ireland, John Stafford was opening a letter bearing the royal cipher. It had been brought by a Queen's messenger, one of a distinguished band of couriers who wore a small, silver greyhound badge. This messenger wore his badge hidden behind his fedora hat band.

He was working with the Fascist Gendarmerie in the counter-espionage Office in Edinburgh and had a pass allowing him unlimited travel in the British Isles. He was on his way to

Cardiff for a meeting with his Welsh Office counterpart and had requested a holiday.

He had just met with Brigadier Wingate and filled him in on New British Police plans to use helicopters equipped with the new portable radar units which could, it was believed, detect people on the ground. They were being developed in a hurry to meet the problem of guerrilla fighters who seemed to be able to strike at will and melt away into the countryside.

"This will be the last time I'll be coming to Wales for a while, but I'm glad I could deliver this to you from the Queen Regent."

John opened the letter and read,

"Major John Stafford, it is my pleasure to write to you and tell you that we are making you a Commander of the Order of the British Empire. Your leadership of the force which rescued my brother-in-law the Duke of Windsor from the Tower of London merits not only this award but my personal gratitude.

I know my husband, the late king, would have been glad to know that his brother is now safe in Canada. The award will be gazetted after the war due to the clandestine nature of your present service. When circumstances allow, we will personally receive you and give you the insignia. Elizabeth Regent."

John stroked his moustache and looked up at the messenger. "I've just been given the OBE."

"Let me be the first to congratulate you,"the messenger said, shaking John's hand. John made a cup of tea and they sat and discussed the war until it was time for the messenger to leave.

"Well I must be going. I'm due in Cardiff."

"All the best. Thank you for bringing the letter." John watched as the courier driving the Rover car changed gears and drove out of site. It was tea time. He opened a tin of sardines, cut up some tomatoes, toasted some bread in front of the coal fire in the fireplace and made some more tea. It was five o'clock.

John reviewed in his mind what was to happen. In a few hours Aubrey and Duncan, back from medical leave, would arrive with the butcher's van. At 2300 hours we expect the fishing trawler from Ireland with a load of ammunition and rations. Rendezvous, unload into the rowboats and shove the ammo under the fake floor of the van. Then back to the our Commando troop in Snowdonia.

He ate, then cleaned his revolver, tommy gun and knife. He checked the batteries in the electric torch and shoved the torch into the inside pocket of the old tweed jacket he wore over his open neck shirt and brown knitted sweater. The revolver was tucked into the jacket pocket. The knife in its leather scabbard he placed into his left work boot that was spattered with mud and sand.

He read a chapter of The Iliad, then went for a walk. Evening had begun. He walked on the sand of Cymyran Bay and looked at the waves of the Irish Sea breaking on the shore. He sat down on a rock by the shore. Contemplating where everyone was in his family, he thought about his wife, Felicity, on a mission to Eire, the Irish Republic.

He wondered how Alan was now that he was working as an instructor in Toronto. Felicity had seen him and learned he'd made it out on the last convoy from Bristol. He looked up at the stars that sparkled in the dark blue spaces between the clouds. His ears pricked up as he heard the distant rumble of heavy guns. The Jerries must be up to something.

When Aubrey and Duncan drove up an hour later, the tide was coming in. They parked the blue van next to Felicity's 1940 Wolseley car, on the seaside of the cottage so it couldn't be seen from the road. Gendarmes made regular patrols along the road on bicycles. They were a bit of a joke to the locals, but the P-38 sub-machine guns strapped on their backs were no laughing matter.

John bounded forward and gripped Duncan's hand in a firm shake. "Good to have you back. You're all right? Feeling better? We've missed you."

"All fixed up. Got a long holiday, didn't I? Although I could think of better reasons to take one." Duncan held up a metal slug. "They dug it out of me. One of two. See." He pulled up his shirt and undervest and showed them the scars in his side.

"We brought some beer," Aubrey announced, cracking open a bottle for each of them, "and some good news and some bad news."

"He'll want the good news first, right, John?" Duncan piped up.

"No, I feel stoic tonight. First the bad news."

"Well, it's mixed really but not good for the Irish. Hitler invaded the Republic today and it could bring the Americans in."

"I hope so," John said. "Too bad for the Irish though. I heard gunfire earlier. Probably the German navy having a go at them. It will be a miracle if the boat makes it over tonight but we should be ready."

"We'll finish this fair dinkum beer and get the boat off the shore," Aubrey suggested.

"Now for the good news," Duncan continued.

John looked expectantly at them. "Well?"

Aubrey put his bottle down and clapped his hands together. "Felicity is on the boat tonight. She's been over in Dublin, for the last week as you know, helping with our pipeline of supplies. We got a radio message in Welsh to tell us she is coming over tonight."

John grinned. "That's wonderful, she does have to get back to her job in London. I hope the Jerries don't sink the boat." He looked thoughtful and rubbed his hand through his red hair.

"Don't worry, those fishermen know a trick or two," Duncan assured him. John pulled himself together and brightened up. "I didn't know you spoke any Welsh, Duncan?"

"Well I've picked up a bit, but one of the sergeants in my platoon is Welsh. You know Jenkins?"

"Yes, his family is from near here, Harlech actually, good cook."

"That's the one. He's recruited quite a few young men and women in the area. We started weekend training like you suggested."

"Good," John said. He put down his bottle and picked up his coat. "Thanks for the good news. It's great to see you both and it will be terrific to see Felicity."

He fished around in his jacket pocket and pulled out a small cribbage board and a pack of cards. "How about some cribbage? Shilling a point, who's the first to take me on?" he asked as he inserted the small pegs at the starting point of the rectangular board.

An hour later, with Aubrey and Duncan a few New British pounds lighter, they were waiting at the beach getting cold in the dark. At full tide they heard a diesel motor, then saw the dark shape of a fishing boat without lights putting into the bay. John flashed a Morse code message by turning the electric torch on and off. It was returned.

"I'll keep watch here then switch with someone next run," Duncan said quietly. John and Aubrey pushed the rowboat into the waves and each taking an oar, put their backs into rowing to the boat as soon as they could. As they came alongside, heaving up and down in the cold salt swell, John could make out Felicity standing over the gunwale and breathed a prayer of thanks. She waved. The Irish fisherman helped Felicity down a rope ladder, then lowered the first wooden boxes of ammunition and rations. John reached up to help her, putting his arm around her. A wave lifted them up, she fell forward into the rowboat and they sat down with a thump. She whispered, "hold me," and John put his arms around her for a moment and held her tight.

Then John and Aubrey pulled for shore looking up when they heard the drone of Luftwaffe bombers droning overhead on a night mission over Ireland.

They wished the crew well as they finished loading the boat for the last time. The Irish captain spoke, "Now we're on the same side. I could see it happening so I could. Those Nazis are even worse than the British," he laughed. "Good luck to you, Major and your good lady. We'll be seeing you, so we will," the fisherman said, slapping him on the shoulder.

"Thank you for helping us, we'll see this through together now. I hope we can continue to get supplies from Ireland. Maybe the Yanks will be delivering the next load."

The crew watched John climb down the ladder to the full rowboat, with Aubrey ready to untie the ropes tethering the rowboat to the trawler. "Let's row like demons," John ordered. By the time they reached the shore to pulled up the rowboat, the fishing vessel had disappeared, and the chugging of her engine faded into the now still night.

With the boxes loaded in the false floor of the butcher's van that Duncan and Aubrey had driven to the cottage they replaced the sides of beef and lamb on their hooks on the ceiling. Duncan climbed behind the steering wheel and Aubrey, clutching a Tommy gun, ducked his way to the rear of the van and lay with his back to the cab, where he was hidden by the hanging carcasses.

He called out to Duncan "I'll be right crooked after an hour of this."

"Don't you mean stiff, you Aussie you?" Duncan joked.

John spoke to Duncan before he and Felicity went into her car. "We'll be just two minutes behind you. We'll have you in sight, but will keep back in case you have trouble."

Twenty minutes later John and Felicity were driving south on the A5. As the approached a roundabout they could see a roadblock set up. Several cars, a cyclist and the butcher's van were halted by the side of the road. Two grey- uniformed German soldiers stood guard as two Gendarmes in black uniforms ordered people out of the vehicles, checked their papers and searched for contraband or Resistance fighters.

"If they suspect anything, we'll have to act," John said to Felicity. "Get your pistol ready. I'll take the Gendarme coming up to us now." He slipped his dark-bladed Commando knife out of the scabbard on his belt with his left hand and reached into his jacket pocket for the wallet containing his identity papers with his other hand.

There was a commotion by the van. Duncan had opened the rear doors and stood back as the Gendarme waved a torch beam over the hanging meat.

The gendarme climbed up into the back of the van and waved at the German guard. He thought there wasn't enough room for him to stand, as he should have been able to in that type of van. The German was shorter and could see no problem. There was an argument. English and German expletives were exchanged.

"So much for British-German friendship," Felicity coolly joked. "When I say 'now'," John said to her, "open the door and shout at everyone to get down, and use your pistol."

The German soldier took his anger out by stabbing at the wooden floor of the van with his bayonet as if wanting to prove there was nothing but road underneath the wooden floor.

The other Gendarme walked towards John and Felicity. John unrolled the driver's window and held out his identification with his right hand. "Good evening, Officer."

"Get out, Sir, and show me your identity papers." At that moment the sound of Aubrey's gunfire from inside the butcher's van rang out and the policeman instinctively swung his weapon back towards the van. John grabbed him by the neck and jabbed the blade between his shoulder blades.

He could hear Felicity shout, "Resistance. Get down!" All but the cyclist had already done so. The bicyclist threw his bike at the second German soldier who was aiming his rifle at John. The soldier's aim was spoilt and the bullet went wide. Felicity levelled her automatic pistol ."Crack!" The German soldier fell onto his knees and then upon his face on the ground.

Aubrey shouted at Duncan, "Where the flaming hell is the other Gendarme?"

Duncan pointed at a figure running down the road across the roundabout, "I'll get him." Aubrey aimed and fired a burst. The policeman ceased running, twitched and fell sideways.

"I'll get his weapon and identity card; they could come in handy," Aubrey said running forward. Felicity picked up dead man's weapon.

"Everyone, help me move this roadblock," John asked . The cyclist, the two motorists, Duncan and Felicity pushed the Gendarme lorry off the road.

"All right to blow it up?" Aubrey asked.

"By all means. Just wait until the civilians are away from it," John ordered. "Better get out of here quickly. Thanks," John said as he thanked the civilians. The cyclist waved goodbye and rode swiftly onto a footpath and through a field, the two civilian cars roared away. They had 'seen nothing.'

As soon as Aubrey had pulled the pins and lobbed two Mills grenades into the enemy vehicle, one after the other, Duncan jumped into the van cab and they were off. Felicity drove her car right behind them. John turned in the front passenger seat, looking back, waiting for the explosions. They came seconds later, angry red balls of heat and flame., consumed themselves by the exploding fuel tank that lit up the sky.

CHAPTER TWENTY THREE THE VISION

"I've got a run in my stocking because of all that," Felicity smirked.

"You're lucky that's all you got," John smiled. "Doesn't it seem a bit odd that we're driving through Wales in the dead of night with a load of Welsh folk costumes in the back seat of your company car while there's a war going on? What are all those Welsh costumes for anyway?"

He started to laugh, then she joined in. It relieved the tension. Still laughing she asked, "Don't you remember my telling you before I left for Ireland that my cover story was I was collecting authentic costumes for the business in London. Are you making fun of my job as a fashion designer for the new British elite? Can I help it if the fashionable ladies in Berlin think it the height to fashion this season to wear dresses inspired by the folk costumes of the peoples of the Greater Reich?

"My dresses fetch a good price. I've got a fashion show next month, perhaps you can come up to London and see it. They'll be modelled on these and others. Next month I go to Paris."

"Well, it would be wonderful to see you but in case you didn't know, Mrs. Stafford, there's a war on."

He put her hand on hers as she shifted gears. "but later on tonight we can just be a young married couple."

They drove past the silent sentinels in the twisting roadways of Snowdonia without further incident and up the A5 to the textile mill that housed his headquarters on the Afon Caseg River. He parked the car in a lay-by, several hundred yards from the mill near a wood.

"We're newly married if any Gendarme stops us."

"How can I forget?"she said.

He kissed her. They walked into the wood and hidden from the road, beneath camouflage netting covered in leaves they found one of the two entrances to the tunnel that led to the textile mill, and allowed Resistance fighters to enter and leave unnoticed in the the gloom of the forest beneath the twin mountains of Carnedd Lleweln and Carnedd Dafydd.

After ensuring Duncan and Aubrey had arrived safely and that the ammo and rations were being unloaded at base camps in the mountains, John and Felicity were able to sleep for a few hours and wake up to a hot breakfast.

Leaving by the exit into the thick wood they walked back to the car in mid-morning, enjoying the singing of birds and the crackle and smell of the damp leaves left over from the autumn. Crocuses poked through the ground cover. Felicity took her young husband's arm and together they looked up at the mountains.

"I don't want to be anywhere else but with you," he said.

"I wonder what the future holds, whether we'll make it through this. Now it looks like the Americans have to come in against Hitler."

"We'll have quite a story to tell our children, won't we?" Felicity said. John arched his ginger eyebrows. "I think we should talk about this, don't you? There's an inn just a few miles away."

Felicity smiled. "O.K. I'll phone the office in Oxford Street and tell them I've got all the costumes I need and will be on my way tomorrow morning."

"Great! I told Duncan and Aubrey I was taking a day's leave."

That night at the inn they enjoyed a romantic dinner of freshly caught trout which they ate by candlelight in a snug wooden corner of the restaurant. As she looked into John's light blue eyes she slipped into a higher level of consciousness, and in her mind's eye saw a vision of brilliant green grass, a hillside. She saw John and herself, standing on the grass. They were older, wearing colourful, strange clothes. They walked with some teenagers, their children she knew instantly.

They turned their eyes up to the sky, shielding them with their hands. A huge, white, delta-winged plane without propellers, with a long pointed nose flew very fast over them. There was a terrific bang in the sky and a screeching, rushing sound as if a thousand lions were leaping through the sky roaring over them.

Yet they were not frightened. It must be a civilian airliner, she thought. The aircraft shot over the fields and out of sight. Then they spread out a blanket on the grass and opened a picnic basket.

It was dark. They were indoors. They were at home, watching a colourful screen while sitting in chairs covered in a kind of plastic leather. A man was reading the news. "*Today, the first supersonic test flight of the Anglo-French supersonic air liner Concorde was successfully made over southern England.*" The screen faded and then she saw only grey, that turned to blue.

She blinked, then she realized it was the familiar blue of John's eyes and jerked back to reality and their own time.

She closed her eyes and her head fell forward a few inches as if she was nodding off to sleep. "Are you all right, Felicity?" John asked gently.

"Yes, I think so, just tired ... mean ... I've just seen the future."

John did not laugh, he had noticed before that her hunches were usually accurate, he asked, "what was it like? Or, maybe I should ask what will it be like?"

She smiled and held his hands. "It's going to be all right. I'll tell you over a cup of coffee. I have a tin of real coffee grounds from a Nazi official who has taken a shine to me, we can have the staff here brew it for us."

"I look forward to that, your story of the future, and later being alone with just you."

CHAPTER TWENTY FOUR   CRY OF THE RAVENS

As Felicity told John of her vision of the future, across the Atlantic the American Congress and Senate were voting to join in the war against the Third Reich. President Roosevelt's passionate speech had brought Senators and Congressmen to their feet, as they furiously clapped their hands and waved their papers. "*First it was Czechoslovakia then Austria, Norway, France, Holland, Belgium, Great Britain and now, now it is Ireland's turn to fall under the shadow of Nazi Germany. I ask, who will be next? I know the answer ... It will be us! Now is the time for Americans to stand alongside those who have fought alone for too long. Now all America is in the fight all the way, for freedom, our homes and civilization as we know it.*"

On the other side of the planet in Sydney, Australia, the Dominion Prime Ministers were meeting with Prime Minister Churchill and his staff. Churchill had just agreed to send 4 divisions of the army raised in Canada to sail for northern Australia and New Zealand and begin the long bloody process of pushing the Japanese out of the Pacific.

The meeting was interrupted by an aide who whispered into Churchill's ear. The British Prime Minister stood up and addressed the other Commonwealth leaders. "I have been informed that President Roosevelt wishes to speak to me on the telephone on a most important matter. Please excuse me."

When Churchill spoke on the scrambler telephone via the cable laid on the floor of the Pacific Ocean to President Roosevelt, he broke down and had to wipe the tears that streamed over his round face. Momentarily his shoulders shook as he entered the room where the Prime Ministers awaited him.

He straightened up and with a great effort spoke in a clear voice. "Gentlemen. The United States is now our ally. She is at war with Nazi Germany. It is now only a matter of time before she is at war with Japan. It will be a long hard road but we are going to win. God be praised."

It was too much for him. He sat and let the tears come. The tears of defeat, and defiance to win against the odds now mingled with those of certain hope. One by one, Fraser of New Zealand; Menzies of Australia; old Boer adversary cum ally,

General Smuts of South Africa; Mackenzie-King of Canada and Chief of the Imperial General Staff, General Brooke, came up to Churchill, shook his hand and thanked the man who had led them out of the darkness into the light of deliverance.

When Churchill died in his sleep of a massive heart attack that night he did it with a smile on his face.

The Labour party leader in the coalition British government in exile, now prime minister , Clement Attlee, released the news to a saddened free world from Ottawa the next day via CBC Radio and broadcast around the free world.

> *The leader of the fight against Fascism, Winston Churchill, died yesterday of a heart attack, without undue pain at 2:13 p.m. Greenwich Mean Time in Sydney, Australia. It is now my duty as prime minister to carry on the great work our leader started in the fight against evil and of the United Kingdom in exile. I promise to serve our Queen Regent and the cause of freedom to the best of my ability. Winston Churchill inspired us with words of courage, he died knowing the tide will turn in our favour. To paraphrase some of his greatest words "He gave us the tools, let us finish the job."*

On his ranch in Alberta, the Duke of Windsor was riding his horse over the Canadian prairie in the hot afternoon sun, inspecting his fences whose shadows lengthened as he rode. He did not yet know of Churchill's passing. Tonight he would be told.

Tomorrow, as scheduled, he would review his new regiment in Edmonton, the "Duke of Windsor's Armoured Regiment". He would take the salute on the reviewing stand, tears in his eyes, as 100 brand new Sherman tanks rumbled past him on their thick caterpillar treads, throwing up dust.

Churchill had been an old friend. The only way he would get through this was to pretend Wallis was with him every step of the way. He suspected he was never going to get over her loss, but strangely he had never felt saner or more sure of himself. He was free. This was where he belonged, under the great blue prairie skies. Now he was alone his horse was his best friend. The Canadian West was where he would stay until he died. At his ranch was the room only he was allowed to enter, the shrine he had built to Wallis.

In Ottawa, in their rooms at the Chateau Laurier Hotel, Princess Elizabeth and Princess Margaret were discussing how they could attend Churchill's funeral planned for next week in Australia. They had jointly presented a new Wellington bomber squadron of the Royal Canadian Air Force with their first colours that afternoon. At dinner in the the squadron's officers' mess the squadron leader had announced Churchill's death and the U.S. entry into the war to a stunned audience.

Tomorrow, Princess Elizabeth would phone Prime Minister Mackenzie King, who had taken an interest in their welfare and become something of a kindly uncle to them. Princess Elizabeth knew she had a good chance of charming Prime Minister King into talking Mr. Attlee into taking them with him to Australia.

Princess Elizabeth knew exactly what to say. "We'll see Australia for the first time, and let the Australians see us. It will show them that they are not forgotten. It will allow us to say goodbye to Mr. Churchill who brought us safely here to Canada. We could fly from San Francisco to Hawaii and to Australia by flying boat."

Defeated, soft hearted Prime Minister King would have no option, but to go to bat for his two favourite princesses.

In Berlin, Adolf Hitler stood before his globe contemplating Rommel's victorious campaign in North Africa. Hitler imagined seizing the Suez Canal and Cairo, then leaping forward to take the oil fields of Iraq. His armies would link up with the victorious Imperial Japanese Army in Delhi. He had only so much time before either Roosevelt or Stalin, or both, attacked, the Gross Reich. He had to grab all he could soon.

It was time for bed. Before he lay down to rest in his simple bedroom, he looked on his bedside table at the small oil painting of a World War One German soldier at prayer. The helmeted face was haggard, expressing determination and grief. A metal label on the 18 inch by 12 inch brown frame gave the title '*Ich hatt einen Kamaraden*' and the artist, Marie Sprenger. 'I had a Friend.' '*Ich hatt einen kamaraden.*' He repeated the words to himself over and over again until he fell into the arms of Morphius.

Ingrid and Heinz cuddled together in their bed in Sweden. The next morning she would grind coffee in the wooden grinder with the metal handle
and they would listen to the radio and hear the news that was tearing around the globe crackling through the airwaves.

Elizabeth the Queen Regent, slept beneath blankets and a tartan cover within Dornoch Castle, safe in the cold Scottish Highlands. Outside her room in the hall a stuffed bear made silent company for a bodyguard sitting on a hard chair trying to stay awake. She dreamt of the Princesses skating on the frozen
Rideau Canal. Their well thumbed letters lay under her pillow beside her revolver.

In the Tower of London, Reinhard Heydrich, Head of the *Sicherheitdienst* SS Security Service, was relishing his third month in residence as Governor of London. He paused his scrutinization of the lists of political prisoners to be rounded up in Ireland by the new SS Einsatz unit in Dublin, time to play the violin later, he mused. After an hour he stood up, tall and black uniformed, he stretched and walked around the room.

He opened the case on the small table and gently drew out his violin and bow and looked out from his window in the White Tower onto the grave on Tower green where Count Von Darmstadt had been given a lavish military burial after the capture of the King and Queen. The flowers he had laid on the grave this afternoon, after visiting the sound proofed interrogation chamber, were visible in the moonlight. He tucked the violin under his chin and began to play with feeling and skill.

As he played a Caprice, a large bird flew from the roof of the White Tower and tore into a rabbit the Tower's eagle handler had left for him. As the notes still echoed around the ancient chamber, Heydrich carefully placed the violin and bow back in their case and walked to his desk where he sat in thought.

"What a shame about Von Darmstadt, he was really enjoying being Governor. I can see why. Still, while I am here I shall do as good a job, better. Lord Eastbourne has asked me to help plan the coronation of the new king-Frederick.

What a relief they had a replacement for Edward VIII in the Hanovarian Prince Frederick who has agreed to be King of Great Britain and leave his home in Germany. This time there shall be no mistakes, there will be ample protection when he arrives to take up residence in the repaired and fortified Buckingham Palace. The coronation will be magnificent, a wonderful opportunity for the SS to display their immaculate precision in front of the world. That new device, what was it?...television the English called it ... so impressive when screens had been set up in Berlin hotels to show the Olympics in '36 ... why not do the same for the coronation? Oh yes, the SS and Gendarmerie uniforms would be most impressive ..."

On the Isle of Wight, cattle cars filled with prisoners shunted into a small railway station near the camp. The trains always arrived at night to disgorge their victims into Camp One.

On the Isle of Man, in the Irish Sea, the first Irish prisoners were arriving at Camp Two.

Deep in the picturesque purple dales of Yorkshire, Charlie Gates lay awake, his room bright with moonlight. He lay on his back, content yet always an alertness coiled up like a spring in his head. He put his hands behind his head listening to Croakey and Jeremiah, through his open window.

An owl hooted and a distant dog barked, the Tower's ravens, called out into the night, patient, biding their time until they would be truly home again. Unable to sleep, Charlie stood up and poked his head through the open window savouring the fresh clear country air, so different from that of London, "You'll be back in the Tower when the war is won my beauties and I shall be with you on that day I swear it."

Eigenschaft des Berlin Nazilagers / New Britain (1941)

CHARACTERS

A list of fictitious and historic characters in the story, fictitious and alternative 'facts' for real people are shown in *italics.*

Attlee, Lord Clement, (1883-1967)-Wartime leader of the British Labour party, Deputy Prime Minister of United Kingdom 1940-1941, *assumed position of Prime Minister of the British Government-in-Exile in Ottawa on the death of Winston Churchill in December 1941, created an Earl by Princess Elizabeth in Ottawa, 1948.*

Beaverbrook, Lord (1879-1964)- Born Max Aitken in New Brunswick, Canada, became British Member of Parliament 1910, owned the widely read British newspapers The Daily Express and Evening Standard, became Minister of Aircraft Production in Churchill's wartime coalition government in 1940, became *Minister of Supply in British Government-in-Exile in Ottawa 1940-1945. Became Governor-General of Canada 1946-1949.*

Carnera, Primo (1906 -1967)-Italian boxer who was 6 feet 5 1/2 inches tall and 266 pounds, he beat Jack Sharkey in 1933 to become the world heavyweight champion. He became a professional wrestler in 1941.

Carol II, King (1893-1953)-King of Romania during the 1930s when Romania experienced economic hardship and the growth of the Fascist Iron Guard. In 1940, Romania decided to side with Hitler after having been left 'in the cold' by the allies. Nazi Germany proceeded to dismember Romania and Carol abdicated in favour of his 19 year old son Prince Michael on 6 September, 1940.

Chamberlain, Neville (1869-1940) - Became British Prime Minister in 1935, and attempted to bring Nazi Germany and Fascist Italy back into the League of Nations and negotiate peace. Chamberlain flew to Hitler's Alpine retreat 15 September, 1938 and secured British and French agreement that Sudetanland (industrialised and well defended western Czechoslovakia) be given to Hitler. Met Hitler in Munich with Mussolini and French Prime Minister Daladier and signed Munich Agreement 30 September,

1938. He was acclaimed by appeasers as a peace maker. Germany invaded the rest of Czechoslovakia March 1939.

Chamberlain realized he had been duped. He proclaimed support for Poland, and after Italy invaded Albania in April 1939 he promised help to Romania, Greece and Turkey if they were attacked by Germany or Italy. It was too late to stop Hitler. He declared war on behalf of Britain when Germany refused to stop its invasion of Poland on 3 September 1939. He resigned as Prime Minister when British and French forces were defeated in Norway 10 May 1940 and died of cancer later that year *in a concentration camp on the Isle of Man.*

Brooke, Field Marshal Sir Alan (1883-1963)-Born in Ulster (N. Ireland) an artillery officer in World War One, in 1937 he commanded the first British Mobile Division. His 2nd Army Corps fought well in France in 1940, he was promoted to General and made Commander-in-Chief, Home Forces. *After the 'Great Evacuation,' he was made CIGS (Commander of Imperial General Staff) in Ottawa for the duration of the war, advising Churchill and Atlee.*

Churchill, Sir Winston (1874-1941)-Greatest Prime Minister of Great Britain, soldier, statesman, orator and historian, son of Lord Randolph Churchill and a beautiful American born in Brooklyn, New York, 'Jennie' Jerome. He was born at his ancestor the Duke of Marlborough's magnificent home, Blenheim Palace. An indifferent student who loved history and all things military, he became a skilled horseman in the 4th Hussars and was posted to the North West Frontier, India where he saw action. He fought in the last major cavalry charge at the Battle of Omdurman in the Sudan and became a war correspondent in the Boer War. Captured by the Boers he escaped, becoming world famous. He was first elected to the British Parliament as a Liberal in 1900, but later became a Conservative. He was First Lord of the Admiralty in World War I but after the debacle of the Gallipoli landings in Turkey he resigned and received a commission as a Major in the front lines in France.

As a back-bench Conservative in the 1930s he wrote a history of the Great War and spoke out against his government's policy of appeasement and German re-armament. Became First

Lord of Admiralty again at outbreak of World War II, replaced Chamberlain as Prime Minister in May 1940.

In May, 1940 he led the British Commonwealth alone against the Axis powers, authorizing the evacuation of British and French troops at Dunkirk June 1940 and British defence against invasion in September.

He masterminded the 'Great Evacuation' of over 1 million allied soldiers and government personnel from Great Britain in mid-October 1940, and set up the British forces and government-in-exile in Canada and established the British resistance network. He worked closely with President Roosevelt to develop a global allied strategy, *persuading America to provide ships, troops and planes fighting under the Union Jack, to defend Hong Kong and Singapore; set up a volunteer U.S. army in Canada* and forged the North Atlantic Defence Alliance (NADO) with Canada and the U.S.

He encouraged Roosevelt to establish the 'Defending Attacked Ships Policy' under which the U.S. Navy protected British and Commonwealth shipping anywhere it was attacked, by sailing alongside convoys.

He allowed the U.S. ownership of airfields and naval bases in the Caribbean, Newfoundland, Fiji, Ascension Island and Ceylon for 99 years in return for rifles, machine guns and ammunition for British defence in 1940, and 50 four stack obsolete destroyers to protect convoys across the Atlantic.

From November 1940 on the following were delivered to British forces in Canada: 300 oil tankers and freighters, 15 submarines, 3 cruisers, 620 B-17, Havoc and Liberator bombers, 776 Tomahawk P-40, Wildcat and Mustang fighter planes, 1,022 Sherman and Honey tanks, 1,860 howitzers, 22,000 lorries/jeeps and an agreement to supply oil without charge for the duration of the war. These weapons became the nucleus of the forces in Canada until British and Canadian designed tanks, aircraft and ships began to roll out from Vancouver, Toronto and Montreal assembly lines in huge numbers to reinforce Commonwealth and Imperial forces around the world.

His inspiring speeches by radio during 1940-1941 kept freedom and hope alive and motivated the allied effort throughout the war. Churchill died of a heart attack from overwork in Sydney, Australia on 26th December, Boxing Day, 1941 the day the U.S.A. declared war on Japan.

He was the first person to be awarded a posthumous knighthood (baronetcy), by Princess Elizabeth in Ottawa in the New Year's Honours list 1942 which was accepted by his widow, Lady Clementine Churchill. The United States Congress made him a posthumous citizen of the United States and the new tank produced in Canada in 1944 *was named the Churchill in his honour. In 1958 the newly built Australian capital, was named Churchill to immortalize how he encouraged Australians to stand against the Japanese Empire.*

Comenici, Josef-Captain *of the Romanian Palace Guard. Hearty, large man with a round face with a large black moustache. A friend to John after he saved Prince Michael.*

Darmstadt, Count Manfred Von (1911-1941)-*Born in the German state of Saxony of aristocratic parents. Attended Heidelberg University, joined the SS in 1935. Led successful attack on the Belgian Eben Emaul fort in May, 1940. Awarded Iron Cross with oak leaf cluster by Hitler. Commanded Operation Checkmate, the capture of the Duke and Duchess of Windsor from the Bahamas August 1940. Led paratroop attack on Windsor Castle 20 September 1940 and escaped with half of the Crown Jewels. Became Governor of London residing in the Tower of London during the occupation. Killed during Operation Lion Heart when the Commandos rescued Edward VIII and Queen Wallis January, 1941.*

Dietrich, Ingrid- *One of Hitler's Wermacht Secretaries at his Chancellery in Berlin, A beautiful blonde born in Vienna in 1920, she falls in love with one of Hitler's translators, Heinz Erhardt. She marries Heinz and to moves with him to Sweden.*

Dowding, Air Chief Sir Hugh (1882-1970)-Commander of RAF Fighter Command 1936-November 1940. He prepared the RAF for the looming confrontation with Germany by speeding up the arrival of the new fighters, the Hurricanes and Spitfires, and building a chain of the new RDF (radar) and observer posts on the southern and eastern coasts of Britain. Information on incoming enemy bombers was relayed to an underground command post at Bentley Prior which dispatched squadrons to attack the enemy.

He refused requests to send extra fighter squadrons to Norway and France and saved Fighter Command for the Battle of Britain. *Unfortunately, the German strategy of attacking the RDF posts and fighter airfields without cease before the invasion, succeeded in destroying many machines, pilots and mechanics. As a result, Fighter Command tried valiantly but ineffectively to destroy the overwhelmingly large German air fleets.*

During the 'Great Evacuation' in October 1940, Dowding ensured the last Spitfires and Hurricanes in factories were flown out before being captured. The famous 'Last of the Few' flew them tirelessly over the evacuation ports of Glasgow, Liverpool, Londonderry and Bristol keeping the Luftwaffe at bay for precious days. Dowding flew to Iceland and commanded the British forces there throughout the war.

Eastbourne, Lord Lancelot (1879-1949)-*Fascist Prime Minister of New Britain appointed by Hitler after the defeat of Great Britain in October 1940 on the advice of British Blackshirt leader Lord Mosley. He collaborated with the Germans convinced that he was saving Britain from Communism and moving it into the future where the Third Reich, Italy and Japan would rule the world.*

Edward VIII (1894-1972)-Popular eldest son of George V and Queen Mary. He was patriotically christened, Edward Albert Christian George Andrew Patrick David, but was known as David to his family and his friends. Attended Oxford University, served in World War I but to his chagrin was not allowed to serve in the front lines. After the war, he made tours around the Empire as a goodwill ambassador and was mobbed and lionized. He showed interest in helping the many unemployed in Britain during the depression but did little to help. He succeeded to the throne on the death of his father and reigned for only 325 days, and was never crowned.

On 10 December 1936 he abdicated (gave up the throne) so he could marry the twice-divorced American, Wallis Simpson. Commonwealth Prime Ministers would not allow him to marry her and remain king.

His brother, Albert and his wife Elizabeth were forced to become King George VI and Queen Elizabeth. Public opinion quickly turned against him.

Edward VIII and Wallis Simpson went to France waiting until George VI and Queen Elizabeth were crowned before they married. They became the Duke and Duchess of Windsor.

They were captured by the Germans and forced to become King Edward VIII and Queen Wallis of an occupied Great Britain, although they were never crowned. Edward VIII was rescued in January 1940 but his wife was killed. He went to live on his ranch in Alberta where he carried out some official duties in Canada until his death in 1972. His body was flown to England and he was buried in the grounds of Windsor Castle..

Elizabeth, Princess (1926-)- Born in London 21 April, 1926, eldest daughter of George VI and Queen Elizabeth, *survived kidnap attempt at Windsor Castle 21 September 1940 by German paratroopers, evacuated with her younger sister, Princess Margaret, first to Wales, then Scotland and to Canada in October 1940.*

She lived in Ottawa with her sister and grandmother, Queen Mary, in the Chateau Laurier Hotel in Ottawa near the Houses of Parliament, for the duration of the war. She visited Australia accompanied by Mrs. Clementine Churchill and Prime Minister Attlee in January 1942, to attend Winston Churchill's funeral in Sydney. A year later she and her sister Margaret made a successful state visit to Washington D.C. as guests of President and Mrs. Roosevelt. She became Princess Regent at the age of 18 in 1944.

Elizabeth, Queen (1900-2002) -Born Elizabeth Bowes-Lyon, the daughter of the Earl and Countess of Strathern on his English estate, brought up at Glamis Castle, Scotland. As a teenager she nursed convalescing officers at the castle during World War I.

After twice turning down his offer of marriage Elizabeth married Bertie, son of George V and Queen Mary at Westminster Abbey 23 April, 1923 in the wedding of the decade.

She left her bouquet of flowers at the grave of the unknown soldier (the body of an unknown British soldier was buried inside the cathedral near the entrance with full honours after World War I), the tradition of brides marrying at the Cathedral leaving their bouquets continues to this day.

She despised Wallis Simpson who caused her husband Bertie to become King George VI. She supported him and helped him not only to cope but excel. She loved Canada, which she toured with George VI extensively in May-June 1939 just before the outbreak of World War Two. She swore never to leave Great Britain during the war and in fact never did leave during that time.

She was wounded by a piece of bomb shrapnel and lost an eye during the Blitz attack on Buckingham Palace which killed Bertie (George VI) 21 September. She was hospitalized in London then evacuated to Edinburgh where she made a rapid recovery. She was made Queen Regent by order-in-council 24 September until Princess Elizabeth became of age at 18.

When Churchill asked the Royal family to go into exile to Canada she refused. She did give permission for her mother-in-law, Queen Mary, and her two children, Princesses Elizabeth and Margaret to leave from Liverpool on the battleship HMS King George V.

Living 'underground' in occupied Scotland she became a legend as the head of the Scottish Resistance, wearing an eye patch over her right eye and proving herself a crack shot against German and New British Fascists who attempted but failed to capture her.

Erhardt, Heinz-*One of Hitler's translators in Berlin, the son of German diplomats in China. Born in 1916 in Shanghai he was studying German literature in Berlin when he was called up for Wehrmacht service. He was assigned to Nazi translation duties since he spoke five languages: English, French, Russian, Chinese and Japanese. He is a German patriot not a Nazi, concerned for the future of his country, he fears that waging a total, global war will destroy any civilization left in the Reich. He marries Ingrid Dietrich, a secretary at the Reich Chancellery and with Hitler's blessing they begin a new life in neutral Sweden where he has a job with his Uncle who owns an export business.*

Gates, Charlie-*Born in Lancashire, England in 1878 served in the Royal Sots Guards, veteran of the Battle of the Somme, World War One . Sergeant-Major Gates later served in India, after retiring from the army as a Warrant Officer he became a Yeoman Warder at the Tower of London in 1934. In 1937 he became Raven Master. In 1940, aged 62, he fought in the Battle of London, was wounded but went back to work in the Tower as the last Warder for the Nazis ,as a member of British resistance. He took the last two ravens and some turf from the Tower to Yorkshire for safekeeping during the occupation where he lived with a new identity.*

Goebbels, Josef (1897-1945)-Minister of Propaganda for the Third Reich, he obtained a doctorate from Heidelburg University, 1921. He became propaganda chief for the Nazi Party in 1930. He devised the greeting 'Heil Hitler' which was to become a common greeting for Nazis, and by extension, many Germans. He also invented the term 'Fuhrer' (leader) to describe Hitler. Goebbels was a masterful speech-maker and made good use of radio, film and newspapers to extol the ideals of the Nazi party.

Guderian, General Heinz (1888-1954)-German General who developed modern tank warfare in the 1930s ironically basing his ideas upon papers written by British officers. During the Polish campaign of 1939 he commanded the 19th Panzer Corps and in France in June 1940, again proved that tanks, air power and motorized infantry could be unstoppable.

During Operation Sea Lion he commanded the 4th Army Group which landed on the east coast of England at Harwich. He teamed up with Rommel's army after the Battle of Hayward's Heath and took Birmingham and the industrial midlands .

Heydrich, Reinhard (1904-1942)-Established the SS Secret Service (Sicherheitsdeinst or SD). He established SS Einsatz (Action Groups) in New Britain and elsewhere to round up those of Jewish descent and other enemies of the Reich to send them to concentration camps. He became the Governor of London after the death of Count Von Darmstadt. Transferred to occupied Czechoslovakia in 1942 he was assassinated by Czech agents trained in Canada.

Himmler, Heinrich (1900-1953)-Second most powerful Nazi after Adolf Hitler. He was made head or Reichsfuhrer of the SS on 6 January 1929. By 1933, this elite Nazi bodyguard was 209,000 strong. **See SS.**

Hirohito, Emperor (1901-1989)-Emperor of Japan 1926-1989, he was the national symbol of Japan, he personally opposed war with Great Britain and the U.S.A. but was not able to overturn the decisions by the military junta that took over the Japanese government in 1931. He tried to avoid war with China in 1937, but was overruled.

Even though he was seen as a god by followers of the Japanese Shinto religion, in reality, he was told what to do by his fascist Prime Minister, General Tojo who advocated military expansion in Asia. Hirohito did manage to postpone hostilities with the United States in early 1941 when an embargo was put upon oil exported to Japan by the United States. However, Tojo and his military junta had their way when the *Japanese attacked Hawaii and San Diego, California on 25th December, 1941.*

Hitler, Adolf (1884-1947)-Born in Austria, he was an artist and would-be architect who joined the German Army in 1914, and served on the Eastern and Western fronts as an infantry message runner. He became a corporal and was awarded the Iron Cross first class for bravery.

He led an aborted putsch (coup d'etat) to seize power in post World War I Munich in Bavaria (Munich Beer Hall Putsch November 9th 1923). He was jailed and there wrote his manifesto *Mein Kampf* (My Struggle). He founded the Nazi party in 1925, an ultra-right wing, patriotic and anti-communist party which combined bully tactics; mesmerizing, well delivered speeches, and ruthlessness in a time of great inflation and uncertainty in Germany. His fascist party was inspired by Mussolini's blackshirts in Italy (**see Fascism, Mussolini**).

Through intimidation and a groundswell of support he was elected Riechkanzellor (Chancellor) of Germany in 1933, and established the Third Reich, making himself and the Nazi party dictatorial rulers of Germany. He proceeded to swiftly re-arm Germany, put the unemployed to work, and manoeuvre to gain back what Germany had given up by losing World War I, blaming that loss not on defeat 'in the field' which was the truth, but unjustly upon Jewish treachery, and defeatism by the German leadership in 1918.

By 1936, he had taken the Rhineland unopposed by Britain and France, and began building the most modern armed forces in the world; by 1938, he had absorbed both Austria and Czechoslovakia into the Third Reich. His plan was to create a world dominated by Nazi Germany in partnership with Fascist Italy and Japan. (**see also Nazi, Third Reich, Treaty of Versailles**)

Hunter, Aubrey-Australian Army Lieutenant, *born in Perth, Western Australia on 11 November, 1915. He was one of five children, the youngest son of third generation Australians of English heritage. Unhappy at school, he ran away and worked in the outback as a sheep sheerer, then lived with Aborigine Bushmen who taught him to live in the desert and play the didgeridoo. He worked his way up through the ranks after joining the Royal Australian Artillery as a Gunner in 1937.*

In 1940 as a Lieutenant in the Australian division stationed in Britain he volunteered for Commando training and met John Stafford, Duncan MacLeod and President Lincoln who become his comrades-in-arms. His distinguishing features are a shock of blonde hair, an irreverent attitude and a didgeridoo, the Australian Aborigine musical instrument strapped to his pack.

King, William Lyon Mackenzie (1874 -1958)-Liberal Prime Minister of Canada during World War II. He was an adroit politician who supported an independent Canada within the Commonwealth. He waited one week before leading Canada into World War II as Britain's ally on September 10th, 1939. A bachelor, he was privately interested in spiritualism. He declared that the allies would win the war because the hands on his office clock on Parliament Hill in Ottawa were at the correct position to indicate success.

He welcomed the Royal family to Ottawa and became something of an uncle to Princesses Elizabeth and Margaret. He also helped the Norwegian, Dutch and Belgian royal families in-exile, as well as the respective governments-in-exile for Great Britain, Czechoslovakia, Poland, Denmark, France, Norway, Holland and Belgium. King worked with Churchill (whom he disliked) and Attlee as well as Roosevelt in developing an allied strategy and *put Canada on a total war footing with compulsory conscription for all able-bodied men and women not working on farms or essential industries in November 1940.*

Le Meseurier, Felicity-*Born in Montreal, Canada 9 February, 1919. Her mother was an American medical doctor Susan Van Dyke from Chicago, who treated her father, Henri Le Meseurier an officer in the Canadian army, while he recuperated from poison gas inhalation on the western front in a hospital in Scotland. He was a veteran of the Canadian victory at Vimy Ridge in 1917 where he became a lifelong friend of John Stafford's father, Colonel Rex Stafford, of the Royal Hamilton Rifles. Consequently, Felicity knew John and his brother Alan, from the summer holidays they shared together as they grew up.*

Felicity, an attractive brunette with green eyes is a fashionable dresser with an interest in art. At the outbreak of war she worked at Windsor Castle helping to store the art there for the duration, during the attack upon Windsor Castle she helped save Princesses Elizabeth and Margaret. She escaped Britain in the 'Great Evac.' and received espionage training in Camp X, Oakville, Ontario.

Aged only 21 she joined Resistance Britain and participated in Operation Lion Heart, she became a spy, posing as a Fashion Designer in occupied London moving in elite fascist circles. Despite living in occupied Britain, she married John Stafford on 21 May, 1941 at Battle, Sussex.

Le Meseurier, Colonel Henri- *Born in 1894 in Montreal, Canadian military attaché at Canada House, London in the 1930s. A Major in World War One in the crack Canadian infantry Regiment the Royal 22nd 'Van Doos' (Vingt Douze), he served on the western front in the Canadian Division. He became friends with John Stafford's father, whom he served with at the Battle of Vimy Ridge. He asked John to spy for Churchill and Lord Beaverbrook in 1938. He was recalled to Ottawa to head the Canadian Military Intelligence department in September 1939.*

Lincoln, Frances-*Born 1901 in Halifax, Nova Scotia the son of a carpenter and lay Baptist Preacher, Samuel, descended from a black slave who came to Canada on the 'underground railway' from the U.S.A. to find freedom in the 1840s. The escaped slave, Noah Richards, changed his surname to Lincoln when that great American President freed all slaves in the United States, he decided however, to stay and raise his family in the country that had accepted him.*

Frances's mother could claim as an ancestor a black soldier, Slocum Archer, a descendant of a tribal Prince from Nigeria, who fought under Cornwallis in the American Revolutionary War and came to Nova Scotia to receive the land grant given by King George III to all loyalists and to retain his freedom.

Although bright, Frances had to leave school to support his family. He joined a boxing club and soon became a pugilist to reckon with. In 1932 he fought the Italian heavyweight Primo Carnera and won.

He joined the British army, trained as a Physical Education instructor and was ordered to teach Commando recruits at Achnarry, Scotland in the summer of 1940. He received permission from the Commandant of the camp to join John Stafford's troop which was ordered to Windsor Castle and stayed with John, Duncan and Aubrey in Red Dragon Commando in Wales, participating in Operation Lion Heart. Soft spoken but a tough soldier, his favourite weapon is the Bren Gun.

MacLeod, Duncan-*Became a Commando attending the training camp in Achnarry, Scotland in the summer of 1940 with John Stafford, Duncan MacLeod and Aubrey Hunter. Born in Edinburgh, Scotland in 1921, at the* *outbreak of war in September, 1939 he tried to join the RAF but failed the medical. He passed his first year pre-medicine courses at the University of Edinburgh but enlisted in the Royal Navy in May 1940 and was accepted, despite his short sightedness which he kept from the medical examiners by memorizing the chart.*

He was commissioned as a Sub-Lieutenant, serving on a destroyer in the Royal Navy and volunteered to be a Commando. He was with John Stafford, Aubrey Duncan and President Lincoln at the Battle of Windsor Castle, at Portsmouth and in the Red Dragon Commando in Wales. He was part of Operation Lion Heart. He wears brown tortoise shell glasses and his intellectual looks cover up a stubborn nature and wiry physique that got him through Commando training.

Margaret Rose, Princess (1930-2002)-Known in the 30's as Margaret Rose, second child of George VI and Queen Elizabeth, and younger sister of Princess Elizabeth (heir presumptive). Born at Glamis Castle, Scotland. *Sent to live at Windsor Castle after the German invasion of France, with her sister, Princess Elizabeth. She survived the German paratroop attack on Windsor Castle and was evacuated to Wales, then Scotland, then to Canada for duration of war. She attended the funeral of Winston Churchill in Australia 3 January, 1942 with Princess Elizabeth. She accompanied Princess Elizabeth on a state visit to Washington D.C. in 1943.*

Mary, Queen (1867-1953)-Remembered for her love of pearl necklaces, upright posture and proper behaviour, she was Queen consort of George V, mother of Edward VIII (Duke of Windsor) and Albert Duke of York (George VI). She saw her eldest son's abdication as a dereliction of duty, and supported her second son who became George VI in 1937. *She left Britain with Princesses Elizabeth and Margaret in October 1940, and lived in Ottawa.*

Michael, King (1921 -)-Son of King Carol III of Romania. In 1938, his father became dictator to take control of a country on the verge of civil war due to the instability caused by the pro-German fascist Iron Guard. King Carol traveled to Western Europe seeking aid and a military alliance, but was turned away empty-handed. The Germans, however, courted him.

Faced with threats from Russia and Hungary, Romania sided with Germany, declaring war on France and Great Britain in May 1940. Hitler forced the King to give up land to Hungary and Carol III was forced to abdicate. Michael became King of Romania at the age of 20, sympathetic to the allies, but forced to reign over a nation governed by fascists allied to the Third Reich until the end of the war when he led his people against the fascists and Romanian communists to establish a democracy.

Montgomery, General Bernard Law, 1st Viscount of the Pyramids (1887-1972)-Descendant of a Norman Baron who accompanied William the Conqueror in his successful invasion of England in 1066. He was a World War I veteran who was the successful commander of the 3rd Division British Expeditionary Force in France in 1940. While Britain braced itself for invasion, he commanded the army in S. E. England. Although a prickly personality he got results and was affectionately known as Monty to his troops who responded to his concern for their welfare.

He defeated the German invasion at the Battle of Dover, September 1940 but was seriously wounded at the Battle of Hayward's Heath just as the German front seemed to be buckling, and the battle was subsequently lost and with it Britain. After recuperating in Gibraltar in 1941 he flew to Cairo to take command of the 8th Army in Egypt.

Mussolini, Benito (1883-1945)-Son of a blacksmith, he was named after the Mexican revolutionary Benito Suarez and became a socialist. He founded a socialist newspaper, was draughted into the Italian army (allied to Britain and France) in World War I he was wounded fighting against the Austrians.

He created the fascist blackshirts who seized power and founded a corporate socialist Italy with himself as 'Il Duce' (The Leader). His aim was to recreate Italy's ancient Roman empire in the Mediterranean. Hitler used him as a model and Mussolini allied himself with Hitler and Japan to form the Axis Alliance. Mussolini over-ran Abyssinia (Ethiopia) in 1936. He declared war against the allies in June 1940, when it appeared Germany was winning.

Raeder, Erich, Gross Admiral (1876-1960)-Commander-in-Chief of the German Navy, organized the building of three *Panzerschrift* (pocket battleships) which broke naval treaties because they were much more powerfully armed and armoured than their size would indicated. By 1939, when promoted to *Gross Admiral* he had a powerful fleet of battleships, cruisers, destroyers and submarines.

Riefenstahl, Leni (1902-)-Talented German dancer and film actress of 1920s who became Hitler's favourite film director. Her 1934 documentary *Triumph Des Willens* (Triumph of the the Will) depicted the terrifying raw power of a Nazi rally at Nurenberg. Her *Olypmpische Spiele* (Olympic Games) documentary of the 1936 Berlin Games included black athlete Jesse Owens and is beautifully filmed. She was cleared of pro-Nazi involvement after World War II and went on to make documentary films in Africa.

Rommel, Erwin General (1891-1958)-German veteran of World War I where he was awarded Germany's highest award, the *Pour la Merite.* He brilliantly led a Panzer division into France in June 1940, and was promoted to Major-General. *Promoted again to General in August 1940, he was given command of the 6th Army Group during Operation Sea Lion.*

His troops took the Isle of Wight and Portsmouth and linked up with the 4th Army Group. He was second-in-command of the German forces at the German victory at Hayward's Heath and led the 6th Army in a left hook around London and teamed up with Guderian's army to invade the industrial midlands.

He was given command of the Afrika Korps in Tripoli in 1941 and ordered by Hitler to take the Suez Canal.

Roosevelt, Franklin Delano, President (1882-1945)-Great American President despite being confined to a wheelchair due to Polio. Of Dutch ancestry, he was Secretary of the U.S. Navy in World War I. As a Democratic President he helped unemployed Americans in the financial depression of the 1930s by establishing government work programs called the 'New Deal'.

He was a good friend to Winston Churchill and a staunch supporter of traditional freedoms against fascism. He supported Britain and Commonwealth short of going to war, *even allowing American ships to fly the RN's White Ensign in the Pacific and help the Royal Navy. He provided arms, ammunition and destroyers to Britain during the Battle of Britain and welcomed Churchill to New York in late 1940. Roosevelt declared war upon Germany and Italy when their invasion of Ireland in June 1941 made this politically possible. He declared war against Japan,*

26 December, Boxing Day, 1941, after Japan invaded Hawaii and bombed San Diego California catching the American armed forces by surprise.

Schwartzkopf, Franz-*Boy in Bavarian family with whom John Stafford stayed in 1938. Aged 15 he was fearful of having to join the Wermacht. John arranged for him to attend a boarding school in England and thus saved him from being forced to fight for the Third Reich.*

Simpson, Wallis Warfield, Queen of occupied Britain (1896 - 1941) -Born Wallis Simpson in Baltimore, Maryland, U.S.A. she was descended from Pocahantas, the native Princess and General Robert E. Lee (a shared ancestor with Queen Elizabeth (wife of George VI). Her father died when she was 5. She was first married to an American naval aviator, Win Spencer, who drank too much and abused her. They were divorced in 1927. She then married an English-American stockbroker, Ernest Simpson, whom she met in New York.

They moved to England in 1933, and moved in social circles that included the Prince of Wales (later Edward VIII). He became infatuated with Mrs. Wallis Simpson and refused to heed advice to drop her. (**see Windsor, Duke and Duchess**)

She went to France when Edward VIII abdicated. They were married there in 1937 and she became the Duchess of Windsor. They lived in exile in Paris. In 1940 they left France via Spain and Portugal for England. She went with her husband to the Bahamas where he was appointed Governor.

In August 1940 she and her husband were kidnapped by the Germans from the Bahamas and brought back to their prewar home in Paris under house arrest. Hitler threatened her and the Duke reluctantly agreed to become King Edward VIII of occupied Britain. She became Queen Wallis. They were to have been crowned in May 1941 but a rescue attempt to free them from the Tower of London ended in her death. Accompanied by her grieving husband her body was taken by Royal Navy submarine to Canada. He went with the body to the private funeral in Baltimore, Maryland.

Stafford, Alan-*Younger twin brother to John by five minutes. Born in Hamilton, Canada 29th July, 1920. Identical to John except he is right handed, has a scar on his chin from an encounter with an ice hockey puck. More athletic than John, he was a champion junior tennis player for Canada and played at Wimbledon in 1939.*

He joined his father's old regiment the Royal Hamilton Rifles as a first Lieutenant in September 1939 and was posted with John as part of the Canadian 3rd Division which sailed for Britain. He fought against the German invasion at Eastbourne and as the army withdrew west to Bristol where he was evacuated.

He volunteered for Commando training when the course was established in New Brunswick in January, 1941. Alan is 6 feet tall like his brother, he also light blue eyes and straight red hair like John but prefers not to grow a moustache,. He has slightly more freckles on his face than John, and weighs ten pounds less. His disposition is easy-going.

Stafford, John-*Eldest son of Colonel Rex Stafford, Colonel-in-Chief of the Royal Hamilton Rifles and his mother Winifred (Lawrence) a distant cousin to Lawrence of Arabia. Older identical twin to his younger brother Alan by five minutes, born 29 July, 1920 in Hamilton, Ontario. Interested in history and archeology in 1937 went to Munich for summer holidays staying with a Bavarian family. After graduation from Westdale Secondary School in June 1938 he decided to stay in Munich for a year studying German and Fencing. He sailed to London en route to Munich, where old family friend, Colonel Le Meseurier asked him to spy while studying in Germany.*

After completing his studies and taking secret photographs of new Luftwaffe aircraft he travelled to Romania where he saved Prince Michael from a Nazi assassination plot. He continued on to Greece, Egypt and Malta where he learned to scuba dive and with a friend in the Royal Canadian Navy thwarted Italian frogmen spying on a British battleship in Valetta Bay. Back in London John reported to Colonel Le Meseurier and began to fall in love with his daughter and friend, Felicity, a year older than himself. He arranged for young Franz Schwartzkopf, of the family he boarded with and befriended, to go to school in England to get him out of Nazi Germany.

While waiting to start second year at the University of Toronto he joined the Royal Hamilton Rifles as a militia Lieutenant and enlisted in the regular force on September 4, 1939 as a Second Lieutenant. Shipped to England with his brother John as part of the 3rd Canadian Division he volunteered to be part of the British Norwegian expeditionary force sent to Narvik, Norway to unsuccessfully stem the German invasion. He was awarded the Military Medal for storming a German machine gun nest and promoted to Captain.

He volunteered for the newly formed Commandos and took the course at Achnarry, Scotland and there met the men who became his team in Red Dragon Commando: Sub-Lieutenant Duncan MacLeod RN, Lieutenant

Aubrey Hunter, Royal Australian Artillery and Sergeant Major President Lincoln.

With the Nazi invasion imminent he was given the rank of acting Major and the 200 men of A troop, 8th Commando. His orders were to drive to Windsor Castle and protect the Princesses. They arrived just in time to beat off a paratroop attack. He took his men to Portsmouth where they retrieved naval munitions from the docks. When Churchill ordered the evacuation John read his sealed orders and led his men to Wales and their new role in Resistance Britain as Red Dragon Commando. He was awarded the OBE for rescuing Edward VIII and Queen Wallis from the Tower of London.

John's characteristics are his light blue eyes, erect stature of 6 feet, solid build, smile, straight red hair and ginger military moustache. He is driven to succeed and is a good shot, especially with the long barrelled Webley and Scott target revolver his father gave him.

Windsor, Duke and Duchess of Windsor-The official title given to Edward VIII after he abdicated in 1936, and his wife Wallis Simpson after they married in 1937. The Royal family, not surprisingly, would not allow the Duchess of Windsor to be called 'Her Royal Highness," a snub that irritated the Duke, although he continued to be called His Royal Highness.

They established themselves in a magnificent mansion in the fashionable area the Bois de Bologne in Paris. In September 1939, the Duke offered himself for military service and he became a British liaison officer with the French army. The Duchess volunteered for work with the Red Cross.

In June 1940, while France was being invaded by Germany, they drove to the Spanish border and stayed in Madrid, then moved on to Lisbon where the Nazis failed in an attempt to ensure they stayed on the continent. An assassination attempt was foiled by MI6.

The Duke and Duchess tried to negotiate with Churchill, who ordered them to Britain. They wanted more financial help, (they already had a comfortable amount) and the HRH designation officially given to Wallis. All they received was a tersely worded telegram to the Duke to obey orders. The Duke hoped to be made a military commander of Wales but instead was appointed Governor of the Bahamas. They left England in the summer of 1940.

In August, 1940 Count Von Darmstadt captured them in the Bahamas and brought them back to France by U-Boat, where they were kept in their old home under house arrest. The Duke met Hitler at the Eiffel Tower. Hitler made veiled threats to the Duke that the Duchess would be harmed. The Duke and Duchess were forced to become the puppet King Edward VIII and Queen Wallis of occupied Britain. Kept as virtual prisoners in the Tower of London, the Commando attack Operation Lion Heart was an attempt to free them and bring them to Canada. (see also Edward VIII; Simpson, Wallis)

Wingate, Major-General Orde (1903-1944)-Born in India, the son of Plymouth Brethren (Puritanical Christians) parents. He served in the British army in Palestine in the 1930s. He gained valuable guerilla warfare experience commanding 'night squads' of Jewish settlers fighting Arab resistance to the new Zionist immigrants settling on Palestinian land. In early 1940, he led an effective guerilla army which returned Abyssinian Emperor Haile Selassie return to his country which had been taken by the Italians. *Churchill ordered him to his occupied homeland in December 1940 to head the British Resistance movement.*

A strong individualist and brilliant soldier, he wore a beard (against regulations) and carried his battered white Wolsley tropical hat with him wherever he went.

GLOSSARY

The alphabetically listed terms and names are explained here are to give some background information to the reader. The data in italics are part of the alternative nature of the novel, the rest in ordinary script are factual. As in the body of the story non-English words are also given in *italics* e.g. *Luftwaffe*

88 mm-Accurate and versatile standard German field gun used for infantry support, anti-tank and anti-aircraft use.

Abdication-The act of renouncing the crown, as Edward VIII did in 1936. He was the first monarch to do so since Richard II in 1399.

Ack Ack-Alliterative allied term for anti-aircraft fire.

Allies-Nations allied against Fascism, initially France, Great Britain and the Commonwealth in World War Two.

Anschluss-Take-over of Austria by the Third Reich, March 1938.

Appeasement-Policy of giving in to dictatorial threats and diplomatic pressure and hoping events will turn out for the best.

ASDIC-Acronym for Allied Detection Investigation Committee, a World War I British-French unit which found a way to locate submarines by sending a pulse of sound that would bounce back when it hit the hull of a U-boat. By 1938, the Royal Navy was using it to detect depth so charges could be set to explode at different depths. The United States improved upon it and called it Sonar.

Axis-Fascist alliance of Germany, Italy and Japan each of which had dictatorships and ambitions to rule the globe.

Battle of Hayward's Heath *-27 September-1 October, 1940. General Montgomery's army (British/Canadian/Australian) fought the combined German 6th and 9th army groups led by Rundstedt and Rommel in East Sussex. Monty's night-time attack resulted in huge German losses; however, when he was seriously wounded and his second-in-command killed in a strafing attack, the Germans regained the initiative and defeated the British army.*

BBC-British Broadcasting Corporation, government run national radio and television service. *Became the New BBC when the fascists took over Britain.*

Black Douglas Commando-*Scottish Resistance unit named after* Sir James Douglas c. 1286-1330, who fought with King Robert the Bruce of Scotland against the English. In 1313 he captured the Castle of Roxburgh by disguising his men as black oxen and became known as 'The Black Douglas'. He fought with Robert the Bruce at Bannockburn and later set out to take that Scottish king's heart to Palestine in a silver casket. However, he died while fighting the Moors in Spain.

Bletchley Park-Site of the British Code and Cipher School 50 miles (80 km.) north west of London. Under the guidance of MI6 was a secret residence of several hundred mathematicians and code experts whose job it was to decipher German and Japanese secret codes such as the German enigma codes. The experts included such geniuses as Alan Turing, who created the first computer.

Blitzkreig-German for 'Lightning War' referring to the quick style of warfare using tanks, aircraft and troops in vehicles, used to great effect by the German Wermacht in 1939-1940. Shortened to 'Blitz' by the Daily Express in the Battle of Britain.

BMW-*Bayern Motoren Werke*- automobile and military vehicle manufacturing company.

Bomber Command-Branch of the RAF comprising of bomber planes.

Bren Gun-best light infantry machine gun ever produced, designed in Czechoslovakia and manufactured in Britain and Canada. Used by British Commonwealth troops in World War II, fired 500 rounds per minute from a detachable curved magazine that fitted on top of the breech, weighed 10.1 kg.

Brian Boru Commando*-Commando resistance unit in Ulster (N. Ireland) named after the ancient King of Ireland* (an ancestor of Queen Elizabeth, wife of George VI). Brian Boroimhe (often spelt and pronounced, Broo) became high king of Ireland in 1002. In 1014, on Good Friday, he destroyed a coalition of enemies near Dublin.

Browning-American small-arms manufacturer producing automatic pistols and belt fed machine guns used in Hurricanes and Spitfires.

Brownshirts-Paramilitary arm of the Nazi party which was 400,000 strong by 1932, they kept order at Nazi meetings and fought in the streets against Communists and other opponents of the Nazis, but were eventually overshadowed by the SS (see SS).

BSA-Pronounced 'Beeza' stands for British Small Arms, a company which made motorcycles and weapons.

Coastal Command- Branch of the RAF dealing with amphibious and other aircraft responsible for defending the air over the ocean surrounding Great Britain and later Iceland and Eastern Canada.

Commandos-British shock-troop unit set up in the summer of 1940 for amphibious attacks against German-held Europe. Volunteers were trained in Scotland, later in Canada, in cliff-scaling, kayaking, unarmed combat and living off the land. Units of Commandos known as *Troops became the initial core of British resistance after the occupation in October 1940.*

Commonwealth-Name given to British Dominions such as Australia, Canada, New Zealand and South Africa given full independence by the Statute of Westminster in 1931, they remained joined in the collective organization called the British Commonwealth. After World War II many colonies of the empire, such as India, were granted independence but chose to join the Commonwealth.

Concentration Camp-First used to describe camps for Boer women and children set up by the British during the Boer War (1900-1901) with poor medical and living conditions. *Konzentrationslager* (slang term was Kz) were set up by the Nazis in Germany (e.g. Dachau) for political prisoners and Jews, who provided slave labour under appalling conditions. Later, more concentration camps such as Auschwitz in occupied Poland, and Belsen were built for the mass extermination of about six million human beings. *Two were established in New Britain (NB). The Isle of Wight off the south coast housed NB Kz1 (Camp One) the Isle of Man in the Irish Sea housed NB Kz2 (Camp Two).* They were labour and extermination camps for Jews, political prisoners, intellectuals, gypsies, Jehovah's Witnesses, homosexuals, captured spies and difficult prisoners of war.

Condor Legion-German Luftwaffe squadrons which flew in the Spanish Civil War for General Franco's Fascist forces.

Cromwell-British code word to be used in event of German invasion 1940, from Oliver Cromwell, Parliamentary General in English Civil Wars 1642-1649 who became Lord Protector during the republican Commonwealth which ended with the return of Charles II.

Drake Commando-South Western English resistance unit named after English explorer, Sir Frances Drake (c. 1543-1596) He built his reputation as a privateer plundering Spanish treasure in the Spanish Main. In 1577 he was backed by Elizabeth I to circumnavigate the globe. He sailed west below South America along the western coast of the Americas to what is now British Columbia., Canada. After almost three years he returned via the Pacific and was knighted by Elizabeth on the deck of his galleon the Golden Hind. In 1587 he destroyed the Spanish fleet assembling in Cadiz to invade England. In 1588 when told the Spanish armada was approaching he finished his game
of bowls first as he waited for the tide to rise. He took a major role in destroying the armada and with it Spanish dreams of invasion.

DSO-Distinguished Service Order. British award for bravery.

Dunkirk-French north western port used as an evacuation point for the British Expeditionary Force and French soldiers late May-early June 1940. 7,000 civilian paddle steamers, ferries, motorboats, yachts, and the Royal Navy brought over 338,000 troops (mostly British with 100,000 French) to Britain in Operation Dynamo.

E-Boat-Short form of *Eilboot* German for 'boat in a rush', fast German navy torpedo boat, known in the German navy as the S-Boot.

Enigma-Name of German coding machine using rotors and electrical plugs which allowed for millions of permutations of letters/numbers. Thanks to the courage of Polish partisans an enigma machine was captured from a German lorry convoy and sent to Britain. The Royal Navy captured code sheets from the German navy. Decoding experts at Bletchley Park were given the task of cracking the code and providing the results, known as Ultra, to Churchill. It took some years to completely crack the enigma code but it engendered the first computers.

Fascism-Anti-communist and patriotic movement founded in Italy during World War I (1914-1918). Benito Mussolini became leader of the fascist Blackshirts and dictator of Italy. Their symbol was the fasces, a bundle of rods with an axe in the middle which was carried before important officials in ancient Rome. The word was used to describe the bellicose, anti-communist regimes of 1920s Italy and 1930s Japan and Germany. Sir Oswald Mosely established the British fascist party, the Blackshirts, in the 1930s. At the outbreak of war he was imprisoned but was released after the Germans entered London and became one of Lord Eastbourne's closest advisors. .

Fascist-Follower of Fascism.

***Fiesler Storch*-**The Stork (Storch) was a German single engined light monoplane used for observing of flying one or two passengers.

Fighter Command-Branch of the RAF utilising fighter planes.

Fuhrer-Leader, a term invented by Josef Goebbels to refer to Adolf Hitler.

Gestapo-Secret police (*Staatspolizei*) in the Third Reich, organized in 1933 but came under the command of Heinrich Himmler in 1936, It was used to terrorize and cow anti-Nazi movements.

Great Evacuation *(Operation Magneto)-The evacuation of the armed services, government officials and scientists and the British gold reserves to Canada. Evacuees included, governments-in-exile of the occupied nations in Europe and their royal families (Netherlands, Belgium, Norway), Princesses Elizabeth and Margaret and their grandmother, Queen Mary.Churchill supervised Operation Magneto which saw one million people and gold reserves sent to Halifax, Nova Scotia and Newfoundland on Royal Navy, ocean liner and merchant marine ships from 15-22 October 1940.*

The Home Fleet provided defence from the Kriegsmarine. 'The Last of the Few' squadrons of 160 speedily trained British, Norwegian, Czech, Dutch, Polish, French, Commonwealth and American volunteer pilots flew the last Spitfire and Hurricane fighters produced by factories before they were over-run by the Wehrmacht. They patrolled the eastern ports of Scotland, Wales, England, and Northern Ireland beating off the Luftwaffe long enough to make the operation a success. They then landed their aircraft on Royal Navy aircraft carriers (miraculously with none crash landing) or flew them to the north of Scotland for refueling and then to Iceland.

Handley Page Hampden-A two engine RAF bomber with a crew of four.

Hawker Hurricane-Sturdy RAF fighter plane with a humpbacked fuselage behind the cockpit canopy, armed with 12 machine guns, four in each thick wing of its monoplane structure, capable of 333 miles per hour.

Heinkel 111 (He 111)-Standard German twin-engined medium bomber with a distinctive plexiglass nose canopy, first flown in Spanish Civil War as part of the Condor Legion, German squadrons flying for Franco's Fascist forces. It could carry a bomb load of up to 5,510 pounds.

HMCS-His (Her) Majesty's Canadian Ship.

HMS-His (Her) Majesty's Ship.

Iron Cross-German decoration for bravery.

Jerry (Jerries)-Nickname for German soldier(s) used by British and Commonwealth troops.

Junkers 87 **(**Ju 87)-Gull-winged dive-bomber which dropped bombs with pinpoint accuracy, slow and an easy target for RAF fighters, nicknamed the Stuka.

Junkers 88 (Ju 88)-Versatile, high-speed, two-engine German bomber. It had a crew of four.

Kreigsmarine-German navy

Lee-Enfield-Standard British Commonwealth infantry rifle .303 calibre.

Liebstandarte-Hitler's personal bodyguard of elite troops formed in 1933.

Lorry (Lorries)-British term for transport truck.

Luger-German officer's pistol with a bullet magazine in its grip.

Luftwaffe-German Air Force, aircraft had black crosses edged with white on wings and fuselages, swastikas were painted on their rudders or tails.

MI6- British secret service operating overseas.

Mauser-German infantry rifle.

Messerschmitt 109 (Me 109) -Excellent, ubiquitous Luftwaffe fighter plane with a top speed of 428 miles per hour, armed with a cannon in its nose with two machine guns on the upper engine cowling in front of the cockpit.

Military Medal-Second highest medal for valour awarded to members of the British and Commonwealth Armies in World War Two.

Nazi-Member of the Nazi party, led by Adolf Hitler, which gained power in Germany in 1933 and created the Third Reich, in which Hitler was dictator as *Reichzchanzler* (Reich Chancellor). A police state was created and submarines, tanks and aircraft built in defiance of the Treaty of Versailles. Revenge for the loss of World War I and the humiliating peace treaty was the motivation for Nazi foreign policy, which wanted to create a German speaking empire and make it the supreme world power by manipulation, coercion or brute force.

The party believed in the mythical supremacy of the Aryan race, supposedly exemplified by the 'master' race (Nordic-Germanic peoples) over the Slavs and Jews. The Nazi party was vehemently anti-Communist but cynically the Third Reich made an alliance with the Soviet Union in 1939, so they could carve up Poland between themselves.

NCO-Non-commissioned officer in army such as lance-corporal, corporal, sergeant, sergeant-major.

OBE-Order of the British Empire, award from the monarch for service.

OKW-*Oberkommando der Wermacht*, German armed forces High Command through which Hitler controlled the army, navy and air force.

Operation Checkmate-*German scheme to kidnap the Duke and Duchess of Windsor from the Bahamas in August 1940 which succeeded under the leadership of Count Von Darmstadt.*

Operation Lion Heart-*British plan to rescue Edward VIII and Queen Wallis from the Tower of London, January 1941. During the rescue Queen Wallis was mortally wounded but Edward VIII and the surviving crown jewels were safely sent to Canada by submarine with Wallis's body.*

Operation Sea Lion-*German plan to invade Great Britain in September 1940.*

Panzer-Short for *panzerkampfwagon* in German for armoured fighting vehicle, also known as PzKw.

Pig-An Italian two man underwater chariot, 6.7 m (22 feet) long carrying detachable explosives in the nose which could be attached to the hull of an enemy vessel and set off. Called a Maile ('Pig') by the Italians. Used by the Italian and British navies in World War Two.

PM-Prime Minister

Pom Pom Guns-Multiple barrel anti-aircraft guns fitted onto Royal Navy vessels not as effective as Bofors guns used by the RN, Army and RAF or their German equivalent. The name derives from the sound of the guns firing.

Pommie-Australian derogatory term for anyone from England.

Pompey-Nickname for the famous southern England naval port, Portsmouth.

Quisling-Term used to denote a collaborator with the enemy. Named after *Vidkun Quisling*, the leader of the Norwegian Fascist Party who became Prime Minister of occupied Norway and an ally of Nazi Germany.

Radar-American term which became the common allied term for RDF radio direction finding, a method of detecting aircraft devised by a Scottish scientist Robert Watson Watt. Radio signals sent by a strong transmitter were reflected by an aircraft up to a range of 100 miles and bounced back to a radio receiver screen. By 1936 the system was practical and a secret chain of RDF or radio location stations were secretly set up under the title, Chain Home Network.

RDF-Radio Direction Finding see Radar

Reich-German word meaning empire.

RCN-Royal Canadian Navy.

RN-Royal Navy.

S-Boat-'Schnellboot'(quick boat), German motor boat similar to American PT boat or British MTB boat, known to the allies as E-Boat .

Sassanach-Scots for foreigner.

Spandau-Ubiquitous German belt fed heavy machine gun, had the unique sound of a woodpecker tapping on a tree when fired.

SS -Initials for *Schutzstaffeln* ('Protective Squadron') formed in 1925 by the Nazi party after the failure of the Munich Beer Hall *Putsch* ('Coup d'etat') in 1923. Under Heinrich Himmler it grew into an elite force of 500,000 men which regarded itself as a racially pure, 'Aryan' force. It formed many divisions of well trained and fanatical troops known as the Waffen SS.

Stuka see *Junkers* 87

Sunderland Flying Boat-Large Royal Air Force flying boat effectively used by Coastal Command in anti-submarine work and to ferry officials. It's long range of up to 2,980 miles made it ideally suited for ocean patrols.

Supermarine Spitfire-Beautifully designed RAF fighter plane with eight .303 machine guns, four in each elliptical wing able to reach a top speed of 448 miles per hour. It's versatility made it more than a match for the Me 109

Third Reich-The German Third Empire (First Empire led by Frederick Barbarossa, Second Empire led by Kaisers Wilhelm I and II), founded by Adolf Hitler and the Nazi party. His dream was for it to last a thousand years, make Germany the predominant world power and eradicate the Jewish 'race' while at the same time promoting the supremacy of the Aryan 'master race'.

Tommy Gun-nickname of American Thompson machine gun made famous 'by 1920s Chicago gangsters' bullet magazines of bullets tended to jam so rectangular magazines replaced them later in the war.

Treaty of Versailles 1919-Peace treaty that ended World War I (Great War) 1914-1918. Germany agreed to pay huge reparation fees (at the same time were loaned a larger amount by the allies). It should be kept in mind that in 1871 Germany forced France to pay huge amounts after France lost the Franco-Prussian War.

The industrial Rhineland was occupied by the British and French. Germany was not allowed an air force, her army was cut to a small size and she could not build any large naval vessels but the military and naval elite planned right after their loss of World War I to circumvent the rules of the treaty. The Nazi party, when it gained power in 1933, aided this subterfuge and after little opposition was voiced in the Reich's reclaiming of the Rhineland in 1936, openly threw off the restrictive treaty obligations and massively prepared for war.

U-Boat-Short form of *Unterseeboot* ('Submarine') in Germany navy.

Vickers Machine Gun-British Commonwealth belt fed heavy machine gun mounted on a tripod used in World War One and World War Two.

VIP-Very important person.

Webley-British small arms manufacturer.

Wellington Bomber-Sturdy two engined RAF bomber by Vickers company which was the mainstay of Bomber Command during the first years of the war. Named after the Duke of Wellington.

Wellington Commando-Name of resistance unit based in southern and south eastern England named for the British Field Marshal and Prime Minister, Arthur Wellesley, 1st Duke of Wellington. Born in Dublin, Ireland in 1769, as a Colonel he won the Battle of Assaye in India in 1803. As Britain's greatest General since Marlborough, he defeated Napoleon's Marshals in Portugal, Spain and France. On 18 June, 1815 he routed Napoleon's army at Waterloo. He became a conservative Prime Minister and later advised Queen Victoria and Prince Albert.

Wehrmacht-German army.

ABOUT THE AUTHOR

Robert Oldham was born in England in 1950 and came to Canada in 1964. He obtained a B.A. in History at the University of British Columbia and a Master of Library Science degree in 1978 from the University of Toronto. He has been a librarian since 1979.

Robert's work 'Smashing Time' was in the final short list for the Commonwealth Short Story Competition in 1997. He has published two mystery short stories and a biographical piece on Canadian General Harry Crerar. He contributed to Berkswell Royal Year 1993/94 and his poems have been published in otobe/ingland, Quarry, Acta Victoriana and the Coach House anthology, This Is My Best. His articles have been published in Monarchy Canada and the Canadian Library Journal.

Besides writing, the author enjoys acting and has performed in various productions such as A Midsummer Night's Dream, Evita and The Madness of George III.